Alphonse Daudet

Sappho - Parisian manners

A Realistic Novel

Alphonse Daudet

Sappho - Parisian manners
A Realistic Novel

ISBN/EAN: 9783337031930

Printed in Europe, USA, Canada, Australia, Japan

Cover: Foto ©Andreas Hilbeck / pixelio.de

More available books at **www.hansebooks.com**

SAPPHO:

A REALISTIC NOVEL.

Trailing on her knees in the mud, lingering in this hollow, she forced him to sit down again.

Frontispiece.

See page 224.

SAPPHO:

PARISIAN MANNERS.

BY

ALPHONSE DAUDET.

SAPPHO:

PARISIAN MANNERS.

A REALISTIC NOVEL.

BY

ALPHONSE DAUDET.

TRANSLATED WITHOUT ABRIDGMENT FROM THE 100TH FRENCH EDITION.

Illustrated

WITH A PORTRAIT OF THE AUTHOR AND THIRTY ENGRAVINGS, FROM DESIGNS
BY MONTEGUT.

LONDON:
VIZETELLY & CO., 42 CATHERINE STREET, STRAND.
1886.

Perth:

S. COWAN AND CO., STRATHMORE PRINTING WORKS.

FOR MY SONS

WHEN THEY ARE TWENTY YEARS OLD.

LIST OF ENGRAVINGS.

ALPHONSE DAUDET.

THE AUTHOR OF "SAPPHO."

"Sappho," is the last work of real import penned by M. Alphonse Daudet, the accomplished author of so many admirable novels. It is one of the few books which have sprung, at a single bound, to fame, having created such a furore in France that more than one hundred thousand copies have been sold there already; and of these, nearly half were disposed of within a month of the original publication. Moreover, the Théâtre du Gymnase—that favoured home of success, as testified by such plays as "The Iron-master," and "Serge Panine"—is at the present moment drawing crowded houses to witness a dramatic version of the story, as prepared by M. Daudet in conjunction with M. Adolphe Belot.

Although several of M. Daudet's previous works—notably "Fromont the Younger, and Risler the Elder," "Numa Roumestan," and "The Evangelist"—have met with a favourable reception in England, but little is known of the author's efforts to attain celebrity, and of the position which he now holds in the French literary world. He was certainly predestined to become a man of letters, for he already wrote clever verses when he was merely thirteen, and two years later, a Lyons newspaper accepted a serial story from his pen. In his earlier days, whilst leading a strangely chequered life, he never lost sight of his intention to become famous, if there is any truth in the following anecdote current in Parisian literary circles. It is said that one cold wintry afternoon, some five-and-twenty years ago, he alighted from a cab, outside one of the best known curiosity shops of Paris, and entering the establishment abruptly asked the dealer if he would purchase a handsome bust in bronze.

"A bust?" answered the shopkeeper. "Pray, whom does it represent?"

"Why myself," retorted Daudet with superb assurance.

"Indeed! Will you kindly tell me your name then? Do you happen to be a celebrity?"

"Not yet; but I mean to be one some day."

"Ah! well," said the dealer with a chuckle, "pray call again when you *are* one, and then, perhaps, I'll buy your bust."

As it happened, however, M. Daudet, although expressing such confidence in himself was not in a position to wait for the day of celebrity he prophesied. Entering the cab again he tried several other curiosity shops, unblushingly offering his bust as that of the great novelist Balzac, but all to no avail ; and, so pressing was his need, that a few hours later he was constrained to part with his effigy for two-and-twenty francs—somewhere about the value of the metal. Then, after paying the cabman his due—half a napoleon—he climbed to his garret in the Rue Jacob, sadly repeating : "How dreadful! Only twelve francs for the image of my glory!"

We all know that M. Alphonse Daudet has since fully redeemed his promise to become a celebrity. As for the bust, it was the work of his intimate friend, the sculptor Clésinger, whom the reader will find portrayed in the pages of "Sappho," under the name of Caoudal. Daudet himself was Jean Gaussin in those times—Jean Gaussin the lover of Fanny Legrand; and uncle Césaire and aunt Divonne are portraits of two of his nearest and dearest relatives. Déchelette, Bouchereau, De Potter, La Gournerie, Alice Doré, and Rosa are in a like manner sketched from life, and the little house at Ville d'Avray, where several scenes of the story are laid, was at one time the residence of M. Alphonse Daudet's brother, Ernest. In point of fact a far healthier memory than that of Sappho attaches to the spot, for it was there that the author first met the charming woman who was to become his wife.

To employ a hackneyed phrase, it may be safely said that Alphonse Daudet's life is in his books, each of which contains an autobiographical element. With the exception of Charles Dickens—between whom and Daudet there are many points of affinity—no other contemporary novelist of note has thrown so much personality into his narratives. M. Émile Zola, mingling a dash of fancy with his earlier ambitions, has certainly sketched himself in the Rougon-Macquart series as "His Excellency Eugène Rougon"—a squat and muscular man, covetous of power, capable of bearing the weight of an empire on his shoulders, full of confidence in himself, and of contempt for the weak—but this is the one solitary instance in which the hermit of Médan figures in his own works. Not so, however, with M.

Alphonse Daudet, who, while his great rival for celebrity observes the doings of others, mainly recounts the adventures in which he himself played a more or less conspicuous part during his earlier years. And herein lies his chief point of contact with that "naturalistic" school, which asserts that the towering giants and rigid statues, the gaudy puppets and bran-stuffed dolls of past fiction should be discarded for human beings, endowed with genuine flesh and blood.

Now all the people who figure in Alphonse Daudet's stories are not mere creations of fancy, but have actually lived ; and he who describes their persons so truthfully and analyses their feelings so delicately, knew them well. In as much as the characters depicted by him are true to life, Daudet is, like M. Émile Zola, a *naturaliste*. But if there are several points of accord there are many more of contrast between these two great novelists. Zola and Daudet are certainly fast friends ; they are both of moderate stature and extremely short-sighted ; they also have the same fondness for the country and rural life ; and curiously enough they neither of them ever passed their *baccalauréat*, that all but elementary examination at which our English bachelors of arts would turn up their noses in contempt. It is true, however, that Daudet was debarred by lack of money from taking the degree, but Zola was plucked twice running, for his " ignorance of literature." *

With regard to the points of contrast, it may be noted that while Daudet is a genuine child of the South, of unalloyed descent, his rival blends a Frankish with a Latin ancestry.

* M. Louis Desprez: " L'Evolution Naturaliste."

The former has been described as an "Arab steed of fine and nervous comeliness;"* and the latter as "a prickly cactus of Provence, sprung up between two Parisian paving-stones."† However that may be, they at least greatly differ in personal appearance. Zola is thickset, broad-shouldered, strong, the picture of good health, with brushy brown hair and beard, full cheeks, a tip-tilted inquisitive nose and pouting lips. Daudet, on the other hand, is of slight and refined build, almost prematurely enfeebled, with long wavy black hair, lustrous gazelle-like eyes, a deep amber complexion, a forked beard, and a sensual mouth. Remember also that M. Zola, the lord of Médan, married a woman of the people, and that his two children are girls; while his rival, M. Daudet, the squire of Champrosay, has a poetess for his wife, and a couple of boys as offspring. And then what a great contrast in their style of writing: Daudet analyses, Zola dissects. The writer of "Nana" rushes into the melee, careless of soiling himself; the author of "Sappho" draws on his gloves before attacking vice. The two novelists, more-over, arrange their daily lives altogether different. Zola rises from bed at an early hour, fresh and ready, and usually finishes his allotted task by noon; Daudet tries to excite himself throughout the day and sits down to write after dinner. "Fromont and Risler," "Jack," "The Nabob," and "Sappho," were all penned between nine at night and five in the morning, like Michelet's histories, Littré's great dictionary, and Coppée's poems!

Few if any contemporary novelists have had so much per-

* M. Zola: "Etude sur Alphonse Daudet."
† M. Louis Ulbach's critique on the "Assommoir."

sonal experience of men and things as has fallen to the lot of M. Alphonse Daudet, who in this respect certainly outvies M. Zola. The space at our command, however, will allow of little more than a glance at the more important incidents of his career. He was born, he tells us, on May 13th, 1840, at Nimes, in Languedoc, where, as in all the other towns of southern France, you will find "a deal of sunshine, no little dust, a Carmelite convent, and two or three Roman monuments." The Daudet family, which had sprung up in the gorges of the Cevennes, amid grey rocks and wild fig-trees, had some pretensions to an aristocratic lineage, and had long been noted for its attachment to the Bourbon kings. At the time of Alphonse Daudet's birth his father carried on business at Nimes as a manufacturer of silk handkerchiefs, but two fires, a strike and a lawsuit, led to ruin ; and the family moved to Lyons, where the future author of "Sappho" was sent to school. It chanced, however, that he had more taste for boating than for syntax, and he has confessed that for a long period he spent six days out of ten on the Rhône, "with a pipe in his mouth and a flask of brandy or absinthe in his pocket." And yet, curiously enough, owing to the family reverses, he was compelled, despite his horror of school-rooms, to make his first real venture in life as an usher, obtaining a situation in that capacity at the college of Alais when he was sixteen years of age. He there endured a twelvemonth's misery, of which he has left us a touching record in "Le Petit Chose ; " but eventually, in the autumn of 1857, his elder brother, Ernest, who was residing in Paris, earning a scanty subsistence by his pen, suggested that he should join him there. Alphonse Daudet was only too glad to avail himself of the proposal, and one raw November morning he arrived, tired, shivering, and hungry, at the Hôtel du Sénat in the Rue de Tournon, where his brother occupied a garret on the fifth floor

A new life now began for young Alphonse—a life of want and effort, mingled with transient gleams of success and periods of youthful folly. His brother was untiring in his solicitude, acting the part of a parent towards him; but youth is wayward, and, besides, the atmosphere of the Hôtel du Sénat—merely a third-rate lodging-house despite its pompous name—was by no means healthy. It was there that Alphonse Daudet fell in with the Bohemian set which he has so cleverly hit off in "Jack;" there that he met Amédée Rolland, Jean du Boys, Charles Bataille, Louis Bouilhet, Louis d'Assas—all those young fellows of promise who were going to carve themselves imperishable names in the world of literature, but who died betimes, mostly killed by their own follies and excesses, by Boulevard and Quartier-Latin life, by that green fiend absinthe, which has so many murders on its conscience. There Daudet also became acquainted with M. Gambetta, then a mere law-student, but already dreaming of the high destiny in store for him.

Ernest Daudet was at this period earning £8 a month on the *Spectateur*, a spirited Royalist newspaper, and this meagre stipend had at first to suffice for the wants of both brothers. Alphonse Daudet has placed it upon record that in those times he often purchased a few sous' worth of bread and sausage, went to bed, and remained there dreaming and composing poetry for two or three days at a stretch. But suddenly the *Spectateur* was suppressed by the Imperial

Government. Ernest Daudet left for Privas to manage a provincial newspaper; and all that he could do for his brother was to recommend him to M. de Villemessant, then editor of the Paris *Figaro*.

Villemessant, one of the founders of contemporary French journalism, was an eccentric, generous, bragging man, with something of Barnum in his nature, and a remarkably keen eye for talent. He at once gave Daudet employment, and the young southerner's contributions, some in verse and others in prose, speedily attracted attention. Moreover, he succeeded in publishing the poems which he had written in the garret of the Hôtel du Sénat, and finally he had the good fortune to be introduced to the Duke de Morny, who greatly appreciated his writings. The duke, aware of Daudet's precarious position, at once offered him a virtual sinecure in the shape of a clerkship in the presidential offices of the Corps Législatif. Daudet, however, was at first afraid to accept, for, bearing in mind his family's long attachment to the Bourbons, he did not care to pass for a political turncoat. "But I am a Legitimist," he stammered in his embarrassment.

"Oh, be whatever you like," replied the duke. "The Empress is even more of a Legitimist than yourself."

After such a reply no further objection could be raised, so that Daudet willingly accepted the offer which so opportunely placed him above want. But, although relieved of the pressure of poverty, with every imperialist drawing-room now thrown open to him, to help him in making his way, he was not to be cured of his partiality for "Bohemia;" and it may safely be said that if his experience at this period subsequently inspired his novel "The Nabob," it also supplied the material for the story of "Sappho."   When we read of Jean Gaussin d'Armandy leaving France for a South American consulate, we are reminded of Alphonse Daudet starting on sick leave for Corsica or Algiers, duly provided with funds by the Duke de Morny.

He certainly wrote a good deal at this period, sending many a delightful sketch of travel from the spots he visited; and, on his return to France, penning several very charming stories and producing some promising little comedies at various theatres; but the flame of Paris has scorched and withered so many budding talents that it is hard to say whether Alphonse Daudet would ever have become the eminent and masterly writer that he is to-day, had it not been for his timely meeting with a good and pure woman. During the summer of 1866 he became acquainted with Mademoiselle Julia Allard, who was not merely a poet's daughter but a poet herself, and early in 1867 they were married.   Thenceforth the shoals and breakers of Parisian life were left behind; the whilom Bohemian was won to the peaceful delights of home, and became happy in the companionship of a faultless wife, in the prattle of his little boys rollicking on his knees.

To the salutary influence of Madame Daudet modern literature is indebted for those masterpieces of fiction which are called "Fromont the Younger and Risler the Elder," "The Nabob," "Kings in Exile," "Jack," and "Numa Roumestan."   M. Daudet has personally paid an eloquent tribute to his wife's accomplishments.   "She is such an artist," he says, "she has had such a share in everything I

have written.   Not a page but she has reperused it, touched it
up, scattered some of her beautiful gold and azure powder
over it.   And withal so modest, so simple, so little of a blue-
stocking ! "

It is not our purpose here to examine M. Daudet's many
works in detail.   Acute sensibility, compassion for all who
suffer, sympathy with the weak—such are the keynotes of
his productions.   His talent, as previously remarked, is
akin to that of our own Charles Dickens, and one cannot
read such books as "Jack" and "Le Petit Chose," without
thinking of "Nicholas Nickleby" and "Oliver Twist."
Moreover, many of his stories, such as "The Nabob,"
"Kings in Exile," and "Numa Roumestan," are more or less
matter of history, and all of them point a salutary and
forcible moral.

"Sappho" is a book which every young man may read
with profit.   Young fellows, fresh to life in a great city,
exposed to its manifold temptations, will find recorded
therein a salutary lesson.   M. Daudet himself dedicates the
volume to his sons "when they are twenty years of age."
Disregarding conventional opinion, he lays his own experience before them, in the hope that, duly cautioned, they
will know how to steer clear of the rocks which he himself
encountered, and reach the haven of life without mishap.

Now-a-days M. Daudet's only desire appears to be to
divide his time between his sons, their mother, and his work.
Barely a week ago M. Philippe Gille, the talented critic and
playwright, pressed him to cancel certain lines which he once
wrote respecting the French Academy.

"Your place is in the Institute of France," said M. Gille.

"You have only to say the word for the doors to fly open."

"No," replied Alphonse Daudet, "I have something very different on my mind. I wish to profit by the few years that may be left to me, to work in freedom, absolutely unfettered. I want to write a fresh study on the young men of the present day; and then I must pen a sketch of the first Napoleon—Napoleon as I understand him, a real southerner. Besides, there is the novel I am now engaged on—"A Rupture in Society," in which, as it happens, I expose some of the jobbery of the elections to the Academy. Finally, and this is my real reason, I have now brought up my elder son; I have gone through my own studies afresh, with him, and my dream is to do the same with his young brother. My delight, too, is in the country with water and cornfields, and the idea of a stroll in the sunlight along a dingle path with my wife and my boys, has far more charms for me than the prospect of forming part of a committee, of ceaselessly crossing the Pont des Arts, and leaving the Palais de l'Institut with a noisy troop. I esteem the Academy, I honour it, but pray never mention it to me again."

SAPPHO.

CHAPTER I.

"Come, look at me, I like the colour of your eyes   What's your name?"

"Jean."

"Only Jean?"

"Jean Gaussin."

"Ah! I see, from the South.   How old?"

"Twenty-one."

"Artist?"

"No, madame."

"Ah! so much the better."

These scraps of conversation, almost unintelligible amidst the shouts, laughter, and music of a costume ball, were interchanged one June night between a pifferaro and an Egyptian peasant woman in the conservatory of palms and tree-ferns which formed the background of Déchelette's studio.

The pifferaro answered the pressing questions of the Egyptian with the frankness of youth, the freedom and relief of a south countryman who had perforce long been silent. A stranger amid all this world of painters and sculptors, lost since his entrance by the friend who had brought him, he had been wandering about listlessly two hours, his fair handsome face tanned and coloured by the sun, his head a mass of curls, close and short like the sheepskin of his costume, whilst a buzz of admiration, of which he seemed barely conscious, followed him.

He was roughly shouldered by the dancers, unmercifully chaffed by young painters about the bagpipes which he carried all awry, and his mountain costume, hot and uncomfortable in the summer night. A bold-eyed Japanese, her hair held up in a knot by steel knives, hummed provokingly: "Ah! he is handsome, he is handsome, the postillion—" whilst a Spanish novio in white silk lace, passing on the arm of an Apache chief, thrust her bouquet of white jasmine rudely in his face.

He did not understand these advances, and feeling extremely ridiculous, took refuge in the cool shade of a glazed corridor, bordered by a broad divan under the greenery. This woman had come immediately and sat down beside him.

Young? Pretty? He could not have told you. The garment of blue woollen stuff displayed her round and delicate arms, and set off her full undulating figure; her small hands loaded with rings, her grey eyes, wide open and thrown into greater prominence by the fantastic ornaments in iron falling over her forehead, formed together a harmonious whole.

An actress, doubtless. Many of them frequented Déchelette's, and this thought did not help to put him at his ease; for that class of person he had a terror. She talked to him, sitting quite close, one elbow on her knee, her head resting on her hand, with a demure sweetness, a slight weariness—"From the South, really? And with such fair hair! What an extraordinary thing!"

This woman had come and sat down beside him.

19.

She wanted to know how long he had lived in Paris, if the examination for the consular service for which he was preparing was very difficult, if he knew many people, and how it was that he was at Déchelette's party in the Rue de Rome, so far from the Latin quarter.

When he mentioned the name of the student who had brought him : " La Gournerie—a relation of the author—she knew him, no doubt "—the expression of her face changed, grew suddenly overcast ; but he paid no attention to that, being of an age when the eyes sparkle and see nothing. La Gournerie had promised him that his cousin would be there, that he would introduce him. " I am so fond of his poetry—I should like to know him so much."

She smiled with pity at his candour, and shrugged her shoulders prettily, at the same time holding aside with her hand the light leaves of a bamboo, and looking towards the dance to see if she could not discover his great man for him.

The ball glittered and swayed to and fro at that moment like a scene from fairyland. The studio, the hall rather, for it was not much used as a workroom, extended to the full height of the mansion, and seemed to make one vast apartment of it. On the light, airy and summer-like hangings, the blinds of fine straw or gauze, the lacquered screens, the multicoloured glass, on the clump of yellow roses which decked the hearth of the lofty Renaissance fire-place, shone the varied and fantastic light of innumerable Chinese, Persian, Moorish and Japanese lanterns, these, in open work of iron, with lancet-shaped interstices like the door of a mosque, those, in paper, coloured to resemble fruit, others, fan-shaped, in the form of flowers, ibises, and serpents. Suddenly gleams of flashing bluish electric light made pale these thousands of lanterns, and blanched as if by moonlight the faces and bare shoulders, the whole phantasmagoria of dresses, feathers, spangles and ribbons which intermingled in the dance, or cast themselves on the Dutch staircase with broad balusters leading to the corridors of the first story, that rose no higher than the necks of the double basses and the frantically waving báton of the leader of the orchestra.

From where he was the young man saw all this through a network of green branches, of flowering creepers, which, mingling with the scene, encircled it, and by an optical illusion threw haphazard among the dancers garlands of wistaria on the silver train of a princess's robe, or bestowed a dracæna leaf as head-dress above the pretty face of a pompadour shepherdess ; and for him all at once the interest in the scene was doubled in the pleasure of hearing from his Egyptian the names, all illustrious and well known, which were concealed under the varied and whimsical costumes.

That whipper-in, with his short whip over his shoulder, was Jadin ; whilst a little further on that country priest's shabby cassock was hiding old Isabey, taller, by a pack of cards in his buckled shoes. Old Corot was smiling from beneath the enormous peak of an old pensioner's cap. She pointed out to him also Thomas Couture as a bull dog, Jundt as a convict warder, Cham as a tropic-bird.

And then a few historical and serious costumes, a plumed Marat, a Prince Eugene, a Charles the First, all worn by quite young painters, showed well the difference between the two generations of artists ; these, serious, cold, with heads like one sees on the Bourse, aged by those peculiar wrinkles due to money cares, those, more mischievous, noisy and overflowing with spirits.

In spite of his fifty-five years and the palms of the Institute the sculptor Caoudal as a mountebank hussar, with his bare arms showing the biceps of a Hercules, and a painter's palette dangling about his long legs for a sabretache, was wriggling through a figure that recalled the days of the Grande-Chaumière, supported by the musician De Potter, who, got up as a muezzin out on the spree, with his turban on one side, was imitating the stomach dance, and bawling out at the top of his shrill voice, " La Allah, il Allah."

These joyous celebrities were surrounded by a large circle of resting dancers; and foremost among them was Déchelette, the master of the house, frowning under a high Persian headpiece, with his small eyes, his Kalmuck nose and his grizzly beard, happy in the gaiety of others, and feeling mightily amused, although he did not show it.

Déchelette the engineer, a figure in the artist society of Paris of ten or twelve years ago, a very good fellow, very rich, with leanings towards art, and the frank manner, the contempt for public opinion which travelling and a single state produce, was superintending at that time the construction of a railway from Tauris to Teheran ; and each year, to recuperate after ten months of fatigues, of nights under canvas, of furious gallops across sands and morass, he came to pass the hot season in this mansion in the Rue de Rome, built after his designs, and furnished like a summer palace, where he gathered about him clever men and pretty women, asking of civilisation during a few weeks the quintessence of everything exhilarating and appetising that it has to give.

" Déchelette has arrived." This was *the* news of the studios directly it was seen that the immense canvas blind which covered the glazed façade of the mansion had been raised like the curtain of a theatre. That meant to say that the ball had opened, and that there would be two months of music and merry-making, dances and junketings, breaking in upon the dull silence of the neighbourhood of

the Place de l'Europe at that season of country visits and
sea baths.

Personally, Déchelette did not figure in the Bacchanalia
which were celebrated at his house night and day. That
indefatigable libertine took his pleasures in a measured
excess, with a vague expression, smiling as if under the influence of haschisch, but with imperturbable coolness and cal-
culation. A most faithful friend, giving with an open hand,
he had, with all his indulgence and politeness, an Oriental
contempt for women; and of all those who came to his
house, attracted by his great fortune or the joyous life led
there, not one could boast of having been his mistress for
more than a day.

"A good sort of fellow, all the same," added the Egyptian,
who had been giving Gaussin these particulars. Then, interrupting herself suddenly, "There is your poet."

"Where ?"

"In front of you, as a rustic bridegroom."

The young man gave vent to a disappointed, "Oh !"
His poet ! That big man, sweating, shining, displaying a
heavy grace in the double-pointed collar and the flowered
waistcoat peculiar to Jeannot. The great despairing cries
of the "Book of Love" came into his mind, the book which
he could never read unaffected ; and then he repeated
mechanically aloud :

> "To animate the proud marble of thy body,
>   O Sappho, I have given my last drop of blood—"

She turned round quickly, her barbarian ornaments jing-
ling :

"What did you say ?"

They were some of La Gournerie's lines, he was surprised
she did not know them.

"I don't care for poetry," she said curtly; and she stood there upright, her brows knitted, looking at the dancers and crushing nervously the beautiful violet bunches of flowers which hung in front of her. Then, and as if the decision cost her an effort, she said: "Good evening," and disappeared.

The poor pifferaro remained quite taken aback: "What is the matter with her? What have I said?" He searched and found nothing, if it were not that he would do well to go home to bed. He picked up his bagpipes mournfully and re-entered the ball-room, less troubled at the Egyptian's departure than at the crowd which he had to thread to gain the door.

The consciousness of his own insignificance among all these celebrities made him feel more timid still. They were no longer dancing; a few couples here and there were footing it desperately to the dying strains of a waltz, and amongst them Caoudal, superb and gigantic, was crashing about, his head high, with a little "tricoteuse," her head-dress floating in the wind, whom he lifted up in his brawny arms.

Through the large window, thrown wide open, at the end of the room came gusts of the pale morning air, shaking the leaves of the palms, flattening the flames of the candles as if to extinguish them. A paper lantern took fire, some sockets split, and all round the room the servants were placing little circular tables, like those outside cafés. They always supped thus, four or five together, at Déchelette's; and kindred spirits were seeking one another and grouping themselves at that moment.

Shouts and wild cries resounded, the "pit—ouit" of the street answering the rattle-like "you-you-you-you," of the Eastern girl; one heard conversations carried on in undertones,

and the voluptuous laughter of women who were being
escorted to their places with a caress.

Gaussin was profiting by this tumult to make his way to
the exit when his friend the student, streaming with per-
spiration, his eyes starting out of his head, a bottle under
each arm, stopped him: "Wherever are you going? I've
been looking everywhere for you. I've got a table and
some women, little Bachellery of the Bouffes—the Japanese,
you know. She sent me to look for you. Come along,
quick!" and he rushed off.

The pifferaro was thirsty; then the intoxication of the
ball tempted him, and so did the pretty little face of the
actress who was making signs to him from a distance. But
a grave, sweet voice murmured in his ear: "Do not go to
them."

His late companion was there, close to him, drawing him
outside, and he followed her without hesitation. Why? It
was not this woman's attractions; he had barely looked at
her, and the other one over there, who was calling him and
arranging the steel knives in her hair, was much more to
his taste. But he obeyed a will stronger than his own, the
impetuous violence of a desire.

"Do not go to them!"

And suddenly they found themselves on the pavement
of the Rue de Rome. Some cabs were waiting in the pale
morning. Some street sweepers and labourers going to their
work looked at this festive, noisy and overflowing house, at
this costumed couple, this Shrove Tuesday masquerade in
the middle of summer.

"To your place or mine?" she asked. Without knowing
exactly why, he thought his would be better, so gave the
distant address to the driver; and on the way, which was
long, they spoke but little. Only she held one of his hands

He lifted her up like a child.

between her own, which he felt were very small and icy cold ; and but for the chilliness of this nervous clasp, he would have thought she slept, leaning far back in the cab, with the moving reflection thrown by the blue blind on her face.

They stopped in the Rue Jacob, before a student's lodging-house. Four flights to mount; it was high and steep. "Would you like me to carry you?" he said laughing, but in a low voice, because of the sleeping house. She scanned him with a searching glance, scornful and tender, a look of experience which gauged him and said clearly : "Poor little fellow."

But he, with one effort, strong in his youth and country training, took her, lifted her up like a child, for he was stout and strapping for all his fair girl's skin, and mounted the first flight in one breath, happy in this weight which two lovely, fresh, bare arms fastened to his neck.

The second flight took longer, was less pleasurable. She let herself go and threw accordingly more weight on him. The iron of her pendants, which at first tickled him slightly, cut gradually and cruelly into his flesh.

At the third flight he panted like a piano-mover ; his breath failed him, whilst she murmured in ecstasy, her eyes half-closed : "Oh ! deary, how nice it is! how happy I feel !" And the last steps, which he scrambled up one by one, seemed to him to belong to a giant staircase whose walls, balusters, and narrow windows turned round and round in an interminable spiral. It was no longer a woman that he was carrying, but something heavy and horrible, which suffocated him, and which he was tempted each moment to let fall, to throw away from him in anger at the risk of brutally crushing it.

Arrived on the narrow landing : "Already !" she said,

opening her eyes. He thought—"At last!" but could not have said it, deadly pale, his hands on his chest which seemed about to burst.

Their whole history, this ascent of a staircase in the dreary grey of the morning.

CHAPTER II.

He kept her two days ; then she went away, leaving him
an impression of soft skin and fine linen. No other information about her but her name, her address, and this :
"When you want me, call me, I shall always be ready."

The tiny, elegant, perfumed card was inscribed :

FANNY LEGRAND,

6 Rue de l'Arcade.

He placed it against his looking glass, between an invitation to the last ball at the Foreign Office and the illumi-
nated and fanciful programme of Déchelette's party, his
only dissipations in fashionable society that year ; and the
remembrance of the woman, which remained a few days
about the fire-place in this delicate and faint perfume, de-
parted at the same time as this did, and Gaussin, an earnest
worker, and distrusting above all the allurements of Paris,
never took it into his head to renew that evening's amour.

The examination at the Ministry was to take place in
November. Three months only remained to prepare for it.
After that would come a course of three or four years in the
offices of the Consular Service ; then he would go away to
some far off country. This idea of exile had no terrors for
him ; for a tradition in the old Avignon family of Gaussin
d'Armandy held that the eldest son should follow what is
styled "the career," with the example, the encouragement,
and the moral protection of those who had preceded him.

For this countryman, Paris was only the first step of a very long voyage, a fact which forbade any close connexion either in love or friendship.

A week or two after Déchelette's ball, one evening as Gaussin, his lamp lighted, his books ready on the table, was beginning his work, there came a timid knock ; and, having opened the door, a woman appeared in an elegant and bright toilette. He recognised her only when she lifted her short veil.

"You see, 'tis I; I have come back."

Then, observing the uneasy and awkward glance which he cast on the work he was engaged upon : "Oh ! I sha'n't disturb you, *I* know what it is." She undid her bonnet, took up a number of the "Tour du Monde," settled herself and did not move again, absorbed apparently in her book ; but each time that he raised his eyes, they met hers.

And truly it required all his courage not to take her at once in his arms, for she was tempting enough, and charming with her little head and low forehead, her short nose, her sensual and full lip, and the supple ripeness of her figure in the robe of Parisian correctness, less terrible for him than her costume of an Egyptian girl.

Having taken her departure early the next morning, she came back several times during the week, and she always entered with the same paleness, the same cold, damp hands, the same voice trembling with emotion :

"Oh ! I know well that I bore you," she said to him, "that I tire you. I ought to be prouder. If you would only believe, every morning, on leaving you, I swear never to come again ; then, in the evening, I am driven back here as if it were a mania."

He looked at her amused, and surprised, in his contempt for women, at this loving persistence. Those he had known hitherto, girls he had picked up at cafés or skating rinks, sometimes young and pretty, always left him disgusted with their stupid laugh, their cook's hands, their coarseness of instincts and conversation, which made him open the window after them. In his innocent belief, he thought all this womankind alike. Accordingly, he was astonished to find in Fanny a truly feminine sweetness and reserve, with this superiority over the women of the middle classes whom he met in the country at his mother's house, that she had a veneer of art, an acquaintance with everything, which made her conversation interesting and varied.

Then she was a musician, accompanied herself on the piano and sang in a rather worn and unequal but well trained contralto voice, some romance by Chopin or Schumaun, country airs, songs of Berri, Burgundy or Picardy of which she had quite a store.

Gaussin, who like the rest of his countrymen was passionately fond of music, that art practised in hours of idleness and in the open air, was enraptured at the sounds as he worked or was lulled in delicious repose. And, coming from Fanny, it had special charms for him. He expressed astonishment that she was not at some theatre, and learnt thus that she had sung at the Lyric. "But not for long, I found it too tiresome."

And truly, in her there was nothing studied, nothing of the actress's conventionalism, not the shadow of vanity or falseness. Only a certain mystery as to her outside life, a mystery kept up even in the hours of passion, and which her lover did not attempt to penetrate, feeling neither jealous nor curious, letting her come at the hour agreed upon without even looking at the clock, ignorant yet of the sensation of expectation, those mighty heart-beats which desire and impatience strike.

From time to time, the summer being very fine that year,
they went about in search of those pretty nooks on the out-
skirts of Paris of which she had an intimate knowledge.
They took their places among the numerous and uproarious
crowds leaving the suburban stations, breakfasted in some
tavern on the wood-side or water's edge, avoiding only certain
too-frequented spots. One day, when he proposed to go to
the Vaux-de-Cernay, she said : "No, no, not there, there are
too many artists there."

And he recollected that this antipathy to artists had been
the beginning of their love. When he asked the reason of
it, she said : "They are such crazy, harebrained fellows, who
always exaggerate everything. They have done me a great
deal of harm."

"And yet," he protested, "art is so beautiful. Nothing
like it for adorning and opening out life."

"I will tell you what is beautiful, darling ; to be simple
and good like you, to be twenty years old, and to be in love."

Twenty ! one would not have said she was more, to see
her so full of life, always at his call, never without a laugh,
taking pleasure in everything.

One evening at Saint-Clair, in the valley of Chevreuse,
they arrived the day before the fair and could not find a
room. It was late, and they would have had to walk three
miles in the dark through the forest to the next village. At
last they were offered a sack bed which was disengaged, at
the end of a barn where some masons were sleeping.

"Let us take it," she said laughing. "It will recall to
me the days of my misery."

She had known misery then.

They groped their way among the already occupied beds
in the great whitewashed apartment, where a night-light
was smoking in a niche in the wall; and all night long,

clasped in one another's arms, they smothered their kisses and laughter, on hearing the snoring, the groaning from fatigue of their companions, whose hob-nails and soiled working clothes were scattered about close by the Parisian's silk dress and dainty boots.

At dawn a cat-hole was opened at the bottom of the great doors, a ray of light was thrown on the sack beds and floor of beaten earth, whilst a hoarse voice cried : " Hullo there ! wake up ! "   Then, in the again darkened barn, began a slow and painful movement, yawnings, stretchings, loud coughs, the mournful human sounds of an awakening dormitory ; and with heavy steps, one by one, the Limousins went silently on their way, never imagining that they had been sleeping close by a pretty girl.

As soon as they had gone, she got up, put on her dress in the dark, twisted up her hair hastily; "Stop there, I'm coming back."   She returned in a moment, with an enormous armful of wild flowers drenched with dew. " Now, we'll sleep," she said, scattering on the bed the fresh, sweet-smelling morning flora which revived the atmosphere around them.   And never had she appeared prettier to him, than coming into the barn, laughing in the dawning of the day, with her light hair flying loose and her wild flowers.

Another time they were breakfasting by the lake at Ville-d'Avray.   An autumn morning enveloped in mist the silent water and the many-tinted forest in front of them ; and alone in the little garden of the restaurant they were kissing each other and eating their fish.   All at once from a rustic arbour built among the branches of the plane-tree at whose foot their table was set out, a loud and bantering voice was heard : " I say, there, when you've done billing and cooing—"   And the leonine face and ruddy beard of Caoudal the sculptor appeared through an opening in the woodwork of the hut.

"I have a good mind to come down and breakfast with you, I feel bored to death like an owl up in my tree."

Fanny, visibly annoyed at the encounter, did not answer; he, on the contrary, jumped at the offer, curious about the celebrated artist, and flattered to have him at his table.

Very coquettish in a seemingly careless get-up, but in which everything was studied, from the white China crape tie to relieve a complexion covered with wrinkles and blotches, to the jacket tightly fitting a still slight figure with prominent muscles, Caoudal seemed older to him than at Déchelette's ball.

But what surprised and even embarrassed him a little was the tone of intimacy which the sculptor adopted towards his mistress, calling her familiarly "Fanny." "You know," he said to her, placing his plate on their table, "I have been a widower for the last fifteen days. Maria has gone off with Morateur. It left me pretty quiet at first. But this morning, on entering my studio, I felt fearfully lazy. Impossible to work. So I left my group and came to breakfast in the country. A deuced silly idea when one's alone. A little longer, and I should have been shedding tears in my plate."

Then, looking at the Provençal whose downy beard and curly hair were the colour of the sauterne in their glasses:

"Youth! Isn't it glorious? No fear of letting that one go. And, what is better, it's catching. She looks as young as he."

"You horrid man!" she said laughing; and her laugh had the ring of those seductions which know not age, the youth of a woman who loves and wishes to be loved.

"Astonishing, astonishing," murmured Caoudal who was

Caoudal appeared through an opening in the woodwork of the hut.

37.

watching her, whilst eating, a shade of sadness and envy playing about the corners of his mouth. "I say, Fanny, do you remember a breakfast here, it's a long time since, forsooth! Ezano, Dejoie, all the lot of us, were here; you fell into the lake. We dressed you up in men's clothes, with the keeper's tunic. It suited you splendidly."

"Don't remember it," she said coldly, and without lying; for these changing and casual creatures never exist but in their love for the time being. No recollection of that which preceded it, no dread of that which may follow.

Caoudal, on the other hand, living in the past, wound off, between the draughts of sauterne, the exploits of his lusty youth; love and drinking, excursions into the country, balls at the Opera, horseplay in the studio, battles fought and won. But on turning towards them, with the gleam in his eyes of the flames which he had stirred up, he found they were hardly listening to him, intent on plucking grapes from one another's lips.

"But all that's not very amusing. I see I weary you. Ah! the devil! It's stupid to be old." He got up, threw away his napkin. "Langlois! charge the breakfast to me," he called out towards the restaurant.

He walked away sadly, dragging his feet, as if eaten up with an incurable disease. For a long time the lovers watched his tall form which stooped under the golden leaves.

"Poor Caoudal! it's true he's nearly done for," murmured Fanny in a tone of tender commiseration; and when Gaussin professed his indignation that this Maria, a common woman, a model, could find amusement in the sufferings of a Caoudal, and prefer to the great artist, whom? Morateur, a little painter, without talent, having nothing in his favour but his youth, she began to laugh: "Ah! how innocent, how innocent!" pulling his head down on her knees with both her hands, she began to inhale, to breathe him, his eyes, hair, all over, like a bunch of flowers.

The evening of that day. Jean for the first time slept at his mistress's, who had been tormenting him on this subject for three months.   "But tell me, why won't you?"

"I don't know, I don't care to."

"When I tell you that I can please myself, that I am free."

And, the fatigue of the country walk coming to her assistance, she lured him to the Rue de l'Arcade, quite close to the railway station.   An old servant, in a peasant's cap, with a crabbed look, came and opened the door on the first floor of a plain but respectable and substantial house.

"It's Machaume. Good day, Machaume," said Fanny, throwing her arms round her neck.   "Here he is, you know, my sweetheart, my king! I've brought him. Quick! light up everywhere, make the house look nice."

Jean remained by himself in a tiny drawing-room, with low arched windows hung with the same common blue silk as covered the sofas and a few lacquered articles of furniture. On the walls, three or four landscapes enlivened the drapery; all were dedicated, "To Fanny Legrand," or, "To my dear Fanny."

On the chimney-piece was a half-size in marble of Caoudal's "Sappho," the bronze counterpart of which is to be met with everywhere, and which Gaussin had seen in his father's study since he was quite a child.   And by the light of the single candle, placed near its base, he perceived the refined and so to say rejuvenating resemblance of this work of art to his mistress. Those lines of the profile, that attitude of the figure beneath the drapery, that tapering roundness of the arms clasping the knees, were well known to him; his eyes fed on them, with the remembrance of more tender sensations.

Fanny, finding him lost in contemplation before the marble, said in an airy way: "There's something of me there, is there not? Caoudal's model was like me." And she immediately took him into her room, where Machaume, looking very cross, was laying the cloth for two on a little round table; all the candles were lighted, even those on the glass door of the wardrobe, and a jolly wood fire, cheerful like the first one of the season, was flaming behind the guard; the room of a woman dressing for a ball.

"I thought we would have supper here," she said, laughing, "we shall be sooner in bed."

Never had Jean seen a room more coquettishly furnished. The Louis XVI hangings, the bright muslin of his mother's and sisters' rooms, gave not the least idea of this padded and quilted nest, where all the wood-work was hidden under delicate satin, where the bed was only a divan broader than the others, spread out at the further end on white furs.

Delicious, this softness of light, of warmth, of blue reflections shining in the bevelled mirrors, after their journey across country, the wetting they had got, the mud on the rough roads in the gathering twilight. But that which prevented him from enjoying all this comfort as a true provincial, was the servant's bad humour, the suspicious look which she fastened on him, so that at last Fanny dismissed her abruptly. "Leave us, Machaume, we will wait on ourselves." And as she slammed the door on going out, "Don't take any notice of her, she's vexed at me for loving you so much. She says I'm wasting my life. These country people, they are so greedy! Her cooking, now, is worth more than she is; just taste this ragout of hare."

She served the dish, uncorked the champagne, forgot to

help herself, in order to watch him eating, the Algerian "gandoura" of soft white wool which she always wore in the house, displaying at every movement her arms up to the shoulder. She reminded him thus of their first meeting at Déchelette's; and, crowded together in the same armchair, eating out of the same plate, they talked about that evening.

"Oh!" said she, "as soon as ever I saw you come in, I felt a liking for you. I wanted to take you, carry you off at once, so that the others should not have you. And you, what did you think when you saw me?"

At first he had been afraid of her; then he felt full of confidence, perfectly at home with her. "By-the-way," he added, "I never asked you. Why were you angry at two of La Gournerie's lines?"

There was the same knitting of the brows as at the ball, then a shake of the head: "Follies! Don't let us talk of them any more." And with her arms around him: "I was a little afraid, myself. I tried to get away, to collect myself, but I could not, I never shall."

"Oh! Never!"

"You will see."

He contented himself for answer with the incredulous smile of youth, without noting the passionate, the almost threatening accent with which this "You will see," was thrown at him. This womanly embrace was so soft, so yielding; he firmly believed he had only to make a sign to free himself from it.

But to what purpose? He felt so happy in the snugness of this voluptuous room, so deliciously overcome by this caressing breath on his eyelids which were closing, heavy with sleep, full of fleeting visions, autumnal woods, meadows, dripping mills, all their day of love in the country.

In the morning, he awoke with a start at Machaume's voice calling out at the foot of the bed, without the least mystery: "He is there, he says he will speak to you."

"What! He will? Am I no longer then in my own house? You have let him in then!"

Furious, she sprang up, flew out of the room, half dressed, her bed-gown open: "Don't move, darling, I shall be back directly." But he did not wait for her, and only felt at his ease when he had got up, dressed himself, and stood firm in his boots.

Whilst picking up his clothes in the hermetically closed room, where the night-light still showed the disorder of the over-night supper, he heard the sound of a terrible quarrel, muffled by the hangings of the drawing-room. A man's voice, irritated at first, then imploring, whose bursts were drowned in sobs, in faint pleadings, alternated with another voice which he did not recognise at first, harsh and hoarse, full of hatred and vile words, flooding in upon his ear like a prostitute's tavern brawl.

All this amorous luxury was tainted by it, soiled, like foul stains on silk; and the woman too was polluted, was on a level with others whom he had formerly despised.

She came in again, breathless, twisting up gracefully her flowing hair: "What a stupid sight, a man crying!" Then, seeing him up and dressed, she gave vent to a cry of rage: "You've got up! Get into bed again at once! I insist upon it!" Then, suddenly appeased, and enfolding him by gesture and voice: "No, no, don't go, you cannot go away like that. In the first place I'm certain that you would never return."

"Of course I should; why not?"

"Swear you are not angry, that you will come again. Oh! I know you so well now."

He swore what she wished, but did not get into bed again in spite of her supplications and the repeated assurance that she was in her own home, free to live and act as she liked. At last she seemed to resign herself to his departure, and accompanied him to the door, having nothing of the raging nymph left in her, on the contrary, very humble, seeking to be pardoned.

A long and profound parting embrace detained them in the ante-room.

"When, then?" she asked, her eyes looking into the depths of his. He was about to answer, to lie, no doubt, in his haste to be outside, when a ring at the bell stopped him. Machaume came out of her kitchen, but Fanny signalled to her: "No, don't open the door." And they stood there, all three, immovable, silent.

A muttered complaint was heard, then the rustle of a letter thrust under the door, and footsteps which descended slowly. "When I told you I was free—look here!" She gave her lover the letter which she had just opened, a poor love letter, very humble, very craving, written hastily in pencil on a table at some café, and in which the wretched man begged for pardon for his morning's folly, acknowledged that he had no claim upon her, beyond what she was good enough to allow him, prayed with clasped hands that she would not exile him for ever, promising to accept anything, resigned to all, only not to lose her, great heavens! not to lose her.

"Just fancy," she said with an evil laugh; and this laugh completed the estrangement of the heart she wished to conquer. Jean thought her cruel. He did not yet know that a woman who loves has no sensibility but for her own love, all feeling of charity, kindness, pity, devotion, absorbed to the benefit of one being, and one only.

"You are very wrong to make fun of it. This letter is horribly beautiful and heart-rending," and then, in a low, serious voice, taking hold of her hands: "Come, why do you drive him away?"

"I don't want him any more. I don't love him."

"And yet, he was your lover. He gave you this luxury in which you live, have always lived, which is necessary to you."

"Deary," she said, in her frank tones, "when I did not know you, I found all that very fine. Now it's a worry, a reproach; my heart revolts at it. Oh! I know, you are going to tell me that in our case it is not serious—that you do not love me. But that's my look-out. Whether you like it or not, I will force you to love me."

He did not answer, made an appointment for next day and went off, bestowing a few louis on Machaume—the contents of his student's purse—in payment of the ragout. All was over now on his side. What right had he to bring trouble into this woman's life, and what could he offer her in exchange for that which he was causing her to lose?

He wrote all this to her the same day, as gently, as sincerely as he could, not telling her, however, he had felt that something bad, something unwholesome existed in their acquaintance—which was but a passing caprice—on hearing after his night of love those sobs of the deceived lover mingling with her laughter and her washerwoman's oaths.

In this great boy, reared far from Paris, in the heart of Provence, there existed some of his father's roughness, and all the tenderness and nervosity of his mother whom he resembled like a portrait. And to safeguard him from the allurements of pleasure, there was also the example of a brother of his father, whose dissipations and follies had half ruined their family and imperilled the honour of their name.

Uncle Césaire! With nothing but these two words and the secret drama which they called up, much more terrible sacrifices could have been imposed upon Jean than that of this slight love affair to which he had never attached much importance. And yet it was more difficult to break it off than he imagined.

Formally dismissed, she returned undiscouraged by his refusals to see her, by the closed door, the inexorable instructions. "I have no self-respect," she wrote. She watched the hour of his meals at the restaurant, waited for him in front of the café where he read the papers. And no tears or scenes. If he was with anyone she contented herself with following him, watching for the moment when he would be alone.

"Will you have me this evening? No? Another time then." She went off with the gentle resignation of a pedlar who shoulders his pack, leaving him in remorse at his harshness and the humiliation of the lie which he stammered out at each meeting. "The examination was near, the time was short. Afterwards, later on, if she were still so inclined." In reality he intended, as soon as he had passed, to take a month's holiday in the South, trusting that during that time she would forget him.

Unfortunately, when the examination passed, Jean fell ill. A chill taken in a corridor at the Ministry, and which he neglected, became serious. He knew no one in Paris except a few students from his own province whom his engrossing connection had kept away and dispersed. Besides, there was need here of a more than ordinary devotion, and from the first evening it was Fanny Legrand who took her place at his bedside, never leaving it for ten days, nursing him

She waited for him in front of the café.

untiringly, without fear or distaste, clever as a trained nurse, with gentle wheedlings which at times in his hours of fever carried him back to a serious illness in his childhood, making him call her aunt Divonne, and say, "Thank you, Divonne," when he felt Fanny's hands on his damp forehead.

"It's not Divonne, it's I; I'm watching over you."

She saved him from mercenary attentions, fires left to go out, diet drinks concocted in the porter's lodge ; and Jean could not get over the feeling of astonishment caused by the alert and ingenious skill of these hands brought up to indolence and voluptuousness. At night she slept for two hours on the sofa—a boarding-house sofa—about as soft as the plank bed of the police station.

"But my poor Fanny, do you never go home ? " he asked her one day. "I'm better now. You must go and re-assure Machaume."

She began to laugh. There had been fine goings-on at home. Machaume was gone, and everything was sold—furniture, clothing, even the bedding. She had only the dress left which she was wearing and a little underlinen saved by her maid. If he sent her away now it would be into the streets.

CHAPTER III.

"I think I've found it this time. In the Rue d'Amsterdam, opposite the railway station. Three rooms and a large balcony. If you like we will go and look at it after you have done at the Ministry. It's high up, five stories, but you can carry me. It was so nice, do you remember?" And delighted at the recollection, she laid herself on his bosom, curled herself up, seeking the old place—her place.

Life had become intolerable for two of them living together in the furnished apartments of the lodging-house, with the disreputable habits, the slipshod women trailing about on the staircase, the partitions of paper, behind which other couples were swarming, the mixing up of keys, candlesticks, boots. Not for her though; with Jean, the roof, the cellar, the sewer even, any quarters would have suited her to roost in. But the delicate instincts of the lover shrunk from certain things which, single, he would have viewed with indifference. These one-night couples annoyed him, seemed to pollute his home, and caused him much the same kind of sadness and disgust as the monkeys in the Jardin des Plantes, parodying all the gestures and expressions of human love. The restaurant too became wearisome to him; the meal which he had to go and get twice daily, down the Boulevard Saint-Michel, in the great room crowded with students, art pupils, painters, architects, who, without being of his acquaintance, knew him by sight for the last year that he had taken his meals there.

He blushed, on opening the door, at seeing all these eyes turned on Fanny; entered with the would-be boldness of quite young men who are escorting a woman; and he was fearful too of meeting one of his chiefs at the Ministry, or someone from his native place. Then there was the question of economy.

"How expensive it is!" she said every time, taking possession of and going through the dinner bill. "If we had a home of our own I could have kept house for three days with this money."

"Well, what is to prevent us?" And then began the search.

The old trap! All are caught in it, the best, the most well meaning, that instinct of what is fitting, that taste for *home* inculcated by familiar training and the warmth of a fireside.

The apartments in the Rue d'Amsterdam were taken at once, and voted charming, despite the fact that the rooms opened one into the other, and that the kitchen and sitting room looked out on a mouldy back-yard whence arose from a neighbouring tavern the fumes of slops and chlorine, and the bed-room on the steep and noisy street, shaken day and night by the jolting vans, drays, cabs, omnibuses, the whistles of arriving and departing trains, all the hubbub of the Western Railway station which reared its glass roofs of the colour of dirty water in front of them. The advantage was in knowing the trains to be at their door, and Saint-Cloud, Ville-d'Avray, Saint-Germain, all the rural stations on the banks of the Seine, almost beneath their balcony. For they had a broad commodious balcony, which owed to the munificence of former tenants a zinc awning painted like striped ticking, dripping and desolate under the winter rains, but which would come in splendidly during the summer for dining in the open air, as in a mountain châlet.

They busied themselves over furnishing. Jean having told them at home of his house-keeping project, Aunt Divonne, who was a kind of house-stewardess, sent him the necessary funds; her letter announced at the same time the early arrival of a wardrobe, a chest of drawers and a large cane arm-chair taken out of the " Windy Chamber " for the Parisian's use.

This room which he could recall at the end of a passage at Castelet—always uninhabited, the shutters closely barred, the door locked—was subject from its position to gusts of the "mistral" which shook it like a light-house chamber. There was heaped up the lumber which each generation relegated to the past in the presence of fresh acquisitions.

Ah! If Divonne could only have known what singular siestas would be taken in the arm-chair, what surah petti-coats and frilled undergarments would fill the Empire chest of drawers! But Gaussin's remorse on this subject was drowned in the thousand little pleasures of setting up house.

It was so jolly, after office hours, in the dusk, setting off on these grand journeys, arm-in-arm, going into some second rate street to choose a dining-room suite, the sideboard, the table and six chairs, or some curtains of flowered cretonne for the windows and the bed. He blindly accepted any-thing; but Fanny had eyes for two, tried the chairs, the leaves of the table, and came out strong in bargaining.

She knew of shops where were to be had at manufacturers' prices a complete set of kitchen utensils for a small family, four iron saucepans, the fifth enamelled for the morning chocolate; nothing of copper, it takes too long to clean. Six metal spoons and forks, with the soup ladle, and two dozen plates of English ware, strong and gay; all this got together, counted and packed like a doll's dinner service. As for the sheets, napkins, toilet and table linen, she knew a dealer—the representative cf a large manufactory at Roubaix—where one could pay so much per month ; and always on the look-out in the shop windows, in search of sellings-off, of those remnants from shipwrecks which Paris is always casting up in the foam of her shores, she discovered in the Boulevard de Clichy the chance of a splendid bedstead, almost new, and large enough to hold the Ogre's seven girls in a row.

He, too, on returning from the office, tried his hand at purchases ; but he knew nothing about it, never knowing how to say no, never going away empty-handed. Having one day entered a second-hand dealer's to buy a cruetstand which she had told him of, he brought home instead of the article, which had been already sold, a drawing-room lustre with pendants ; a particularly useless acquisition, since they had no drawing-room.

"We will put it in the verandah," said Fanny, to console him.

And the fun of taking measures, the discussions as to the position of the furniture, and the cries, the mad laughs, the gesticulations, when it was found that in spite of all their precautions, in spite of the complete list of indispensable purchases, there was always something forgotten.

Thus, the sugar-grater. Fancy anyone starting housekeeping without a sugar-grater !

Then, everything bought and put in its place, the curtains hung, a wick in the new lamp, what a glorious evening when they moved in, the minute review of the three rooms before going to bed, and how she laughed whilst she showed him a light to bolt the door by. "Another push—another, make everything fast. Let's be really and truly at home."

Then began a new and delicious life. On leaving his work he came in quickly, anxious to be home with slippered feet by the fireside. And in the black, splashing street he pictured to himself their warm, lighted room, enlivened by his old country furniture which Fanny had foretold would be rubbish, and which turned out to be very handsome and ancient ; the wardrobe especially, a gem in the Louis XVI style, with its painted panels representing Provençal fêtes, shepherds in flowered jackets, dances to the flute and tabourine. The presence of these out-of-date antiquities, familiar to his childish eyes, recalled his father's roof, consecrated his new home the comfort of which he was enjoying.

As soon as he rang the bell, Fanny opened the door, neatly dressed, coquettish, "all there," as she said, in her dress of black woollen stuff, very-plain but fashionably made—the simplicity of a woman who had been used to dressing well— her sleeves turned up, and protected by a large white apron ; for she did the cooking herself, and contented herself with a charwoman for the rough work which chaps or spoils the shape of the hands.

She was very clever at it too, knew a quantity of recipes, dishes peculiar to the North or the South, varied as her repertory of popular songs which, dinner over, the white apron hung up behind the closed kitchen door, she chanted in her languishing and passionate contralto.

Below, the street murmured, the traffic rolled along. The cold rain tinkled on the zinc verandah ; and Gaussin, his feet on the fender, stretched out in his easy chair, watched the window-panes of the station opposite, and the clerks bending over their work by the white light of the large reflectors.

He was happy, he let himself be lulled. In love ? No ; but grateful for the love with which he was surrounded, for this invariable fondness. How had he been able so long to deny himself this felicity, in the fear—which he laughed at now—of captivation, of an obstacle of some sort? Was his life not more seemly now than when he wandered from one woman to another, imperilling his health?

No danger for the future. In three years' time, when he went away, the rupture would take place of itself, without a shock. Fanny was forewarned; they used to talk together about it, as about death, a fatality, distant but inexorable. But he had in his mind the great grief they would be in at home on learning that he was not living alone, his stern and passionate father's anger.

But how could they know? Jean saw no one in Paris. His father, " the consul " as they called him in the country, was kept at home all the year round superintending the large estate which he cultivated, and sustaining a fierce struggle with his vines. His mother, utterly helpless, could not take a step nor make a movement without assistance, leaving to Divonne the ordering of the house, the care of his little twin sisters, Marthe and Marie, whose unlooked-for birth had for ever robbed her of all strength. As for Uncle Césaire, Divonne's husband, he was a great child who was not allowed to travel alone.

And Fanny knew all the family now. When he received a letter from Castelet, at the bottom of which the twins had added a few lines of their large writing, she read it over his shoulder, was moved with him. Of her own existence he knew nothing, never inquired. His was the beautiful, unconscious egoism of youth, without jealousy, without a care. Full of his own life, he let it overflow, thought aloud, abandoned himself, whilst she remained silent.

Thus the days, the weeks, passed in a happy calm, troubled for a moment by a circumstance which moved them much, but in different ways. She believed herself enceinte and imparted the news to him with such joy that he could not but share it. At heart, he was afraid. A child at his age! What should he do with it? Should he recognise it? And what a tie between this woman and him! What a complication of the future!

On a sudden, his eyes saw the chain, heavy, cold and riveted. At night he could sleep no more than she; and side by side in their great bed, they dreamt, with eyes open, a thousand miles from one another.

Happily, this false alarm was not renewed, and they betook themselves again to their peaceful and delightfully shut-in existence. Then, the winter over, and the real sun at last come back, their room became gayer still, larger by the balcony and awning. In the evening they dined there beneath the green-tinted sky, across which darted the twittering swallows.

The warm air rose from the street, together with all the sounds from the neighbouring houses; but the slightest breath of wind was for them, and they forgot themselves for hours, their knees touching, conscious of nothing more. Jean recalled similar nights on the banks of the Rhone, dreamt of distant consulates in very hot climates, of the decks of departing vessels where would blow the same long-drawn breaths of wind as were now agitating the curtain of their tent. And when the words trembled on her lips: "Do you love me?" he always returned from far off to answer: "Oh! yes, I love you." See what it is to get hold of them so young; they have too many things running in their heads.

On the same balcony, separated from them by the iron-work garlanded with twining flowers, cooed another couple, Monsieur and Madame Hettéma, very fat married people,

On the same balcony cooed another couple.

whose kisses sounded like smacks. Wonderfully matched, with a similarity in age, taste and heavy appearance, it was touching to hear these lovers drawing towards the close of their youth, singing together sentimental old romances, in low tones, whilst leaning over the rails :

> " But I can hear her sighing in the shade,
>   'Tis a sweet dream, oh ! let me sleep again ! "

Fanny liked them, she would willingly have made their acquaintance. Sometimes even the lady and she exchanged the smile of loving and happy women over the blackened hand-rail ; but the men, as is always the case, were more stiff, and did not speak.

Jean was returning from the Quai d'Orsay one afternoon, when someone called him by name at the corner of the Rue Royale. It was a lovely day, and Paris was opening out in the hot glare at this corner of the boulevard which on a fine evening, towards the fashionable hour in the Bois, has not its equal in the world.

" Sit down there, beautiful youth, and have something to drink ; it does my eyes good to look on you."

Two great arms collared him from under the awning of a café encroaching on the pavement with its three rows of tables. He allowed himself to be persuaded, flattered at hearing all this crowd around him, country people, foreigners, striped jackets and round hats, curiously whispering Caoudal's name.

The sculptor sitting with a glass of absinthe before him, which went well with his military figure and his rosette of officer of the legion of honour, had next to him Déchelette, the engineer, arrived the day before ; always the same, sunburnt and yellow, his prominent cheek-bones throwing up his good-natured little eyes, his greedy nostril sniffing Paris.

As soon as the young man was seated, Caoudal, pointing to him with a comical transport, exclaimed :

" Isn't he handsome, that creature there ? To think that I was once his age, and curly like that. Oh ! youth, youth."

"Still on the same subject ? " said Déchelette, greeting his friend's hobby with a smile.

" My dear fellow, don't joke. All that I have, that I am, medals, crosses, the Institute, the whole bag of tricks, I would give them all for that hair and sunburnt face." Then, turning to Gaussin, with his abrupt manner :

" And Sappho, what have you done with her ? One never sees her now."

Jean opened his eyes, not understanding.

" Are you no longer with her ? " And, seeing his astonishment, Caoudal added impatiently : "Sappho, come—Fanny Legrand—Ville d'Avray."

" Oh ! that's all over long ago."

How came he to tell this lie ! From a kind of shame, of uneasiness at this name of Sappho given to his mistress ; a distaste for talking about her with other men ; perhaps, too, a desire to hear things that one would otherwise not have mentioned before him.

" What ! Sappho ! She is still on the go?" asked Déchelette carelessly, full of the intoxication of again seeing the steps of the Madeleine, the flower market, the long line of boulevards between two rows of green.

" Don't you remember her at your place last year ? She looked superb in her Egyptian peasant's costume. And one morning that autumn, when I found her breakfasting at Langlois's with this pretty boy, you would have thought her a fifteen days' bride."

" How old is she then ? From the time one has known her—"

Caoudal threw up his head to calculate: "How old! How old? Let's see, seventeen in '53, when she sat to me for my statue, it's now '73. So count for yourself." All at once his eyes sparkled: "Ah! if you had seen her twenty years ago, tall, slender, with arched lip, fine forehead. Such arms, shoulders still a trifle thin—but that suited the ardent Sappho. And as a woman, a mistress! What rapture to be drawn from that fleshly form, what sparks from that flint; a key-board where never a note was wanting. The whole gamut! as La Gournerie used to say."

Jean deadly pale, asked: "Was he too one of her lovers?"

"La Gournerie? I should think so; I suffered enough through him. Four years we lived together as man and wife, four years I tended her, slaved to satisfy her every caprice; singing-masters, music-masters, riding-masters, masters for everything. And when I had got her well-polished, licked into shape, cut like a precious stone, emerged from the gutter out of which I had lifted her one night, in front of the Bal Ragache, that infernal botcher of rhymes came and took her from under my nose, at the hospitable table where he dined every Sunday!"

He breathed hard as if to drive away this old love sore, which vibrated still in his voice: then he resumed more calmly:

"After all, his rascality profited him nothing. Their three years of life together were like hell. This poet with the insinuating manners was mean, vicious, mad. They used to comb one another, you should have seen! When one went to see them, one found her with a bandage over her eye, he with his face scratched and clawed. But the beauty of it was when he wanted to leave her. She stuck to him like a teazle, followed him, hammered at his door, waited for him stretched on his mat. One night in the middle of winter, she waited five hours for him outside the Farcy's where the whole troop of them had gone up. A pitiful tale! But the elegiac poet remained implacable up to the day when, to get rid of her, he put the matter in the hands of the police. Ah! a nice gentleman; and as a final wind-up, a thank-offering to this beautiful girl who had given him the best of her youth, her intelligence and her flesh, he poured out on her head a volume of spiteful drivelling verses, curses, lamentations, 'The Book of Love,' his best work."

Motionless, his back stiff, Gaussin listened, sipping through a long straw the iced drink before him. Some poison, surely, they had given him which froze his heart and stomach.

He shivered in spite of the glorious weather, he saw a pale vision of shadows which came and went, a water-cart standing in front of the Madeleine, and the crossing and re-crossing of carriages rolling over the soft roadway, silently as if upon cotton wool. No longer a sound in Paris, nothing beyond what was being said at this table. Now Déchelette was speaking; it was he who was pouring out the poison:

"What fearful things are these ruptures!" and his quiet and scoffing voice assumed an expression of gentleness, of infinite pity. "Two persons have lived together for years, slept together, mingled their dreams, their sweat. They have had no secrets, no possessions apart from one another. They have assumed the same habits of living, of speaking, the same features even. They are bound together hand and foot, regular glutination in fact! Then suddenly they leave one another, are torn apart. How do they do it? How have they the courage? For myself I could never do so. Yes, deceived, insulted, befouled, with ridicule and filth, if the woman wept and said to me: 'Stay,' I should not go. And that is the reason why, when I take one, it is always by the night. No morrow, as they used to say in old France, or else, marriage. It is decisive and fitter."

"No morrow, no morrow—it is very fine for you to talk. There are women one cannot keep only for a night. That one for instance."

"I did not give her a minute's grace," said Déchelette with a placid smile which the poor lover thought revolting.

"Then that was because you were not her fancy, otherwise—She is a girl who, when she loves, sticks tight. She has domestic tastes. But then, no luck in that line. She takes up with Dejoie, the novelist; he dies. She is passed on to Ezano; he marries. Then appears on the scene handsome Flamant, the engraver, formerly a model, for she has always had a rage for talent or beauty, and you know his dreadful story."

"What story?" asked Gaussin in a choking voice, and he set himself to draw at his straw again, whilst listening to the love-drama which was one of the sensations of Paris a few years ago.

"'The engraver was poor, madly in love with this woman; and, from fear of dismissal, to keep her in luxury he forged some bank-notes. Discovered almost immediately, arrested with his mistress, he got off with ten years' imprisonment, she with six months at Saint-Lazare, her innocence having been proved."

And Caoudal reminded Déchelette, who was present at the trial, how pretty she looked in her little prison cap, and cheeky, not snivelling, faithful to her lover to the last. And her answer to the old owl of a judge, and the kiss which she threw to Flamant over the cocked hats of the gendarmes, calling out to him in a voice which would have melted a stone, "Keep up your spirits, deary; the happy days will come back, we shall love one another again!" All the same, it had rather sickened her of her domestic tastes, poor girl.

"Since then, launched into the gay world, she took lovers by the month, the week, and never artists. Oh! artists; she had a horror of them. I was the only one, I really believe, that she continued to see. From time to time she came and smoked a cigarette in my studio. Then months passed without my hearing of her, until the day I found her at breakfast with this pretty child, eating grapes from his lips. I said to myself, 'Sappho is bitten again.'"

Jean could listen to no more. He felt the steeping poison was killing him. After freezing just before, he now felt flames in his chest, mounting to his head which buzzed and seemed about to split like a metal plate at a white heat. He crossed the road, reeling under the wheels of the vehicles. Coachmen called out. The idiots! who were they shouting at?

Passing along the Madeleine market he was annoyed at the smell of heliotrope, his mistress's favourite scent. He hastened to escape it, and furious, torn by emotion, he thought aloud : "My mistress! yes, a nice baggage, Sappho, Sappho. To think that I've lived a year with a thing like that!" He repeated the name in his fury, remembering having seen it in scurrilous prints, among other prostitutes' nick-names, in the grotesque Court Guide of fast life : Sappho, Cora, Caro, Phryne, Jeanne de Poitiers, Le Phoque.

And with the six letters of her hateful name, all this woman's life passed in disgusting review before his eyes. Caoudal's studio, the scenes with La Gournerie, the night-watches before the dirty lodgings or on the poet's door-mat. Then the handsome engraver, the forgeries, the assizes, and the little prison cap which suited her so well, and the kiss thrown to her forger—"Keep up your spirits, deary."

Deary ! the same name, the same caress she bestowed on him. What a disgrace ! Ah ! he would sweep away this filth. And always this smell of heliotrope which pursued him in a twilight of the same pale lilac as the tiny flower.

All at once he perceived that he was still pacing the market like the deck of a vessel. He resumed his way, arrived in one breath at the Rue d'Amsterdam, fully decided to drive this woman from the place, to throw her out on the staircase without explanation, hurling after her the insult of her name. At the door he hesitated, reflected, took a few more steps. She would cry, sob, let loose in the house all her vocabulary of the pavement, as before in the Rue de l'Arcade.

Write ? Yes, that would be better ; settle the affair in a few savage words. He entered an English tavern, deserted-looking and depressed beneath the gas which was being lit, sat down at a sticky table, near the sole customer, a girl with a death's head who was devouring smoked salmon without drinking. He ordered a pint of ale, did not touch it, and began a letter. But too many words were crowded in his head, all wanting to come out at once, and which the decomposed and clotted ink traced as slowly as it would.

He tore up two or three commencements, was going away finally without writing, when, in a low tone, close to him, a full and greedy mouth asked timidly, "You are not drinking, may I ?" He made a sign of assent. The girl threw herself on the ale and finished it in one long draught, which showed the distress of the unhappy creature who had just enough in her pocket to satisfy her hunger without moistening her mouth with a little beer. A feeling of pity came over him which appeased him, enlightened him suddenly as to the miseries of a woman's life. He set himself to judge more humanely, to reason with his unhappiness.

After all, she had not lied to him, and if he knew nothing of her life it was because he had never troubled himself about it. What had he to reproach her with? Her term at Saint-Lazare? But since she had been acquitted, carried in triumph almost on coming out—with what then? Other men before him? Did he not already know that? Why should he have a greater spite against her because the names of those lovers were well known, celebrated, because he might meet them, speak to them, look at their portraits in the shop-windows? Was he to consider it a crime that she had preferred those?

And at the bottom of his heart there reared itself an evil, an unspeakable pride, at sharing her with those great artists, at telling himself that they had found her beautiful. At his age one is never sure, never certain. One loves woman, loves Love; but perception and experience are wanting, and the young lover who shows you the portrait of his mistress seeks a look, an approbation, to reassure him. Sappho's figure seemed magnified, surrounded by a halo, since he knew he rsung by La Gourneric, immortalised by Caoudal in marble and bronze.

But suddenly, seized with rage again, he left the seat on the distant boulevard where his meditation had cast him, in the midst of the cries of children, the gossiping of workmen's wives in the dusty June night; and he set off walking again, talking out loud, furiously. A pretty thing, the bronze of Sappho, the bronze of commerce, dragged about everywhere, hackneyed as the tunes on a street organ, like the word itself, Sappho, which, coming down to us through the mist of ages has had its former beauty clogged with obscene legends, and from being the name of a goddess has become that of a disease. How disgusting, good heavens!

Thus he walked along, by turns calm or furious—in this

She had gone to bed, tired of waiting.

68.

whirl of diverse thoughts and feelings. The boulevard became dark, deserted. A sickly faintness floated in the close atmosphere, and he recognised the gates of the large cemetery where he had come the year before with all the youth of Paris to the unveiling of a bust by Caoudal on the tomb of Dejoie, the novelist of the Latin quarter, the author of "Cenderinette," Dejoie! Caoudal! The strange sound which these two names had had for him for the last two hours! how false and mournful seemed the story of the student and the little home, now that he knew the sad facts beneath the surface, that he had learnt from Déchelette the fearful name given to these marriages of the pavement.

This darkness, deeper from the near presence of death, terrified him. He retraced his steps, brushing against bloused figures prowling about, silently as the wings of night, draggled skirts at the doors of dens whose rough window-panes became for the time magic-lantern slides showing couples passing, embracing. The time? He felt broken down like a recruit after drill, and his grief, deadened, flown to his legs, he was conscious only of his stiffness. Oh! to go to bed, to sleep. Then on waking, coldly, without anger, he would say to the woman, "I know what you are; it is not your fault, nor mine, but we can live together no more. Let us separate." And, to put himself beyond pursuit, he would go and embrace his mother and his sisters, shake off in the breeze of the Rhone, in the free and invigorating "mistral," the pollution and horror of his bad dream.

She had gone to bed, tired of waiting, and was sleeping in the full light of the lamp, an open book before her on the coverlet. His entry did not wake her, and, standing at the bedside, he looked at her curiously, as at a fresh woman, a stranger whom he had found there.

Beautiful, oh! beautiful, the arms, the neck, the shoulders

like fine amber, firm, without spot or blemish. But upon
those eyelids, reddened, maybe by the novel she was reading,
maybe by the uneasiness, the waiting, upon those features
relaxed in sleep and from which had disappeared the ardent
desire of the woman craving to be loved, what weariness, what
confessions ! Her age, her history, her excesses, caprices,
affections, and Saint-Lazare, the blows, the tears, the terrors,
all were there open to his gaze ; and the violet bruises of
pleasure and sleeplessness, and the pout of disgust drooping
the lower lip, used up, worn out, like the fountain where all
the parish has drunk, and the incipient bloating loosening
of the flesh for the wrinkles of old age.

That treachery of sleep, enveloped in the silence of death,
it was grand, sinister ; a field of battle by night, with all the
horror which is seen and' that which is imagined in the
ghostly shadows.

And all at once there came over the poor child an
immense, a suffocating desire to weep.

CHAPTER IV.

They were finishing dinner, the window open, and the twittering swallows saluting the failing light. Jean did not speak, but he was going to do so, and always of the same cruel thing which haunted him, and with which he had tortured Fanny ever since the meeting with Caoudal. She, seeing his eyes cast down, the falsely indifferent air which he wore, read and anticipated him:

"Listen, I know what you are going to say to me. Spare us it, I entreat you, since all that is dead, since I love no one but you, that there is no one but you in the world—"

"If it was only dead as you say, all that past—" and he looked into her beautiful grey eyes changing at every impression "—you would not keep things which recall it, yes, there, in the wardrobe."

Her grey eyes were black now.

" You know then ? "

All that litter of love-letters, portraits, those glorious archives of her past life, saved from so many wrecks, must she then destroy them all ?

" At least you will trust me afterwards ? "

And on his incredulous smile she ran to fetch the lacquered box, whose chiselled ironwork amongst the delicate piles of her underlinen had so puzzled her lover during the last few days.

" Burn, tear, they are yours."

But he did not hurry to turn the little key, looked at the

cherry trees with fruit in pink mother of pearl, the flights
of storks incrusted on the lid which he opened suddenly.
All sorts of sizes and writing, coloured paper with illumi-
nated headings, old yellow notes broken at the folds, pencil
scrawls on leaves of note-books, visiting cards, all in a heap,
in no sort of order, like a drawer constantly rummaged and
turned over, and into which he too was now plunging his
trembling hands.

"Hand them to me. I will burn them before your eyes."

She spoke feverishly, kneeling in front of the grate, a
lighted candle on the ground at her side.

"Give them me."

But he said : "No, wait." And then, lower, as if ashamed :
"I want to read."

"Why? You will only give yourself more pain."

She thought only of his suffering, and not of the indelicacy
of giving up thus the secrets of passion, the heart's confessions of all those men who had loved her; and coming
nearer, still on her knees, she read at the same time as he,
watching him from the corners of her eyes.

Ten pages, signed La Gournerie, 1861, in a long feline
hand, in which the poet, sent to Algiers to write the official
and lyrical account of the voyage of the Emperor and
Empress, gave his mistress a glowing description of the
fêtes.

Algiers, overflowing and swarming, a true Bagdad of the
"Arabian Nights;" all Africa gathered together, crowded
about the town, beating against its doors as if to burst them
in like a simoon. Caravans of negroes and camels laden
with gum, tents of dressed hides, an odour of human musk.
Amidst all this menagerie encamped by the sea-shore, dancing
at night around huge fires, dispersed every morning on the
arrival of the chiefs of the South, like Eastern kings with

Oriental pomp, discordant music, reed flutes, harsh little drums, the "goum" surrounding the tricoloured standard of the Prophet; and behind, led by negroes, the horses destined as presents for the "Emberour" clothed in silk, caparisoned in silver, shaking bells and embroideries at each step.

The poet's genius made all this life-like and present; the words sparkled on the page like unmounted stones which jewellers value on a piece of paper. Truly she might be proud, the woman at whose feet these riches were thrown. Must she not have been loved, since, in spite of the strangeness of these fêtes, the poet thought but of her, was dying to see her.

"Oh! last night I dreamed I was with you on the great divan in the Rue de l'Arcade. You were naked, mad, crying out with joy under my caresses, when suddenly I awoke with a start to find myself rolled in a rug on my terrace, beneath the starry sky. The muezzin's cry was wafted from a neighbouring minaret like a bright and limpid stream of fire, voluptuous rather than imploring, and, my dream over, it was still you whom I heard."

What evil impulse urged him to continue reading in spite of the horrible jealousy which blanched his lips and caused him to clinch his hands. Gently, coaxingly, Fanny tried to take the letter from him; but he read it to the end, and after that, another, then another, letting them fall one by one to the ground with scorn and indifference, without heeding the flames which flared up in the fire-place, fed by the great poet's flowing and passionate effusions. And occasionally, as his exaggerated love boiled up in the heat of Africa, the lover's lyrics were polluted by some gross obscenity which would have surprised and scandalized the worldly ladies who read the "Book of Love," with all its

refined feeling, immaculate as the silver horn of the Jung-
frau.

Miseries of the heart! It was these passages which Jean
lingered over the most, these blots on the page, without
suspecting the nervous twitchings which each time disturbed
his face. He had even the courage to sneer at this post-
script, which was appended to a glowing description of a
fête of Aïssaouas: "I have been reading my letter over
again; really there are some very good things in it; put it
on one side for me, I may be able to 'make some use of it."

"A gentleman who was not in the habit of wasting anything," said he, passing on to another sheet in the same
handwriting, where, in the icy tone of a man of business,
La Gournerie demanded the return of a book of Arab songs
and a pair of rice-straw slippers. It was the liquidation of
their love-affair. Ah! he had known how to break off; he
was strong, that one.

And, without a pause, Jean continued draining this morass,
from which arose a close and unwholesome emanation. At
night-fall he had put the candle on the table, and was
running through some short notes, illegibly traced as with a
stiletto, by great fingers which in the savageness of desire
or anger tore and mauled the paper. The first days of the
connexion with Caoudal, assignations, suppers, country excursions, then quarrels, suppliant returns, laments, coarse and
vulgar insults suddenly mingled with jokes, funny expressions,
pitiful reproaches, all the weakness laid bare of the great
artist at the time of dismissal and abandonment.

The fire took it all, thrusting out great red tongues of
flame where were smoking and shrivelling the flesh, the
blood, the tears of a man of genius; but what mattered it
to Fanny, solely engrossed by the young lover whom she
was watching, and whose ardent fever was scorching her

through their clothes? He had just discovered a pen-and-ink portrait signed Gavarni, with this dedication—" To my friend, Fanny Legrand, in a tavern at Dampierre one rainy day." An intelligent and melancholy head, with hollow eyes, something bitter and worn looking about it.

" Who is this ?"

" André Dejoie.   I wanted to keep it because of the signature."

" Keep it, you are welcome to it," he said, but in such a strained, such an unhappy voice, that she took the drawing and threw it, torn to pieces, on the fire, whilst he buried himself in the novelist's correspondence ; a heartrending story dated from sea-side winter resorts and mineral springs, where the writer, sent thither on account of his health, grew desperate over his physical and moral afflictions, racking his brain to find there an idea far away from Paris, and mingling together orders for medicine, prescriptions, anxieties about money or work, the sending of proofs, the renewing of bills, with ever the same cry of longing for and adoration of Sappho's beautiful body which the doctors forbade him to approach.

Furious and unsparing, Jean murmured :

" But what on earth ailed them all to run after you like that ? "

That to him was the sole meaning of these despairing letters, confessing the disorder of one of those glorious existences which young men envy and of which romantic women dream.   Yes, what ailed them all ? What had she given them to drink ? He experienced the fearful anguish of a man, who, himself bound, sees the woman he loves outraged before his eyes ; and yet he could not make up his mind to empty out, at one go, with eyes shut, what remained in the box.

Now came the turn of the engraver, who, wretched, unknown, without other notoriety than that of the "Police Gazette," only owed his place in the shrine to the great love which had been borne him. Disgraceful, these letters dated from Mazas prison, and stupid, awkward, sentimental like those of a conscript to his rustic sweetheart. But one was conscious of an accent of sincerity in his passion running through the romantic effusions, a respect for the woman, a forgetfulness of self, which distinguished him, the convict, from the rest; for instance, when he asked Fanny's pardon for the crime of having loved her too well, or when writing from the Palais de Justice just after his sentence, he expressed his joy at knowing his mistress was acquitted and free. He complained of nothing; he had spent in her company, thanks to her, two years of happiness so perfect, so profound, that the memory of it sufficed to fill his life, to soften the horror of his fate, and he ended by asking her a favour:

"You know I have a child in the country, whose mother has long been dead; he lives with an old relation in such an out-of-the-way spot that they will never know of my affair. The money which I had left I sent them, telling them that I was going on a distant voyage. And it is to you that I look, my darling Nini, to inquire from time to time after this unhappy little fellow, and to send me news of him."

As a proof of Fanny's interest, followed a letter of thanks, and another, quite recent, dated barely six months back: "Oh! how good of you to come. How pretty you looked, how good, beside my prison jacket, of which I was so much ashamed!" And Jean broke out savagely: "You have continued to see him, then?"

"At intervals, out of charity."

"Even since we have lived together?"

A bright glare lighted up the room.

"Yes, once, only once, in the visitors' room; one only sees them there."

"Ah! you are a kind soul."

This idea that, in spite of their connection, she visited this forger, exasperated him most of all. He was too proud to own it; but a packet of letters, the last, tied with a blue ribbon over the fine, slanting writing, a feminine hand, let loose all his wrath.

" I shall be changing my tunic after the chariot-race,— come to my dressing-room—"

"No, no, don't read that !"

She rushed at him, seized the whole bundle, and threw it on the fire before he had time to understand, even on seeing her at his knees, reddened by the reflection of the flames and the shame of her confession.

"I was so young—it's Caoudal, that great fool—I did whatever he wished."

Then only he understood, and became deadly pale.

"Ah! yes, Sappho—the whole gamut." And spurning her with his foot like an unclean beast: "Get away, don't touch me, you fill me with disgust."

Her cry was drowned in a fearful thunder-clap, quite close and prolonged, whilst a bright glare lighted up the room. Fire! She sprang up terror-stricken, took up mechanically the water-bottle left on the table, emptied it upon the mass of paper whose flames had set on fire the last winter's soot ; then followed the water-can, the jugs, and seeing herself powerless, the flames darting out into the middle of the room, she ran to the balcony crying, " Fire ! fire !"

The Hettémas came first, then the door porter, and the police. Someone cried out:

" Let down the register ! Get out on the roof ! Water, water ! No, a blanket !"

E

Mournfully they stared at their invaded and soiled room; then, the alarm over, the fire extinguished, the black crowd below under the street lamp dispersed, the neighbours re-assured, the two lovers, in the midst of this mess of water, wet soot, and overturned furniture, felt disheartened and low-spirited, without strength to renew their quarrel or to clear up around them. Something sinister and vile had entered into their existence ; and, that evening, forgetting their old repugnance, they went and slept at a lodging-house.

Fanny's sacrifice was not destined to have any effect. Entire sentences retained in his memory out of these de-stroyed and burnt letters haunted the lover's mind, mounted in blood to his face like certain passages in bad books. And these old lovers of his mistress were almost all celebrated men. The dead ones rose up again ; the living ones—one encountered their names and portraits everywhere. They were talked about before him. And each time he felt an uneasiness, as of a family tie painfully broken.

As the pain sharpened his senses and his eyes, he began soon to note in Fanny the trace of former influences and the expressions, ideas, and habits which she had retained from them. That way of thrusting out the thumb as if to fashion, to form, the object of which she was speaking, with a " You can just picture it," belonged to the sculptor. From Dejoie she had caught the mania of clipping her words, and had learnt all the popular songs of which he had published a collection celebrated in every corner of France ; while she had taken from La Gournerie his haughty and scornful in-tonation and the severity of his judgments on modern literature.

She had retained all these characteristics, each succeeding one being placed above the last by that same phenomenon of stratification which enables one to recognise the age and changes of the earth by the different geological layers; and possibly she was not so intelligent as she had seemed to him at first. But really it was not a question of intelligence; for had she been outrageously stupid, vulgar, and ten years older, she would have held him by the strength of her past, by that vile jealousy which was devouring him, and of which he could neither satisfy the irritation nor the malice bursting out on every occasion one against another.

Dejoie's novels were no longer popular, the whole edition was knocking about in the second-hand book-stalls at five sous a volume. And that old fool Caoudal longing for love at his age! "You know he has no teeth left. I was looking at him at that breakfast at Ville d'Avray. He eats like a goat with the front of his mouth." His talent, too, had forsaken him. What a fiasco his Nymph was at the last salon! "It didn't hold together"—an expression he had got from her—"it didn't hold together"—and she from the sculptor. When he was thus pulling to pieces one of his past rivals, Fanny agreed with him, to please him; and one might have heard this raw youth, ignorant of art, of life, of everything, and this shallow girl with a polish of the wit of these famous artists, judging them with an air of superiority and doctorally condemning them.

But Gaussin's deadly enemy was Flamant the engraver. All he knew about him was that he was very handsome, fair like himself; that he was called "deary;" that he was visited on the quiet; and that when he attacked him like the others, calling him "the sentimental convict," or "the handsome prisoner," Fanny turned away her head without a word. Presently he accused his mistress of preserving an affection for this thief; and it became necessary for her to explain, gently, but with a certain firmness:

"You know well, Jean, that I love him no longer, since I love you. I never go to see him; I do not answer his letters; but you shall never make me speak evil of the man who adored me to madness, even to crime." On this open-speaking—her best quality—Jean did not persist; but he suffered from a jealous hatred, sharpened by uneasiness, which brought him home sometimes to the Rue d'Amsterdam in the middle of the day. "Supposing she had gone to see him!"

He always found her there in their little home, domesticated, indolent as an Eastern woman, or else at the piano giving a singing lesson to their fat neighbour, Madame Hettéma. They had formed an acquaintance since the evening of the fire with these placid and plethoric good people, living in a perpetual current of air, doors and windows open.

The husband, a draughtsman at the artillery museum, brought his work home; and each week-day evening—on Sunday all day—one could see him bending over his trestle table, sweating, puffing, in his shirt sleeves, waving his wrist-bands to make the air circulate, with a beard up to his eyes. Near him, his fat wife in a short jacket was steaming away too, although she never did anything; and to cool their blood, from time to time they sang one of their favourite duets.

The two establishments were soon on an intimate footing. In the morning, about ten, Hettéma's loud voice called outside the door: "Are you ready, Gaussin?" And their offices being near each other, they walked there together. Very dull, very vulgar, a few degrees lower in the social scale than his young friend, the draughtsman spoke but little, sputtered as if he had as much beard in his mouth as on his cheeks; but one felt that he was a good sort of man, and

He found her at the piano.

Jean's moral disorder had need of some such companionship. He was glad of it, especially on account of his mistress living in a solitude peopled with souvenirs and regrets more dangerous, perhaps, than the existence which she had voluntarily renounced, and who found in Madame Hettéma, forever preoccupied about her husband, and the savoury surprise which she was preparing for his dinner, and the new song which she would sing him during dessert, a respectable and healthy connection.

And yet, when the friendship became intimate to the point of giving and receiving invitations, he had a scruple. These people must think they were married; his conscience revolted at the deceit, and he charged Fanny to tell her neighbour, so that there should be no misunderstanding. This amused her very much. Poor child! such simple ideas occurred to no one but him. "But they have never believed for one moment that we were married. They think nothing of it! If you only knew where he picked up his wife! Your saint next door is quite as bad as I am. He only married her to have her all to himself, and you see the past troubles him but little."

He could not get over this. A former gay woman, this worthy body with her bright eyes, a childish smile on her fat face, and her drawling provincialisms, and for whom novels were never sufficiently sentimental nor words select enough! And he, the husband, so calm, so secure in his amorous happiness! He looked at him walking at his side, his pipe between his lips, with little sighs of contentment, whilst he himself was always brooding, always being devoured with impotent rage.

"You will get over it, deary," said Fanny to him softly at those times when one keeps nothing back; and she soothed him, tender and charming as on the first day, but with a certain abandonment about her which Jean could not define.

It was her freer manner and her way of expressing herself, a consciousness of her power, strange and unasked-for confessions as to her past life, debaucheries, and follies. She refrained no longer from smoking now, rolling in her fingers, leaving about on all the furniture, the eternal cigarette which beguiles the prostitute's day ; and in their discussions she expressed the most cynical theories on life, the baseness of men and the roguery of women. There was a change even in the expression of her eyes, dimmed with their stagnant moisture through which now flashed a libertine laugh.

And the intimacy of their love was transformed too. Reserved at first before her lover's youth whose first illusions she respected, the woman no longer laid any restraint on herself after having seen the effect of her rudely discovered past, on this boy the unhealthy fever with which she had fired his blood. And the wayward caresses so long held back, all those delirious words which her clinched teeth had checked, she poured them forth now, showed herself off, abandoned herself in the fulness of her amorous and practised courtesanship, in all the horrible glory of Sappho.

Modesty, coyness, where was the use of them? Men are all alike, mad after vice and corruption, this youth like the rest. To stuff them with what they love is still the best way to keep them. And whatever she knew, those depravities of pleasure with which she had been inoculated, Jean learnt them in his turn, to pass them on to others. Thus the poison travels, breeds, blasting body and soul, like those torches of which the Latin poet speaks, which went from hand to hand through the stadium.

CHAPTER V.

IN their bedroom, by the side of a beautiful portrait of Fanny by James Tissot, a relic of the girl's ancient splendours, there was a Southern landscape, all black and white, clumsily taken in the sun by a country photographer.

A rocky steep terraced with vineyards, shored up with banks of stone : then, above, behind the rows of cypresses protecting it from the north wind, and nestling under a little wood of bright-coloured pines and myrtles, the great white house, half farm, half château, with a broad flight of steps, Italian roof, escutcheoned doors in the red walls of the Provençal "mas," perches for the peacocks, a fold for the flocks, the black bay of the open sheds with their glistening ploughs and harrows. The ruins of ancient ramparts, an enormous tower, sharply cut out against the cloudless sky, overlooked the whole, with a few roofs and the Roman belfry of Châteauneuf-des-Papes where the Gaussins d'Armandy had lived from time immemorial.

Castelet, farm and estate, rich in its vineyards which are as famous as those of La Nerte and Hermitage, was handed down from father to son, joint-tenanted by all the children, but always worked by the younger son, in consequence of the family tradition of entering the eldest in the consular service. Unfortunately, nature often thwarts such plans, and if ever there was a being incapable of managing an estate, or of managing anything, that being was Césaire Gaussin who at twenty-four inherited this heavy responsibility.

A libertine, a frequenter of village gaming-houses and brothels, Césaire, or rather "Le Fénat," the ne'er-do-weel, the good-for-nothing, to give him his youthful cognomen, was a striking instance of the contradictory type which appears from time to time in the most austere families, to which it acts as a kind of safety-valve.

In a few years of improvidence, of stupid waste, of disastrous gambling at the clubs of Avignon and Orange, the farm was mortgaged, the reserve stock of wine exhausted, the coming harvest sold in advance; then, one day, on the eve of final seizure, Le Fénat forged his brother's signature and drew three bills payable at the Hong-Kong consulate, convinced that before their maturity he would obtain the money to withdraw them; but they arrived in due course at his eldest brother's with a distracted letter acknowledging the ruin and the forgery. The consul hastened to Châteauneuf, remedied this desperate situation with the aid of his savings and his wife's dowry, and seeing Le Fénat's incapacity, he resigned his career which had opened brilliantly and became simply a vine-grower.

A true Gaussin was he, with a mania for tradition, violent and calm, like extinguished volcanoes which still keep threatening an eruption, hardworking too, and very clever at cultivating. Thanks to him, Castelet prospered, increased by all the land up to the Rhone, and as luck always brings luck in this life, little Jean made his appearance under the myrtles of the estate. During this time, Le Fénat wandered about the house, crushed under the burden of his fault, hardly daring to lift his eyes towards his brother whose scornful silence overwhelmed him; he could only breathe freely when out in the fields, or hunting, or fishing, wearing out his grief with absurd tasks, picking up snails, trimming splendid walking-sticks of myrtle or reeds, and breakfasting

Le Fénat was thoroughly at home in these village adventures.

alone out of doors off a roast of small birds which he cooked
on a fire of olive stumps in the middle of the common.   In
the evening, returned to dinner at his brother's table, he
never uttered a word, in spite of the indulgent smile of his
sister-in-law, who pitied the poor creature and furnished him
with pocket-money unknown to her husband, who kept a
tight hand over Le Fénat, less on account of his past follies
than of those to come ; and, in fact, the grand freak having
been set straight, the elder Gaussin's pride was put afresh to
the proof.

Three days a-week there came to Castelet to do needlework a pretty fisher-girl, Divonne Abrieu, born amongst the
osier beds on the banks of the Rhone, a true water-plant,
with long and undulating stem.   Beneath her "catalane"
in three pieces encircling her small head, and whose strings
thrown back allowed one to admire its junction with the
neck, which, like her face, was slightly sunburnt as far as
the delicate flesh of the throat and shoulders, she reminded
one of some "donc" of the ancient Courts of Love formerly
held all around Châteauneuf, at Courthezon, at Vacqueiras,
in those old donjons whose ruins are scattered about the
hills.

This historical souvenir had nothing to do with Césaire's
love ; he was a simple soul, destitute of ideality and reading ;
but, small himself, he liked big women, and was smitten
from the first day.   Le Fénat was thoroughly at home in
these village adventures : a quadrille at the dance on Sunday,
a present of game, then at the first meeting in the open fields
the fierce onslaught amongst the lavender or hay.   It
happened that Divonne did not dance, that she took the
game back to the kitchen, and that, strong as one of those
white and flexible riverside poplars, she sent the seducer
rolling ten yards away.   Since then she had kept him at a

distance with the point of her scissors hanging from her girdle by a steel ring, and caused him to fall desperately in love, so much so, that he ta'ked of marriage and confided in his sister-in-law. She, having known Divonne from her infancy, and that she was of a serious and delicate disposition, thought at the bottom of her heart that this misalliance might be the saving of Le Fénat; but the consul's pride revolted at the idea of a Gaussin d'Armandy marrying a peasant. "If Césaire does it, I will see him no more." And he kept his word.

Césaire, having married, left Castelet and went to live on the banks of the Rhone with his wife's parents, on a little allowance which his brother made him and which his indulgent sister-in-law brought him every month. Little Jean used to accompany his mother in her visits, delighted at the Abrieus' hut, a sort of smoky rotunda, shaken by the north wind or the "mistral," and supported by a single beam, upright like a mast. The open door looked upon the little jetty where the nets were dried, and where the bright and enamelled silver of the scales shone and danced; below were two or three large boats heaving and creaking at their fastenings, and the great river, joyous, broad, shining, beat back by the wind against its islands tufted with pale green. And Jean, still a child, first acquired there his taste for distant voyages and for the ocean which he had never yet seen.

This exile of uncle Césaire lasted two or three years, and would never have ended, perhaps, had it not been for a family event, the birth of the little twins, Marthe and Marie. The mother fell ill from the effects of this double birth, and Césaire and his wife had permission to come and see her. The reconciliation of the brothers followed, unplanned, instinctive, from the all-powerful ties of blood; the couple came to live at Castelet, and as an incurable anæmia, complicated soon by rheumatic gout, rendered the poor mother immovable, Divonne found herself charged with the ordering of the house, the superintendence of the feeding of the little ones, of the numerous household, with visiting Jean twice a week at the college at Avignon, without reckoning that the care of her patient required her attention at all hours.

A careful and sensible woman, she supplied the education which she lacked by her intelligence, her peasant's shrewdness, and the remnants of learning which remained in the cowed and disciplined Le Fénat's brain. The consul trusted her with all the expenses of the house, which had become very heavy with increased charges, and receipts—diminishing from year to year—swallowed up by the disease among the vines. All the plain had been attacked, but the home close was still clear, and it was the consul's anxious care to save it by means of investigations and experiments.

This Divonne Abrieu—who remained faithful to her head-dress and her seamstress's ring, and behaved herself so modestly in her situation of housekeeper and lady's companion—preserved the family from embarrassment in those critical years, always surrounded the sick woman with the same costly attentions, reared the little ones at their mother's side as young ladies, paid Jean's allowance regularly, first at college, then at Aix, where he went to study law, and finally at Paris, where he went to complete his education.

By what miracles of care and watchfulness she managed it all no one knew any more than herself. But every time Jean thought of Castelet, lifted his eyes to the faint and faded photograph, the first face recalled, the first name pronounced was Divonne, the large-hearted peasant, who was, he felt, on guard at his home and sustaining it by the power of her will. Since the last few days, however, since he knew what his mistress was, he avoided pronouncing this revered name, like that of his mother, and of all his friends, in her presence; even the look of the photograph troubled him, astray and out of place as it was on this wall above Sappho's bed.

One day, on coming home to dinner, he was surprised to see the table laid for three instead of two, more still on finding Fanny playing cards with a little man whom he did not recognise at first, but who, on turning round, showed the bright, wild-goat's eyes, the large nose dominating the tanned and good-looking face, the bald head and conspirator's beard of Uncle Césaire. At his nephew's exclamation, he remarked, without throwing down his cards: "You see I'm not at all dull. I'm having a game of bezique with my niece."

His niece!

And Jean, who had so carefully kept the secret from every-one! This familiarity was distasteful to him, as were also the remarks which Césaire threw out in an undertone whilst Fanny was busying herself about dinner. "My congratula-tions, youngster; what arms, what eyes, a morsel fit for a king!" Things were much worse when at table Le Fénat began to talk without any reserve about affairs at Castelet, about what brought him to Paris.

The pretext for the journey was some money he had to receive: eight thousand francs which he had lent in former days to his friend, Courbebaisse, and which he never expected to see again, when a notary's letter informed him of Courbe-baisse's death—the deuce!—and the repayment of his eight thousand francs awaiting him. But the true motive, for the money could have been sent to him, "The true motive is your mother's health, my poor boy. Since a short time back she has grown much weaker, and now sometimes her head fails her, she forgets everything, even to the little ones' names. The other evening, after your father had left her room, she asked Divonne who that good gentleman was who came to see her so often. No one has noticed this yet but your aunt, and she only told me to make me decide on coming to consult Bouchereau about the health of the poor woman whom he attended formerly."

"Have you ever had madness in your family?" asked Fanny in a pompous and solemn manner, after the style of La Gournerie.

"Never," said Le Fénat, adding with a malicious smile that he had been rather that way inclined in his youth, "but my madness was not unpleasing to the ladies, and I did not require to be shut up."

Jean looked at them, heart-broken. To the grief which the sad news caused him was added an oppressive uneasiness at hearing this woman talk of his mother, of the infirmities of her critical age, in the unrestrained language and with the experience of a matron, her elbows on the cloth, and rolling a cigarette. And the other, talkative and imprudent, let his tongue wag and discussed all the family private affairs.

Ah! the vineyards, the vineyards were done for. The home close itself would not last much longer; half the vines were diseased and one only preserved the rest by a miracle, tending each bunch, each grape, like sick children, with expensive drugs. The worst of it was, that the consul persisted in continuing to plant fresh vines which the worm attacked, instead of devoting all this good land lying useless, covered with diseased and discoloured branches, to the culture of olives and capers.

Fortunately, he, Césaire, had a few acres on the banks of the Rhone, which he was treating with immersion, a splendid discovery, feasible only in the low-lying lands. Already a good vintage encouraged him—a thin and not very generous wine—"frog's wine," as the consul disdainfully called it; but Le Fénat was obstinate too, and with Courbebaisse's eight thousand francs he was going to buy La Piboulette.

"You know, youngster, the first island on the Rhone, below Abrieu's—but this between ourselves, no one at Castelet must suspect anything yet—"

"Not even Divonne, uncle?" asked Fanny, laughing.

At his wife's name Le Fénat's eyes moistened.

"Oh! Divonne, I do nothing without her. Besides she believes in my idea, and would be so happy if her poor Césaire rebuilt the fortunes of Castelet after having begun the ruin of them."

Jean shuddered; was he then going to confess, relate the lamentable history of the forgeries? But the Provençal, all affection for Divonne, began to talk of her, of the happiness she gave him. And so pretty too, so splendidly put to-gether.

"Look here, niece, you are a woman, you should know something about it."

He handed her a photograph, which he took from his pocket-book, and which he always carried on him.

By the filial way in which Jean spoke of his aunt, by the motherly advice written in the peasant's awkward and shaky hand, Fanny had pictured to herself one of the poor Seine-et-Oise cottars, and was astounded at this pretty face with its regular features thrown out by the close white head-dress, this elegant and supple figure of a woman of thirty-five.

"Yes, very pretty," she said, pursing her lips and in a strange tone.

"And so splendidly put together!" said the uncle, who liked the illustration.

They went out on the balcony. After a sultry day, from which the zinc of the verandah was still hot, there was falling from a stray cloud a fine rain which freshened the air, tinkled gaily on the roofs and splashed the pavements. Paris was rejoicing beneath this shower, and the movement of the crowd, of the vehicles, all that rising murmur intoxicated the countryman, stirred up in his head, empty and unsteady as a bell, recollections of his youth and of a three months' stay which he had made thirty years before with his friend, Courbebaisse.

What revels, my children, what times we had! And their visit to the Prado one night in mid-Lent, Courbebaisse as Chicard and his mistress, the Mornas, as a vendor of songs— a costume which had brought her luck, as she became a music-hall celebrity. He, the uncle, had in tow a little darling they called Pellicule. And, a boy again, he laughed all over his face, hummed dance-music, seizing his niece by the waist. At midnight, when he left them for the Hôtel Cujas, the only one he knew in Paris, he sung at the top of his voice on the staircase, blew kisses to his niece who was lighting him, and called out to Jean:

"Take care of yourself, you know!"

As soon as he had gone, Fanny, whose face still wore a pre-occupied look, went quickly into her dressing-room, and through the open door, whilst Jean was going to bed, she began in almost a careless tone of voice:

"I say, she's very pretty, your aunt; I don't wonder now that you used to talk so often about her. I suppose you made poor Fénat's horns grow, he has a head for that."

He protested indignantly. Divonne! a second mother to him, who, when he was a child, tended him, dressed him. She had saved him from an illness, from death; no, never had the temptation to commit such a base act occurred to him.

"Go along, go along," continued the woman's harsh voice, her mouth full of hair-pins, "you will never make me believe that with those eyes and that fine figure of which that idiot talked, his Divonne can have had no desire towards you with your pretty fair face and girl's skin. Look you, on the banks of the Rhone or anywhere else, we are all alike."

She spoke from conviction, believing all her sex yielding to every caprice, vanquished by the first desire. He protested, but ill at ease, racking his memory, demanding of himself, whether the light touch of an innocent caress had ever warned him of any danger; and, although finding nothing, the purity of his affection remained affected, the unspotted cameo scratched as if with a nail.

"I say, look, the head-dress of your country."

On her beautiful hair, gathered into two long pleats, she had pinned a white neckerchief which resembled pretty closely the "catalane," the cap in three pieces of the girls of Châteauneuf; and standing in front of him in the milk-white folds of her night-dress, her eyes glittering, she asked:

"Am I like Divonne?"

Oh! no, not in the least; she was only like herself in this little cap, recalling the other one, that of Saint-Lazare, which made her look so pretty, they said, as she threw a parting kiss to her convict in open court: "Keep up your spirits, deary, the happy days will come back."

And the recollection of this pained him so much, that, his mistress in bed, he extinguished the light quickly, so as not to see her any longer.

Early the next morning the uncle arrived uproariously, flourishing his stick and calling out: "Now then, you children," in the brisk and patronising voice in which Courbebaisse had spoken long ago, when he came and found him in Pellicule's arms. He appeared still more excited than the day before; the Hôtel Cujas, no doubt, and above all the eight thousand francs put away in his pocket-book. The money for La Piboulette, well yes, but he had surely the right to spend a few louis of it to stand his niece a breakfast in the country!

"And Bouchereau?" remarked his nephew who could not stay away from his office two days running. It was settled that they should breakfast in the Champs-Elysées, and that the two men should go afterwards to the consultation.

That was not what Le Fénat had longed for; the arrival at Saint-Cloud in style, the carriage full of champagne; but they had a charming repast all the same on the restaurant terrace, overshadowed by acacias, and which was filled with the sounds of a morning rehearsal at the neighbouring music-hall. Césaire, very talkative, very polite, put on all his airs and graces to dazzle the Parisian lady. He hit off the waiters, complimented the cook on his sauce; and Fanny gave vent to stupid and forced laughter at some private supper-room joke which pained Gaussin, as also the intimacy growing up between the uncle and niece over his head.

One would have said they were friends of twenty years' standing. Le Fénat who grew sentimental over the wine at dessert talked of Castelet, of Divonne, and also of his little Jean; he was glad to see him with her, a steady woman, who would not allow him to go wrong. And he gave her bits of information and advice as to the young man's somewhat gloomy character and the way to manage him, as if to a young bride, tapping her on the arm, his speech thick, his eyes dead and running.

He got sober at Bouchereau's. Two hours' waiting on the first floor in the Place Vendôme, in those huge, lofty and cold rooms, full of a silent and agonised crowd; the hell of suffering, of which they traversed successively all the circles, passing from room to room to the sanctum of the celebrated doctor.

Bouchereau, with his prodigious memory, remembered Madame Gaussin perfectly, having come to a consultation at Castelet ten years before, at the beginning of her illness ; he asked for an account of the different phases of it, read over again the old prescriptions, and at once reassured the two men as to the disorder of the brain which had lately shown itself, and which he attributed to the employment of certain drugs. And whilst immovable, his great eyebrows knitted over his sharp and searching eyes, he wrote a long letter to his colleague at Avignon, the uncle and nephew listened, holding their breath, to the scratching of his pen which by itself drowned all the murmur of fashionable Paris ; and suddenly there appeared to them all the might of the modern physician, the greatest priest, supreme belief, invincible superstition.

Césaire went out serious and chilled :

"I am going back to the hotel to pack my portmanteau, the air of Paris is not good for me—see ? If I were to stop here I should make a fool of myself. I shall catch the seven o'clock train. Make my excuses to my niece, eh ?"

Jean took good care not to detain him, fearful of his childishness and levity ; and in the morning on waking, he was congratulating himself on knowing that his uncle was at home, safe, with Divonne, when he saw him appear, crestfallen, his clothes in disorder :

"Good heavens ! uncle, what has happened ?"

He sunk into a chair, speechless, motionless, at first, but recovering himself by degrees he confessed to meeting one of his old friends, a too plentiful dinner, the eight thousand francs lost in a gambling hell the night before. Not a sou left. Nothing ! How could he go home and tell this to

Divonne? And the purchase of La Piboulette. Suddenly, seized with a sort of frenzy, he covered his eyes with his hands, thrust his thumbs into his ears and, yelling, sobbing, completely beside himself, the south countryman gave vent to his feelings and expressed his remorse in a general confession of his whole life. He was a shame and disgrace to his friends; men like himself ought to be killed like wolves. Without his brother's generosity where would he be? In prison among thieves and forgers.

"Uncle, uncle," said the unhappy Gaussin trying to stop him.

But his uncle, wilfully blind and deaf, took a kind of pleasure in this public confession of his crime, related even to its smallest details, whilst Fanny looked at him with a pity mingled with admiration. He at any rate was a scapegrace of the kind she liked; and moved with compassion she was thinking of some means to help him. But which? She had seen no one for a year; Jean had no friends. Suddenly a name came into her head: Déchelette! He must be in Paris at that moment, and he was such a good-hearted fellow.

"But I hardly know him," said Jean.

"I will go myself."

"What! you would?"

"Why not?"

Their eyes met, and they understood one another. Déchelette too had been her lover, the lover of a night whom she hardly remembered. But he never forgot one of them; they were all in order in his head, like the saints in a calendar.

"If you don't like it—" she said rather awkwardly. But Césaire who during this short debate had left off yelling, turned anxiously towards them with such a look of despair-

ing supplication that Jean gave in and unwillingly consented.

How long the hour seemed to the two of them, distracted
by thoughts which they could not avow, leaning over the
balcony watching for her return.

"He lives some distance away then, this Déchelette?"

"Not at all, in the Rue de Rome, close by," answered
Jean furiously, he too thinking that Fanny was a very long
time getting back. He tried to quiet himself with the
engineer's motto in love, "no morrow," and the scornful
manner in which he had heard him speak of Sappho as a
past member of the gay throng; but his lover's pride took
offence, and he could almost have wished that Déchelette
would find her pretty and desirable. Ah! How this old
madman had opened all his old sores.

At length they saw Fanny's mantle turning the corner of
the street. She entered beaming :

"It's done ; I've got the money."

Uncle Césaire wept for joy with the eight thousand
francs spread out before him, and wanted to give a receipt,
settle the interest and the date for repayment.

"It is needless, uncle, I never mentioned your name.
It's to me that he lent the money, to me you owe it, and
for as long as you please."

"Such services, my child," answered Césaire, transported
with gratitude, "are repaid by eternal friendship." And in
the station whither Gaussin accompanied him to make
certain this time of his departure, he repeated with tears in
his eyes : "What a woman! What a treasure! You must
make her life happy, won't you?"

Jean remained very vexed at this incident, feeling his
chain, already heavy, grow tighter and tighter, and two
things getting confused which his native delicacy had

Good evening ; going on all right ?

always kept separate and distinct : his family and this connection. Now, Césaire kept his mistress informed of his
work, of his plantings, gave her the news of Castelet ; and
Fanny criticised the consul's obstinacy in the matter of the
vines, talked about his mother's health, irritated Jean with
her solicitude or her misplaced advice. No sort of allusion
to the service she had rendered, nor to Le Fénat's ancient
escapade, that blemish on the house of Armandy, which the
uncle had let out before her. Once only she made it the
excuse for a repartee under the following circumstances :

They were coming home from the theatre, and were
getting into a cab, in the rain, on a cab-rank on the boulevard. The cab, one of those old "growlers" which only ply
after midnight, took a long time to start, the driver asleep
and the beast shaking its nose-bag. Whilst they were
waiting in the cab, out of the rain, an old cabman who was
putting a new lash on his whip calmly came up to the door,
his bit of whip cord between his teeth, and said to Fanny in
a cracked voice reeking of drink :

"Good evening ; going on all right ?"

"Hullo ; you !"

She gave a little start, recovered herself quickly, and in a
low voice, to her lover : "My father !"

Her father ! this ruffian in a long livery frock-coat, soiled
with dirt, the metal buttons torn off, and showing in the
gaslight a face bloated and sodden with drink, in which
Gaussin fancied he saw a resemblance on a hideous scale to
Fanny's regular and sensual profile, her large, voluptuous
eyes ! Without troubling himself about the man who
accompanied his daughter, and as if he had not seen him,
old Legrand told her the news of the family. "The old
woman's been at the Necker hospital for the last fortnight,
she's in a bad way. Go and see her one Thursday, it'll give

her some pluck. For my part, fortunately, I've a famous
carcase, always in good condition. But trade's bad. If you
wanted a good driver by the month, it would be just the
thing for me. No? So much the worse, then, and good-
bye till next time."

They touched one another's hands ; the cab moved off.

" Well, would you believe it?" murmured Fanny ; and
all at once she began to tell him a long story about her
family—a thing she had always avoided, " it was so ugly,
so vulgar," but they knew one another better now ; they
had no need for secrets. She was born at the Moulin-aux-
Anglais in the suburbs, of this father of hers, an old dragoon,
who drove a stage between Paris and Châtillon, and an inn-
servant, between two shifts at the counter. She had never
known her mother who had died in giving birth to her ;
but her father's employers, good sort of people, made him
own the little one and pay the nurse. He dared not refuse
for he was deeply indebted to them, and when Fanny was
four years old he took her with him on the coach like a little
dog, perched up under the hood, amused at rolling thus
along the roads, looking at the light from the lanterns,
running along on either side, at seeing the backs of the
horses steam and pant, and at going to sleep in the dark, in
the breeze, with the sound of the bells in her ears.

But old Legrand soon got tired of this forced paternity ;
little as it cost he had to feed and dress the brat. Then
she stood in the way of his marriage with the widow of a
market-gardener on whose melon frames and rows of cab-
bages along his route, he had an eye. She had at that
time a firm belief that her father wanted to lose her ; it was
the drunkard's fixed idea to get rid of her at any hazard,
and if the widow herself, the good Machaume, had not taken
the little girl under her protection—

" By-the-bye, you know her, Machaume," said Fanny.

" What! the servant I saw at your place—"

"She was my step-mother. She had been so kind to me when I was young that I took her, to get her away from her blackguard of a husband who, after having squandered all her property, beat her cruelly, made her wait upon a slut with whom he lived. Ah! poor Machaume, she knows what a handsome man costs. Well! when she left me, in spite of all I could say to her, she hastened to make it up with him, and now she's in the hospital. What times he's having without her, the old rascal! how filthy he was! what a scampish look! he only cares for his whip, did you notice how straight he held it? Too drunk to walk, he would carry it in front of him like a taper, and lock it up in his room; it was the only decent thing he had about him. 'Good whip, good lash,' that's his motto."

She talked carelessly about him, as of a stranger, without disgust or shame; and Jean was horrified at hearing her. That father! That mother! what a contrast to the consul's stern face and Madame Gaussin's angelic smile! And, understanding suddenly all that was contained in her lover's silence, all the revulsion against this social quagmire with which he was polluted through her. "After all," said Fanny philosophically, "one meets that kind of thing in every family, one can't be responsible for it; I've my father, Legrand; you've your Uncle Césaire."

CHAPTER VI.

"My dear child, I am writing to you, trembling still with the anxiety we have all been in : the twins disappeared, away from Castelet during the whole of one day, one night, and the morning of the next day !

"It was on Sunday at breakfast-time that the little ones were missed. I had dressed them nicely for the eight o'clock mass where the consul was going to take them, then I thought no more about them, as I was kept at your mother's side, who, as if feeling the misfortune which was hanging over us, was more nervous than usual. You know she has always been like that since her illness, foreseeing what is about to happen ; and the less she is able to move the more her brain works.

"Your mother in her bedroom, luckily; you can see us all in the dining-room waiting for the little ones ; we shouted for them all over the farm, the shepherd blew his great horn with which he calls back the sheep. Then Césaire went in one direction and I in another, Rousseline, Tardive, all of us rushing about Castelet, and each time, on meeting : 'Well?' 'We've seen nothing.' At last we dared not ask any more ; with beating hearts we looked in the wells, under the high windows of the loft. What a day ! And I had to go up to your mother's room every moment, smile tranquilly, explain the absence of the little ones, saying I had sent them to pass the Sunday at their aunt's at Villamuris. She appeared to believe it ; but later in the evening whilst I was attending

They gently grounded among the reeds.

to her, watching through the window the lights which were flickering in the plain and by the Rhone in search of the children, I heard her crying softly in bed; and when I questioned her: 'I am crying at something which is being concealed from me, but which I have nevertheless guessed—' she said in her childish voice which has come back to her from much suffering; and without speaking any more we both of us gave ourselves up to our own grief.

"Well, my dear child, not to dwell on this painful story, on Monday morning our little ones were brought back to us by some workmen whom your uncle employs on the island, and who had found them on a heap of vine-shoots, pale from cold and hunger and the night in the open air, on the water. And this is what they told us in the innocence of their little hearts. For a long time past the idea had troubled them to do as did their patron saints, Marthe and Marie, whose story they had read—set off in an open boat without sails or oars, or provisions of any sort, and spread the gospel on the first shore whither God's breath should waft them. On Sunday then after mass, unloosing a fishing-boat and kneeling at the bottom like the holy women, whilst the current carried them away, they gently grounded among the reeds of La Pibou-lette, in spite of the heavy volume of water at this season, the wind, the 'révouluns.' Yes, God took care of them and it is He who brought them back to us, the pretty creatures! having rumpled their Sunday frocks a little and spoilt the covers of their prayer-books. We had not the heart to scold them, and received them with kisses and open arms, but the fright we have had has made us all ill.

"The one most affected is your mother who, without us saying anything about this to her, has felt, as she says, death pass over Castelet, and she, ordinarily so quiet, so cheerful, is attacked by a sadness which nothing can drive away, though your father, myself, and everyone surround her with our loving attentions. And if I told you, my Jean, that it is after you especially that she pines and yearns. She dare not own it before your father who wishes you to be left to your work, but you did not come home after the examination as you promised. Give us a surprise at Christmas ; and let our invalid put on her old smile again. If you only knew how you will regret that you did not devote more of your time to the old folks when you had the chance."

Standing at the window through which the sluggish light of a foggy winter's day was filtering, Jean read this letter, enjoying its rustic fragrance and the dear souvenirs of love and sunshine.

" What's it all about, let me see ? "

Fanny had just awoke in the yellow light admitted by the drawn curtain, and, still heavy with sleep, she stretched out her hand mechanically towards the packet of " Maryland " which was in its usual place at her bedside. He hesitated, aware of the jealousy which tore his mistress at the sole name of Divonne ; but how hide the letter whose origin and shape she recognized ?

At first the little girls' adventure touched her, as, leaning on the pillow with a cloud of brown hair about her, her arms and neck exposed, she read the letter through whilst rolling a cigarette ; but the last part roused her to fury, and tearing up and throwing the letter about the room : " Holy women be damned ! All inventions to drag you home ! She misses her handsome nephew this—"

He tried to stop her, to prevent the filthy word which she screamed out, and many others with it. Never had she behaved so coarsely before him, in this flood of obscene rage, this rent sewer letting loose its slime and stench. All the foul language of the ex-prostitute and street arab causing her neck to swell, her lip to hang.

It was easy to see what they were all after down there. Césaire had been talking, and the family was conspiring to break off their connection, to entice him into the country with pretty Divonne as a bait.

" In the first place, know, that if you go, I will write to your cuckold—I will warn him—Ah, but—!" As she spoke she gathered herself up spitefully on the bed, pale, her cheeks sunken, her features enlarged, like a savage beast ready to spring.

And Gaussin recollected having seen her thus in the Rue de l'Arcade ; but it was directed against him now, this wild hatred which tempted him to fall upon his mistress and beat her, for in these loves of the flesh, where esteem and respect for the being loved are as nothing, brutality is present always in quarrels as in caresses. He was afraid of himself, so rushed away to the office, and, as he walked along, he felt disgusted at this life which he had made for himself. This would teach him to put himself in the power of women like this ! What insults, what horrors ! His sisters, his mother, no one was spared. What ! not even the right to go and see his relations ! What prison was he shut up in then ? And, all the history of their connection coming up before his eyes, he saw how the Egyptian's beautiful bare arms, twined round his neck the evening of the ball, had fastened there despotically and fiercely, separating him from his friends, from his family. Now, however, his resolution was taken. That very evening, cost what it might, he would leave for Castelet.

Some business transacted, his leave from the office obtained, he went home early, expecting a terrible scene, prepared for anything, even a rupture. But the affectionate greeting which Fanny gave him at once, her swollen eyes and her tear-stained cheeks, hardly left him the courage of his will.

"I am going this evening," he said stiffly.

"You are right, deary ; go and see your mother, above all—" she approached him coaxingly—"forget that I was naughty ; I love you too much, it's my folly."

All the rest of the day, packing his portmanteau with coquettish solicitude, putting on all the sweetness of the old days, she kept up this repentant attitude, possibly in the hope of detaining him. But yet she never once said to him, "Stay !" and when at the last moment, having lost all hope at the sight of the final arrangements, she nestled and pressed closely to her lover, trying to impregnate him with herself, with her adieu, her kiss, during his journey and absence, only murmuring the while : "Tell me, Jean, you are not angry with me ?"

Oh ! the delight the next morning at waking up in his childhood's little room, his heart still warm from the affectionate embraces, the joy at his arrival, at finding in the same place, on the mosquito curtain of his narrow bed, the same shaft of light which his past awakenings always sought there, at hearing the cries of the peacocks on their perches, the pulley of the well creak, the quickly pattering feet of the sheep, and, when he had fastened the shutters back against the wall, at seeing the lovely warm light coming in in floods as through a sluice-gate, and the wonderful horizon of sloping vineyards, of cypresses, olive trees and glistening pine woods losing themselves in the distance beyond the Rhone under the deep and pure sky, without a trace of mist in spite of the early hour—a green sky, swept all night by the "mistral" which was still filling the immense valley with its strong and cheerful breath.

Jean compared this awakening with those at the other place, under a sky as foul as his love, and felt happy and free. He went downstairs. The house, white from the sun, was sleeping still, with the shutters all closed as if they were eyes ; and he was thankful for a moment alone—to collect himself—in this moral convalescence which he felt beginning within him.

He took a few turns on the terrace, ascended a steep path in the park, or what they called the park, a grove of pines and myrtles growing at hazard on the rough hillside of Castelet, intersected by rough paths slippery with dry pine spikes. His dog, Miracle, very old and lame, had come out of his kennel, and was following silently at his heels; they had so often taken this morning walk together before !

At the entrance to the vineyards, whose great cypresses enclosing them were nodding their lofty heads, the dog hesitated ; he knew how uncomfortable the ground covered with a thick layer of sand—a new device against the phylloxera to which the consul was giving a trial—would be to his old paws, not less than the steep gradients of the terrace. The pleasure of following his master decided him nevertheless ; and at each obstacle there were painful efforts, timid whines, halts and sprawlings like a crab on a rock. Jean did not look at him, being solely taken up with the new Alicante vine-stock of which his father had given him a long account the day before. The stocks appeared to be of a fine growth on the level and glistening sand. At last the poor man was going to be repaid for his desperate pains ; Castelet might revive when La Nerte, Hermitage, all the great vineyards of the South, had perished !

A little white cap rose suddenly in front of him. It was Divonne who was the first in the house to rise ; she had a pruning-knife in her hand, and something else which she

threw away, and her cheeks, usually so pale. blushed scarlet :
" It's you, Jean ? you frightened me.   I thought it was your
father."   Then recovering herself, she kissed him :   " Did
you sleep well ?"

" Very well, aunt; but why did you fear my father's coming ?"

" Why ?"

She picked up the vine-root which she had just torn up.

" The consul told you, did he not, that this time he was
sure of succeeding ?   Well, look ! behold the beast."

Jean looked at the small yellowish moss fretting the wood,
the imperceptible mouldiness, which, spreading from one to
another, has ruined entire provinces.   And it was an irony
of nature, on this splendid morning, under the life-giving
sun, this tiny atom, destructive and indestructible.

" This is the beginning.   In three months the whole
home close will be eaten up, and your father will begin over
again, for he has set his pride on it.   It will be new plants,
remedies, until—"

A despairing gesture ended and emphasised the sentence.

" Really ! it has come to that ?"

" Oh ! you know the consul.   He says nothing, gives me
the housekeeping money every month as usual ; but I can
see he is anxious.   He goes off to Avignon, to Orange : it is to
procure money."

" And Césaire ?   The immersions ?" asked the young man
in consternation.

God be thanked all was going on well there.   They had
had fifty barrels of ordinary wine the last vintage ; and this
year would produce double.   As a consequence of this success, the consul had made over to his brother all the vineyards in the plain, which hitherto had lain fallow, rows of
dead posts like a country cemetery, and now they had all

been under water three months. And, proud of her husband's, her Fénat's work, the Provençal shewed Jean from the elevated spot where they stood great ponds dammed up with chalk, like at the salt works.

"In two years that growth will yield; so also in two years will La Piboulette, and again the island of Lamotte, which your uncle bought without saying a word. Then we shall be rich, but we must hold on till then, and every one must contribute and make a sacrifice."

She spoke so cheerfully of sacrifice, as a woman who found nothing astonishing in it, and with such a moving impulse that Jean, struck with a sudden idea, answered in the same voice: "Sacrifices shall be made, Divonne."

That same day he wrote to Fanny that his parents would not be able to continue his allowance, that he would be reduced to his salary, and that under these circumstances their living together would be impossible. It was breaking off earlier than he had intended, three or four years before the foreseen departure ; but he relied on his mistress accepting these grave reasons, pitying him and his trouble, and aiding him in the painful accomplishment of a duty.

Was it really a sacrifice ? Was he not on the contrary pleased to end an existence which seemed to him odious and unwholesome, especially since he had returned to nature, to his family, to simple and pure affections ? His letter written without a struggle or a pang, he counted—to defend him from the furious answer, full of threats and extravagances which he foresaw—on the honest and faithful tenderness of the kind hearts which surrounded him, the example of his father, upright and proud amongst them all, on the open smile of the little "saints," and also on the great peaceful horizon, healthy with the air from the mountains, the lofty sky, the rapid and hurrying river ; for when he thought on his passion, on all the vile things of which it was made up, he seemed to be issuing from a pernicious fever such as one catches from the exhalations of marshy ground.

The deed done, five or six days passed in silence. Morning and evening Jean went to the post and returned, much troubled, with empty hands. What was she doing? What decision had she taken, and, in any case, why did she not write? He thought of nothing else. And at night when every one at Castelet was asleep with the lulling sound of the wind in the long corridors, they talked of it, Césaire and he, in his little room.

"She is capable of coming herself," said his uncle; and his anxiety increased for this reason that he had been obliged to put in the envelope of the fatal letter, two bills, at six months and a year, settling his debt and the interest. How should he meet these bills? How explain to Divonne? He shuddered at the mere thought of it, and pained his nephew when, the sitting over, with his great nose projecting, and shaking his pipe, he said to him sadly: "Well, good night; at all events you have acted right in the matter."

At last the answer arrived, and at the first lines: "My dear old man, I did not write before because I wanted to prove to you, otherwise than by words, how much I understand and love you—" Jean stopped, surprised like a man who hears a symphony when he is fearing a jig. He turned quickly to the last page where he read "—remain until death your dog—who loves you, whom you may beat, and who embraces you passionately—"

She had not received his letter then! But, read line by line, and with tears in his eyes, there was no doubt about its being an answer, saying that Fanny had long expected the bad news, the distress at Castelet bringing about the inevitable separation. She had at once set about looking for employment, in order no longer to be a charge on him, and had happened on the management of a hotel in the Avenue du Bois-de-Boulogne on behalf of a very rich lady. One hundred francs a month, board and lodging, and her liberty on Sunday.

"You understand, old man, one whole day every week to love one another, for you are still willing, are you not? You will recompense me for the great effort I am making, in working for the first time in my life, for this slavery by night and day which I am accepting, with humiliations which you cannot picture, and which will weigh very heavily on my mania to be independent. But I feel an extraordinary satisfaction in suffering for love of you. I owe you so much; you have made me understand so many good and honest things of which no one had ever spoken to me! Ah! if we had only met before! But you were in long clothes when I was lying in men's arms. But not one of them can boast of having inspired me with such a resolution in order to keep to him a day longer. You can come back as soon as you like now; the rooms are ready for you. I have collected all my things; that was the hardest of all; routing out drawers and keepsakes. You will only find my portrait, that will cost you nothing; only kind looks which I beg for on its behalf. Ah! deary, deary. Well, if only you will keep Sunday for me, and my place on your breast—my place, you know—" and then dotings and coaxings, the voluptuous licking of a mother cat, and words of passion which made the lover rub his face against the glossy paper, as if it contained for him a warm, human caress.

"She says nothing about my bills?" asked Uncle Césaire, timidly.

"She sends them back to you. You are to pay her when you are rich."

His uncle gave a sigh of relief, his temples wrinkled with happiness, and with wise-looking gravity, he exclaimed, in his loud Southern accents :

"Would you like me to tell you? That woman is a saint."

Then passing to another order of ideas, with that inconstancy, that lack of logic and memory, one of the ludicrous points in his nature : "And what passion, my boy, what fire! My mouth is parched at the thought of it, as when Courbebaisse read me the Mornas's correspondence."

Once more Jean had to submit to the first journey to Paris, the Hôtel Cujas, Pellicule; but he did not listen, leaning out of the window opening on the hushed night, bathed in the light of a full moon, so brilliant that the cocks were deceived, and saluted it as the dawning day.

So then, it was true, this redemption by love of which poets talk; and he had a feeling of pride at thinking that all those great, those celebrated men who had been loved by Fanny before him, far from reforming her, had thrust her down deeper still, whilst he by the sole force of his goodness would, perhaps, rescue her from vice for evermore.

He was grateful to her for having hit upon this middle course, this half separation by which she would learn new habits of work so difficult to her indolent disposition ; and he wrote the next day in the paternal tone of an old gentleman to encourage her reform, to express his uneasiness at the kind of hotel she was managing, the people who came there ; for he mistrusted her indulgence, and the facility with which she would say, in yielding herself up : "What would you? I can't help it."

By return of post, with the docility of a little girl, Fanny drew a picture of the hotel, a real family hotel inhabited by foreigners. On the first floor some Peruvians, father and mother, numerous children and servants ; on the second, some Russians and a rich Dutch coral merchant. The rooms on the third floor lodged two riders at the Hippodrome, swell Englishmen, highly respectable ; and a most interesting little family, Mademoiselle Minna Vogel, a zither player from Stuttgard, and her brother Léo, a poor little consumptive fellow, obliged to leave off his clarionette lessons at the Paris Conservatoire, and whom his elder sister had come to nurse, without other resource beyond what was produced by a few concerts to pay for their lodging and keep.

"One could not imagine anything more touching or proper, as you see, my dear old man. As to myself, I pass for a widow, and am shown the greatest possible consideration. I would not permit that it were otherwise ; your wife must be respected. When I say 'your wife' do not misunderstand me. I know that you will go away some day, that I shall lose you, but after that, never another ; I shall remain yours for ever, retaining the recollection of your caresses and the good instincts which you have roused in me. It seems very comical, does it not? Sappho virtuous! Yes, virtuous when you will no longer be there ; but for you I remain as you have loved me, frenzied and ardent — I adore you —"

Suddenly Jean was seized with an immense wearied sadness. These returns of the prodigal son, after the joys of arrival, the feast of the fatted calf and the loving attentions, always suffer by comparison with the delights of a wandering life, the bitter acorns and the lazy flock. It is a disenchantment with regard to things and beings suddenly losing their specious attraction. The Provençal winter mornings had no longer for him their healthy cheerfulness, nor the hunt along the banks after the pretty reddish-brown otters its attraction, nor shooting ducks in old Abrieu's pond. Jean found the wind disagreeable, the water rough, and the walks among the flooded vineyards very tiresome, with his uncle explaining his system of sluices, dams and supply-trenches.

The village, which he had visited during his joyous walks of the first few days, old huts, some of them empty, reminded one of the death and desolation of an Italian village; and when he went to the post he had to linger on the tottering doorstep of each, and listen to the everlasting repetitions of these old men, bent like trees exposed to the wind, wearing pieces of knitted stockings on their arms, and of these old women with their chins the colour of yellow box-wood under their close-fitting caps, with their little eyes glittering and dancing like those of lizards in old walls.

Always the same lamentations over the death of the vines, the failure of the madder, the disease of the mulberry-trees, the seven plagues of Egypt ruining this beautiful country of Provence; and, to avoid them, he returned sometimes by the shelving lanes which run along the ancient walls of the Château des Papes, deserted lanes choked with brush-wood, with those great "herbes de Saint-Roch" which cure diseases of the skin, well placed in this middle-age nook, under the shadow of the enormous ruin rising high above it.

Then he would meet the Curé Malassagne coming from mass and descending the hill with furious strides, his bands askew, his cassock held up in both hands because of the briars and teazles. The priest would stop and thunder against the impiety of the peasants, the infamy of the Town Council; he hurled his malediction on the fields, the beasts, and the men, wretches who did not go to church, who buried their dead without the sacraments, tried to heal themselves by magnetism, spiritualism, to spare themselves the priest and the doctor.

The priest would stop and thunder against the impiety of the peasants.

Jean would return to Castelet and stow himself in the hollow of a rock.

"Yes, sir, spiritualism! that is what our peasants have come to. And you wonder that the vines are diseased!"

Jean, who had Fanny's letter open and glowing in his pocket, would listen with an absent look, escape the priest's homily as quickly as possible, return to Castelet and stow himself in the hollow of a rock, in what the Provençals call a "cagnard," sheltered from the wind which whistles all around, and concentrating the sun's rays reverberating from the stone.

He would choose the one furthest off, the wildest one, surrounded by brambles and kermes oaks, and throw himself down to read his letter; and little by little, from the delicate scent which it gave out, the loving words, the scenes which it conjured up, there would steal over him a sensual intoxication which hastened his pulse, caused an hallucination which wiped away as useless ornament the river, the bosky islands, the villages in the hollows of the Alpilles, the whole curve of the immense valley where the gusts of wind pursued the dust, and rolled it along in clouds. He was far away, in their room, in front of the railway station with its grey roof, a prey to those mad caresses, those furious desires, which made them cling to each other with the contortions of drowning persons.

All at once there are steps on the path, ringing laughs. "He's there!" His sisters appear, their little bare legs in the lavender, led by old Miracle, quite proud at having tracked his master, and wagging his tail victoriously; but Jean would kick him away, and decline the timid offers to play hide-and-seek or race. And yet he loved them, these little twin sisters doting on their brother who was always so far away; and he had made a child of himself to please them since the moment of his arrival, amused himself at the contrast between these pretty creatures, born at the

same time and yet so unlike each other. The one, tall,
dark, with curly hair, at once mystical and wayward; it
was she who, carried away by the priest's readings, had had
the idea of the boat, and this little Egyptian Marie had
persuaded the fair Marthe, who was soft and gentle, like her
mother and brother.

But how horribly out of place, whilst he was dwelling on
his memories, to see the coaxings of these little children
mingling with the coquettish perfume from his mistress's
letter. "No, leave me, I must work." And he would go
into the house with the intention of shutting himself in his
room, when his father's voice would call him as he passed.

"Is that you, Jean? come and listen to this."

The post brought fresh reasons for moroseness to this
man, already gloomy by nature, retaining from the East a
habit of silent gravity broken by abrupt recollections—
"When I was consul at Hong-Kong—" which burst out like
the crackling of fagots on a large fire. While he listened to
his father reading and discussing the morning papers, Jean
would look at Caoudal's Sappho on the chimneypiece, her
arms clasping her knees, her lyre at her side—"the whole
gamut"— a bronze bought twenty years before, when they
were adorning Castelet, and this hackneyed bronze which
sickened him in the shop-windows of Paris gave him here in
his loneliness an amorous feeling, a desire to kiss those
shoulders, to embrace those cold and polished arms, to have
said to him : "Sappho, for *you*, but for you only !"

The tempting image would rise when he left the room,
walk with him, echo the sound of his steps on the great
stately staircase. It was Sappho's name which the pendulum
of the old clock sang in measure, which the wind murmured
through the cold flagged corridors of the estival dwelling,
her name which he found in all the books of the country

library, old volumes with red edges, preserving between the leaves the crumbs of his childhood's luncheons. And this oppressing memory of his mistress pursued him even into his mother's room where Divonne was doing the invalid's hair, brushing back the beautiful white tresses from her face, which remained calm and rosy, in spite of varied and perpetual tortures.

"Ah! here's Jean," his mother would say. But, with her bare neck, her little cap, her sleeves turned up for this toilet of which she had the sole charge, his aunt reminded him of other awakenings, conjured up his mistress again, leaping out of bed in the clouds of her first cigarette. He was angry with himself for such thoughts, in this room above all! Yet what could he do to escape them?

"Our child is no longer the same, sister," Madame Gaussin would say sadly. "What is the matter with him?" And together they would search for the reason. Divonne racked her innocent head, she would have liked to question the young man; but he seemed to fly from her now, to avoid being alone with her.

Once, having watched him, she came and surprised him in his nook, in the fever of his letters and evil dreams. He rose, looking sulky. She detained him, and sat down by him on the warm stone: "You love me no longer then? I'm no longer your Divonne to whom you used to tell all your troubles?"

"Yes, yes," he stammered, confused by her tender manner, and turning away his eyes, that she should not see in them anything of what he had been reading, cries of love, despairing appeals, the frenzy of a distant passion.

"What ails you? Why are you so sad?" murmured Divonne with wheedlings of voice and gesture, such as one has for children. He was still her little one, still

ten years old to her, the age when little men get their
freedom.

He, already ardent from his reading, was carried away by
the overpowering charms of this beautiful body so near his
own, by this fresh mouth with its colour heightened by the
breeze which disturbed her hair and blew it over her forehead
in delicate waves in the Parisian fashion. And Sappho's
lessons, "all women are alike, in the presence of a man they
have but one idea in their heads," caused him to see a chal-
lenge in the peasant's happy smile, in her gesture to detain
him in tender conversation.

All at once he felt an evil temptation rush upon him;
and the effort which he made to resist it shook him in a
convulsive shudder. Divonne was frightened to see him so
pale, his teeth chattering. "Ah! poor boy, he has got a
fever." With a movement of unreflecting kindness she took
off the large neckerchief she had round her to put it on him;
but suddenly seized, enfolded, she felt the burning of mad
kisses on her neck, her shoulders, on all the glistening flesh
which had just burst forth in the sun. She had not time to
cry out nor to defend herself, perhaps she had not even a
just idea of what had passed. "Ah! I'm mad, I'm mad."
He was rushing, already far off, over the common, the
stones of which were rolling with a sinister sound under
his feet.

At breakfast that day Jean announced that he was going
away the same evening, recalled by an order from the
Minister. "Going away, already! but you said— you have
only just come." And then there were cries and beseechings.
But he could no longer remain with them, since among all their
fondnesses the agitating and corrupting influence of Sappho
intervened. Besides, had he not made a great sacrifice in
giving up living with her? The complete separation would

bring itself about later ; and he would come back to love and embrace those dear ones without shame or fear.

It was night, the house asleep, the lights out, when Césaire returned from seeing his nephew to the train at Avignon. Having given the horse his corn, and having scrutinised the sky—that look at the weather-signs, of men who live by the soil—he was going into the house, when he saw a white form on one of the seats on the terrace.

" Is that you, Divonne ? "

"Yes, I was waiting for you."

Being very busy all day, separated from her Fénat whom she adored, they would meet thus in the evening to talk, or take a walk together. Was it the short scene between Jean and herself, understood, and more so than she cared for, now that she had thought it over, or the emotion at having seen the poor mother weeping silently all day ? Her voice was strange, her mind disturbed to an extent extraordinary with her, the calm woman of duty. " Do you know anything? Why did he leave us so suddenly ? " She did not believe this story of the Minister, suspecting rather some evil attachment which was dragging the boy far from his family. So many dangers, so many fatal meetings in that ruinous Paris !

Césaire, who could hide nothing from her, acknowledged that there was in fact a woman in Jean's life, but a good creature, incapable of estranging him from his relations ; and he spoke of her devotion, the touching letters she had written, praised above all the courageous resolution which she had taken of working, a thing which seemed quite natural to the peasant woman : " For after all, one must work to live."

" Not a woman of that kind though," said Césaire.

" Was it a good-for-nothing then with whom Jean lived ? And you went to see him there ? "

"I swear to you, Divonne, that since she has known him there is no chaster, no better woman. Love has reformed her."

But Divonne did not understand these subtle distinctions. For her, this lady came under the head of what she called "bad women," and the thought that her Jean was the prey of such a creature filled her with indignation. If the consul should come to know of it !

Césaire tried to calm her, and his jolly and rather sensuous face all wrinkles, assured her that at the boy's age he could not do without a woman. "Well then, let him marry," she said with a touching conviction.

"After all they are no longer together, it's always something."

Then, in a grave voice, she said : "Listen, Césaire ; you know that they say : 'The evil that a man does lives after him.' If, as you say, Jean has really lifted this woman out of the mire, he has very likely soiled himself sadly in the task. Possibly he has made her better and more virtuous ; but who can tell whether the evil that was in her has not corrupted our child to the heart ?"

They returned towards the terrace. A peaceful and clear night over all the silent valley where nothing was moving but the gliding moonlight, the swelling stream, the ponds like plashes of silver. One breathed the quiet, the remoteness from all, the profound repose of dreamless slumber. Suddenly the up-train going at full speed made its rumbling sound heard along the banks of the Rhone.

"Oh, Paris !" said Divonne, shaking her fist towards the enemy on whom the country vents all its anger, "Paris ! what do we give you and what do you send us back ?"

They had taken each other's hands.

CHAPTER VII.

It was cold and foggy, an afternoon dusky at four o'clock, even in the broad avenue of the Champs-Elysées, where the carriages were rolling along with a deadened sound. Jean could with difficulty read at the end of a little garden, with open gate, the large painted letters, above the mezzanine floor of a house which had the luxurious and quiet appearance of a villa: "Furnished apartments, family boarding-house." A brougham was waiting close to the pavement.

Having opened the door of the office Jean saw her at once, she whom he sought, sitting in the light of the window, turning over a large account-book opposite another woman, tall and elegant, a handkerchief and a little reticule in her hands.

"What can I do for you, sir?" Fanny recognised him, rose, dumbfounded, and passing in front of the lady: "It's the youngster," she said in a low voice. The other examined Gaussin from head to foot, with that superb coolness which experience gives, and then added aloud, without embarrassment: "Embrace, my children. I am not looking at you." Then she took Fanny's place and continued checking the accounts.

They had taken each other's hands, were whispering empty phrases: "How are you?" "Pretty well, thanks." "Then you started yesterday evening?" But their strained voices gave the words their true significance. And, seated on the sofa, recovering herself a little: "You did not recognise my mistress?" asked Fanny in an undertone, "yet you have seen her before, at Déchelette's ball, as a Spanish bride; rather a faded bride."

"Then it is—"

"Rosario Sanchès, De Potter's woman."

This Rosario, Rosa for short, whose name was written on all the looking-glasses of the night restaurants, and always with some obscenity beneath it, was an ex-performer at the Hippodrome, celebrated in the fast world for her cynical brazenness and her smart sayings, which were very much in vogue among club-men whom she managed like her horses.

A Spaniard from Oran, she had been handsome rather than pretty, and her coal black eyes and eyebrows joining in one straight line, were still sufficiently attractive by gaslight; but here, even in this failing light, she had her fifty years stamped on her harsh, expressionless face, with its wrinkled skin yellow as the lemon of her native land. Intimate for years with Fanny Legrand, she had chaperoned her in gay life, and her name alone horrified the lover.

Fanny, who understood the trembling arm, tried to excuse herself. To whom could she apply to find a situation? She was very much embarrassed. Besides, Rosa was keeping quiet now; rich, very rich, living in her mansion in the Avenue de Villiers or at her villa at Enghien, receiving a few old friends, but one lover only, always the same one, her musician.

"De Potter?" asked Jean. "I thought he was married."

"Yes, married, and the father of a family. It seems even that his wife is pretty; that did not prevent him from returning to his old flame; and if you could but see how she speaks to him, how she treats him. Ah! he is badly bitten, that one." She pressed his hand in tender reproach.

The lady at that moment interrupted her task, and

addressed her reticule which was moving about at the end of its cord.

"Come, do keep still." Then, to the manageress, in a tone of command: "Give me a bit of sugar for Bichito, quick!"

Fanny rose and brought the sugar, which she held near the mouth of the reticule with little coaxings and childish expressions. "Look at the pretty creature," said she to her lover, showing him, all surrounded with wadding, a kind of large lizard, unshapely and rough, crested, serrated, its hooded-head of shivering and gelatinous flesh; a chameleon sent to Rosa from Algeria, and which she was preserving in the Parisian winter by dint of attentions and warmth. She adored it as she had never done a man; and Jean recognised at once, from Fanny's fond endearments, the position which the horrible beast held in the house.

The lady closed the book, in readiness to start. "Not bad for the second fortnight. Only, look sharp after the candles."

She threw her look of ownership round the neat well-kept little room, its furniture covered with stamped velvet, blew a little dust off the yucca of a round table, noticed a hole in the lace curtains; after which she said to the young people, with a knowing look: "No nonsense, children; the house is very respectable," and getting into the carriage which was waiting at the door, she went off for her drive in the Bois.

"Isn't it a bore?" said Fanny. "I have them down on me, she or her mother, twice a week. The mother is more awful, more skinflint still. I must love you, indeed, to stop in this den. Well, you are here at any rate. I have got you again! I was so afraid—" Standing up, she folded him in a long embrace, lip to lip, satisfying herself from the trembling caress that she was still all to him. But people were passing backwards and forwards in the passage, and they had to be on their guard. When the lamp was brought, she sat down in her usual place, with some work in her hands ; he close to her, as if he were a visitor

"Am I changed, eh ? Am I little enough like myself ?"

She smiled, showing her crochet-work which she set about with the awkwardness of a little girl. She had always detested needlework ; a book, her piano, her cigarette, or her sleeves rolled up for the confection of some dainty, she had never employed herself otherwise. But here, what was there to do ? The drawing-room piano ? She could not dream of such a thing all day, being forced to remain in the office. Novels ? She knew more than they had to tell. In default of the prohibited cigarette, she had taken to this lace which occupied her fingers, and left her at liberty to think, understanding now the taste women have for these trifling occupations which formerly she despised.

And whilst she was catching up her thread clumsily, with a carefulness resulting from inexperience, Jean looked at her sitting in her plain dress, her little stiff collar, her hair lying flat on the antique roundness of her head, and her look, so straightforward and rational. Without, in all their luxurious adornment, the crowd of fashionable women rolled by, perched up on their phaetons, going back towards the noisy boule-vards ; and Fanny did not seem to have a regret for this glaring and triumphant vice in which she could have borne her part, but disdained it for his sake. If only he would consent to see her from time to time she would accept gladly this life of slavery, would even find an amusing side to it.

All the lodgers adored her. The women, foreigners, without taste, consulted her about their toilet purchases. In the morning she gave singing lessons to the eldest of the little Peruvian girls, and whether it was a book to read or a play to see, she advised the gentlemen, who treated her with every respect, every attention; one especially, the Dutchman on the second floor. "He seats himself where you are, remains in contemplation until I say to him: 'Kuyper, you bother me.' Then he says, 'pien,' and goes off. It was he who gave me this little coral brooch. You know, it's worth about five francs; I accepted it for the sake of peace."

A waiter entered carrying a loaded tray which he placed on one side of the table, moving back the green plant a little. "I dine here all alone an hour before the table-d'hôte." She pointed out two dishes on the long and plentiful bill of fare. The manageress had only a right to two dishes and soup. "Isn't she stingy, that Rosario? However, I prefer dining there; I need not talk, and I can read your letters which keep me company."

She interrupted herself again to get a tablecloth, some table napkins; she was disturbed at every moment, an order to give, a cupboard to open, a claim to satisfy. Jean saw that he would be in her way if he remained longer; moreover, her dinner was being served; it was so pitiful, the little soup tureen holding one portion, which was smoking on the table, giving them both the same thought, the same regret of their old tête-a-têtes!

"Till Sunday, till Sunday," she murmured softly, as she dismissed him. And as they could not kiss because of the servants, the lodgers, who were coming downstairs, she had taken his hand, pressing it long against her heart to make the caress enter there.

All the evening, all night, he thought of her, pained at her humiliating slavery under that horrid woman and her great lizard; then the Dutchman made him feel uneasy, too, and until Sunday he hardly lived. In reality, this half separation, which was going to soften the shock of the final one, was for her as the cut of the pruner's knife which re-animates the worn-out tree. They wrote one another almost every day affectionate notes like those that lovers scribble in their impatience; or else, after his work was over, they had a pleasant chat in her office during the hour of needlework.

She had said at the hotel, speaking of him, "One of my relations," and under cover of this vague description, he was able sometimes to pass the evening in her room, feeling a thousand leagues from Paris. He made the acquaintance of the Peruvian family, with its innumerable young ladies, dressed up in gaudy colours, ranged round the drawing-room like birds on a perch. He listened to Mademoiselle Minna Vogel's zither, herself garlanded like a hop-pole, and saw her consumptive brother following passionately with his head the rhythm of the music, and running his fingers over an imaginary clarionette—the only one he was allowed to play. He played whist with Fanny's Dutchman, a great, bald numbskull, with a sordid look, who had navigated all the oceans of the world, and who, when one asked him for some information about Australia, where he had just passed some months, answered, rolling his eyes: "Just guess the price of potatoes at Melbourne," having never been struck but by this one fact—the dearness of potatoes in all the countries he visited.

Fanny was the soul of these assemblies, talked, sang, played the well-informed and worldly Parisian; and what remained in her of Bohemia or the studio, escaped the notice of these foreigners, or seemed to them the height of taste. She dazzled them by her familiarity with the celebrities of art and literature, gave the Russian lady, who doted on Dejoie's works, information as to the novelist's habits in writing, the number of cups of coffee which he drank in a

night, the exact and ridiculous sum which the publishers of
" Cenderinette " had paid him for the masterpiece which was
making their fortune. And his mistress's success made
Gaussin so proud that he forgot to be jealous, would have
given his word upon it, if anyone had cast a doubt.

Whilst he admired her, in this quiet drawing-room lighted
by the shaded lamps, pouring out tea, accompanying the
young girls' songs, giving them the advice of an elder sister,
it was a singular sensation to him to picture her widely
different when she arrived at his place on Sunday morning,
wet through, shivering, and without even approaching the
fire, which was blazing in her honour, undressing hastily, and
slipping into the large bed by the side of her lover. Then
what embracings, what long caresses, in which all the
restraints of the week were avenged, this privation of each
other which kept their amorous desires alive.

The hours passed, were lost count of; they did not stir
from bed until evening. There was no temptation to be
elsewhere, no pleasure, no one to see, not even the Hetténas,
who, from motives of economy, had decided on living in the
country. The little breakfast made ready, they listened
languidly to the roar of the Parisian Sunday in the muddy
streets, the whistle of the trains, the rolling of the loaded
cabs, and the rain falling in large drops on the zinc of the
balcony, the quick throbbing of their breasts beating time
to this absence of life, without a notion of the hour, till dusk.

The gas, which was being lit opposite them, threw a pale
ray of light on the hangings; they had to get up, Fanny
being obliged to be in at seven. In the half-light of the
room, all her annoyances, all her disgusts, came upon her
again, more weighty, more cruel, as she put on her boots,
still wet from her walk, her petticoats, her working dress,
the black uniform of poor women.

And to increase her grief, there were all the beloved objects around her—the furniture, the little dressing-room of the happy days. She tore herself away: "Come!" And in order to remain longer together, Jean escorted her; keeping close to each other they walked slowly up the Avenue des Champs-Elysées, whose double row of gas-standards, with the Arc de Triomphe at the end, far off in the shade, and two or three stars peeping out in a bit of sky, formed the basis of a diorama. At the corner of the Rue Pergolèse, close to the hotel, she lifted her little veil for a last kiss, and left him, lost, disgusted with his rooms, to which he went home as late as possible, cursing his poverty, almost angry with them at Castelet for the sacrifice which he was imposing on himself for their sakes.

For two or three months they dragged on this existence, which became at last absolutely insupportable, Jean having been obliged to restrict his visits to the hotel, on account of some servants' gossip, and Fanny more and more exasperated at the avarice of the Sanchès, mother and daughter. She thought silently of setting up their little home again, and suspected that her lover, too, was relenting; but she preferred that he should be the first to speak.

One Sunday in April, Fanny arrived more gaily dressed than usual, in a round hat, a spring costume, very simple— she was not rich—but showing off her graceful figure.

"Get up, quick, we are going to lunch in the country."

"In the country?"

"Yes, at Enghien, with Rosa. She has invited both of us." He said "No" at first, but she insisted. Rosa would never forgive a refusal. "You can well consent for my sake. I think I do enough."

It was on the borders of the lake at Enghien, with an

The meal had begun when they arrived.

144.

immense lawn sloping down to a little bay where some yawls
and gondolas were lying, a large cottage, wonderfully
decorated and furnished, whose ceilings and mirror panels
reflected the glittering water, the superb elms of a park
which was already budding forth in early foliage and lilac
flowers. The correct liveries, the walks which not a twig
disfigured, did honour to the double supervision of Rosario
and old Pilar.

The meal had begun when they arrived, a wrong direction
having sent them wandering for an hour round the lake,
amongst lanes running between high garden walls. Jean's
confusion was complete at the cold reception of the mistress
of the house, furious at having been kept waiting, and the
extraordinary appearance of the old witches, to whom Rosa,
in her trooper's voice, introduced them. Three "élégantes,"
as the gay ladies are called among themselves, three old
baggages who were amongst the glories of the Second
Empire, and owned names as famous as those of a great poet
or a victorious general—Wilkie Cob, Sombreuse, Clara
Desfous.

Elegant they certainly were still, bedizened out in the
latest fashion, in spring colours, deliciously dressed like dolls
from collar to boots ; but so faded, painted, made up ! Sombreuse, without eyelashes, her eyes lifeless, her lip hanging,
fumbling about for her plate, her fork, her glass ; Desfous,
enormous, blotchy, a hot-water bottle at her feet, spreading
out on the cloth her poor gouty twisted fingers with their
sparkling rings, as difficult to get on and off as the rings of
a puzzle. And Cob, very thin, with a girlish figure, which
rendered more hideous her gaunt head like a sick clown's
under its shock of towy hair. Ruined and sold up, she had
been to Monte-Carlo to venture a last throw, and had
returned without a sou, madly in love with a handsome

croupier, who would have none of her ; Rosa, having offered her a home, was keeping her, and taking great credit to herself on the strength of it.

All these women knew Fanny, and greeted her patronizingly. "How are you, little one?" The fact was that, with her dress at three francs a yard, without other jewellery than Kuyper's red brooch, she had the air of a recruit among these horrible veterans in gallantry, who were made to look more spectral still by this luxurious setting, by all the light reflected from the lake and the sky, entering loaded with spring fragrance by the dining-room doors.

Old mother Pilar was there, too, the "chinge," as she even called herself in her Franco-Spanish jabber, a true baboon, with colourless and shrivelled skin, a savage malignity on her grinning features, her grey hair cropped close like a boy's, and a great blue sailor's collar over her old black satin dress.

"And lastly, Monsieur Bichito," said Rosa, concluding the introduction of her guests, and showing Gaussin a heap of rose-coloured wadding, amidst which the chameleon was shivering on the cloth.

"Well, and what about me, am I not to be introduced?" inquired, in a tone of forced joviality, a great fellow, with grizzly moustaches, very correctly got up, but rather stiff in his fancy waistcoat and high collar.

"Yes, what about Tatave?" said the women, laughing. The mistress of the house named him carelessly.

Tatave was De Potter, the clever composer, the popular author of "Claudia" and "Savanarola," and Jean, who had only caught glimpses of him at Déchelette's, was surprised to find in the great artist such a cold manner, his face, as it were, a wooden mask, harsh and expressionless, colourless eyes revealing a mad, incurable passion which for years

past had bound him to this vile woman, made him leave
wife and children, to remain a hanger-on in this house
where he squandered part of his large fortune, his profits from
the theatres, and where he was treated worse than a servant.
It was something to see Rosa's bored look when he began
speaking, and the scornful manner in which she silenced
him; and, taking her cue from her daughter, Pilar never
failed to add, in a decided tone:

"Shut up, my boy."

Jean had her as his neighbour, and those old chops,
grunting as she chewed her food like some animal, that inquisitive glance into his plate, put to torture the young
man, already embarrassed by Rosa's patronizing tone as she
chaffed Fanny about the musical evenings at the hotel, and
the simplicity of those poor greenhorns who took the
manageress for some lady of quality who had fallen on evil
days. The old circus lady, bloated with unhealthy fat,
with uncut stones worth ten thousand francs in each ear,
seemed to begrudge her friend the renewal of youth and
beauty which her young and handsome lover had communicated to her; and Fanny did not lose her temper, but on the
contrary she amused all the table, made fun of the lodgers,
of the Peruvian who confessed to her—rolling the whites of
his eyes—his desire to know a "grande coucoute," and the
speechless courting, as he puffed like a seal, of the Dutchman, gasping behind her chair: "How much should you say
potatoes cost in Batavia?"

Jean was far from laughing, for his part; and Pilar also,
being too much taken up with keeping an eye on her
daughter's silver plate, or, having espied a fly on a dish in
front of her or on her neighbour's sleeve, suddenly making
a dash at it, and presenting it, jabbering fond words, "Eat,
mi alma; eat, *mi ccrazón,*" to the hideous little beast

stretched out on the cloth, withered, wrinkled, shapeless as Desfous's fingers.

Occasionally, having put them all to flight, she saw one on the sideboard or the glass door-panel, and jumped up and captured it triumphantly. This performance, constantly repeated, annoyed her daughter, who was evidently very nervous that morning.

"Don't be getting up at every moment, it's wearying."

With the same kind of voice, but in which the accent was more marked, the mother answered: "You are stuffing yourself, why should he not eat?"

"Leave the table or keep quiet, you worry us."

The old woman retaliated, and they began to abuse one another like pious Spaniards, mixing up the devil and hell with the language of the gutter.

"*Hija del demonio.*"

"*Cuerno de Satanás.*"

"*Puta!*"

"*Mi madre!*"

Jean looked at them terrified, whilst the other guests, accustomed to these family scenes, went on quietly eating. Only De Potter interposed out of consideration for the stranger.

"I say, come, don't quarrel."

But Rosa turned on him passionately: "Mind your own business; nice manners! Can't I speak? Go home to your wife and see if I'm there! I've had enough of your fried whiting's eyes, and the three hairs you've got left. Take them back to the silly fool, it's time you did!"

De Potter, rather pale, smiled.

"And I have to live with this thing!" he muttered in his moustache.

"This thing's as good as that," she yelled, her whole body

stretched over the table. "The door's open, you know; so take your hook, out you go!"

"Come, come, Rosa," implored the poor spiritless eyes. And mother Pilar, going on with her meal, said with such a comical indifference : "Shut up, my boy!" that every one burst out laughing, even Rosa, even De Potter, who kissed his still chiding mistress, and to complete his forgiveness caught a fly and presented it tenderly by the wings to Bichito.

And this was De Potter, the glorious composer, the pride of the French school! How did this woman retain her hold on him, by what sorcery, aged as she was by vice, coarse, with her mother who was her double in vileness, showing her such as she would be in twenty years, as if seen in a mirror globe?

Coffee was served by the lake, in a little rock-work grotto, lined inside with bright silks watered by the movement of the ripples close by; one of those delicious lovers' nooks invented by the stories of the eighteenth century, with a mirror in the ceiling which reflected the attitudes of the old hags reclining on the broad divan in the languor of digestion, and Rosa, her cheeks flushed beneath the paint, lying on her back, and stretching out her arms to her musician, as she exclaimed :

"Oh! my Tatave! my Tatave!"

But this tender warmth evaporated with that of the chartreuse; and the idea of a row on the lake having struck one of the ladies, she sent De Potter to get the boat ready.

"The cutter, you know, not the pair-oar."

"Suppose I tell Désiré?"

"Désiré is having his lunch."

"The reason is that the cutter is full of water; it must be baled out, it is a long business."

" Jean will go with you, De Potter," said Fanny, who foresaw another scene.

Seated opposite one another, their legs wide apart, each
one on a seat of the boat, they baled busily without speaking, without looking at one another, as if lulled by the
rhythm of the water falling from the two scoops. Around
them a large catalpa cast its fragrant shade, and was reflected on the dazzling water.

" Have you been long with Fanny ?" asked the composer
all at once, leaving off his work.

" Two years," said Gaussin, rather surprised.

" Only two years ! Then what you see to-day may be of
some use to you. I have lived with Rosa twenty years. It's
twenty years ago that on my return from Italy, after my
three years defrayed by the 'Prix de Rome,' I went to the
Hippodrome one evening and saw her standing upright in
her little chariot, flying round the track, towering above me,
whip in air, with her barred helmet and her coat of gold
mail fitting close to her figure down to her thighs. Ah, if
any one had told me—"

And, setting to work to bale again, he related how at
home they had only laughed at this connection at first ;
then, when the matter became serious, how many efforts,
prayers, sacrifices, his parents would have made to effect the
separation. Two or three times the girl left him by dint of
money, but he always rejoined her. " Let us see what
travelling will do," his mother had said. He travelled,
returned, and took her to live with him again.' Then he let
himself be married : a pretty girl, a rich dowry, the promise
of becoming a member of the Institute among the wedding
presents. And three months afterwards he forsook the new
home for the old one. " Ah ! young man, young man."

He told the story of his life in a dry voice, without a

muscle animating his face, stiff as the starched collar which held it so erect.   And boats passed loaded with students and girls, overflowing with song, with youthful laughter and transport.   How many among these unconscious youths might well have stopped and learned the fearful lesson !

In the kiosk, during this time, as if the word had been passed to bring about their separation, the old "élégantes" were reasoning with Fanny Legrand.

"A pretty boy, hers, but not a sou.   What would it lead to ?"

"But since I love him !"

Rosa shrugged her shoulders.   "Let her be, she will go and miss her Dutchman as I have seen her miss all her grand opportunities.   After the Flamant affair she did try to become practical, but here she is now more foolish than ever."

"*Ay ! vellaca*," grunted mamma Pilar.

The Englishwoman with the clown's head interposed with the horrible accent to which she had so long owed her success :

"It's very nice to love for Love's sake, little one ; it's a very fine thing Love, you know, but one should love money too ; for myself, now, if I was still rich, do you think my croupier would say I was ugly ?"   She bounded with rage, raising her voice to a screech: "Oh ! that was too horrible. To have been a figure in the world, known everywhere, like a monument, a boulevard ; so well known that there was not a cabman who, when you said, 'Wilkie Cob,' did not know at once where to drive.   To have had princes for footstools, and kings who, if I spat, said spitting was pretty ! And then to come to this filthy blackguard who would have nothing to do with me because I was ugly ; and I had not even enough money for one night of him !"

And irritated at the idea that she could have been found ugly, she opened her dress abruptly:

"The face, yes, I sacrificed that; but there! the throat, the shoulders.   How white, how firm!"

She shamelessly exposed her witch's flesh, still miraculously young after thirty years in the furnace, and surmounted by a head faded and deathly, from the neck upwards.

"The boat is ready, ladies!" cried De Potter; and the Englishwoman, fastening her dress again over what remained to her of youth, murmured with a comical despair :

"I could not, though, go walking about stark naked!"

In this scenery, worthy of the brush of a Lancret, where the coquettish whiteness of the villas dazzled one amidst the young foliage, with the terraces, the lawns enclosing the little lake all glistening in the sun, what an embarkation was that of all these worn-out Venuses! the blind Sombreuse, and the old clown, and the paralytic Desfous, leaving in their wake the musky perfume of powder and paint.

Jean was sculling, his back bent, ashamed and fearful lest anyone should see him, and attribute to him some low function in this sinister allegoric bark.   Happily, he had opposite him, to refresh his heart and eyes, Fanny Legrand, seated in the stern near the tiller which De Potter held—Fanny, whose smile had never seemed to him so youthful, by comparison no doubt.

"Sing us something, little one," said Desfous, softened by the spring day.

In her expressive and deep voice Fanny began the barcarolle from "Claudia," which the composer, stirred by the remembrance of this, his first great success, followed, imitating with closed lips the orchestration, that undulation which gives to the melody the sparkle of dancing waves. At this hour, amid this scenery, it was delicious. Some one called "bravo" from a neighbouring terrace ; and the Provençal, keeping time with his sculls, felt a thirst for this divine music from his mistress's lips, a temptation to place his mouth to the source, and to drink in the sun, his head thrown back, for ever.

Suddenly, Rosa furiously interrupted the melody in which the blending of the voices enraged her. "Hullo! you there, when you've done warbling in one another's faces. Do you think your doleful ditty is entertaining? That's enough of it. Besides, it's late ; Fanny must get back to the shop."

And with a violent gesture she pointed to the nearest landing-stage.

"Bring the boat up there," she said to her lover, "they will be nearer to the station."

It was a brutal leave-taking ; but the ex-circus lady had accustomed those about her to such manners, and no one ventured to protest. The couple chucked out on the bank, with a few cold words of politeness to the young man, and some orders in a hissing voice to Fanny, and the boat pushed off amidst screams and disputes, which terminated in an insulting burst of laughter, sounding clearly over the water to the two lovers.

"Do you hear—do you hear?" said Fanny, pale with rage, "she's laughing at us."

And all her humiliations, all her grievances rising up at this last insult, she told him of them as they walked back to the station—owned things even which she had always concealed. Rosa sought only to estrange her from him, to facilitate opportunities to deceive him. "What has she not said to make me take the Dutchman? Just now they were all at me about it. I love you too much, you know. That does not suit her, with her vices, for she has vices—all the vilest, the most monstrous. And it's because I will no longer—"

She stopped, seeing him very pale, with trembling lips, like the evening when he was turning out the letters.

"Oh ! don't be afraid," she said, "your love has cured me of all those horrors. She and her filthy chameleon disgust me."

"I will not have you stop there any longer," said her lover, sick with horrible jealousy. "You earn your bread at that place at too heavy a cost. You shall come back to me, we shall get on somehow or other."

She was waiting for it, this cry—had long invoked it. Yet she resisted, saying that it would be very difficult to keep house on his three hundred francs from the Ministry, and that they would very likely have once more to separate. "And I suffered so much on leaving our poor little home !"

There were seats at intervals under the acacias which bordered the road, with the telegraph wires covered with swallows ; and in order to be able to talk better they sat down, arm-in-arm, very much agitated.

"Three hundred francs a month," said Jean ; "but what do the Hettémas do who have only two hundred and fifty ?"

"They live in the country, at Chaville, all the year round."

"Well, let us do the same ; I don't care for Paris."

"Really ? Will you ? Ah ! deary, deary !"

People were passing along the road, a crowd of donkeys carrying a post-nuptial party. They could not embrace, and remained immovable, sitting close to one another, dreaming of a happiness renewed in the summer evenings with their rural sweetness, their warm stillness enlivened in the distance by the sound of the shooting-galleries and organs of a suburban fête.

CHAPTER VIII.

THEY took up their quarters at Chaville, between the lower
and upper town, by the side of the old forest road which is
called the Pavé des Gardes, in an old hunting-lodge close to
the wood. Three rooms hardly larger than those in Paris,
with their old furniture still, the cane arm-chair, the painted
wardrobe, and nothing to adorn the frightful green paper in
their bedroom but Fanny's portrait; for the photograph of
Castelet had had its frame broken in moving, and was
fading away in some dark corner.

They hardly alluded to poor Castelet since the uncle and
niece had broken off their correspondence. "A nice sort of
friend," she said, remembering the way Césaire encouraged
their first separation. The little ones alone supplied their
brother with news. Divonne wrote no longer. Perhaps
she bore ill-will towards her nephew; or guessed that the
bad woman had come back to open, and make comments on,
her poor motherly letters with their great rustic hand-
writing.

At times they could have imagined themselves still in the
Rue d'Amsterdam, when they awoke at the singing of the
Hettémas, who had become their neighbours once more, and
the whistling of the trains which were perpetually passing
on the other side of the road, and were visible through the
branches of a large park. But instead of the pale glass roof
of the western station, its curtainless windows showing the
shadows of the clerks bending over their work, and the

noisy uproar in the steep street, they enjoyed the green and silent expanse beyond their own little orchard surrounded by other gardens, by little houses in clumps of trees sloping down to the bottom of the hill.

In the morning, before starting, Jean breakfasted in their little dining-room, whose window opened on the broad paved road covered with grass and bordered with hedges of strong-smelling hawthorn. It was by this way that Jean got to the station in ten minutes, skirting the rustling and tuneful park ; and when he came home this murmur became hushed as the shadows from the copses were cast on the mossy green road, purpled by the setting sun, and the cuckoo-calls in every corner of the wood answered to the trills of the nightingales in the ivied trees.

But no sooner had they got settled, and their surprise at the quietness of everything around them passed away, than the lover was seized again by fits of barren and brooding jealousy. His mistress's quarrel with Rosa, her departure from the hotel, had brought about between the two women an explanation, the monstrous insinuations of which had revived his suspicious and restless anxieties ; and when he went off and saw from the train the low house with its ground floor surmounted by a round dormer-window, his eyes tried to pierce the walls. He said to himself : "Who knows?" And the thought pursued him, buried in his papers at the office.

On his return, he made her render an account of her day, of her simplest acts, her thoughts, usually not worth mentioning, but which he drew from her by suddenly asking, "What are you thinking of?" ever dreading that she was regretting something or someone belonging to that horrible past, which she always owned to with the same unhesitating frankness.

The Hettémas set to work at watering.

158.

At least, when they met only on Sunday and were eager for one another, he did not devote his time to these reproachful and minute moral investigations.   But together, with the continuance of their joint existence, they were tortured even in their caresses, in their most tender embraces, stirred by dull anger, by a painful consciousness of the irreparable : he, struggling to impart to this woman, satiated with love, a sensation hitherto unknown ; she, ready to sacrifice herself to give him a pleasure which had not belonged to a dozen others, failing, and weeping in impotent rage.

Then a healthy change came over them ; possibly the satiety of the senses in the warm envelopment of nature, or more simply, the neighbourhood of the Hettémas.   It is certain that of all the families living in the suburbs of Paris not one, perhaps, enjoyed to the full like this one the joys of a country life, of going about threadbare, with hats of bark, the wife without stays, the husband in tatters ; of taking, when they rose from table, the crusts to the ducks, the parings to the rabbits, then weeding, raking, grafting, watering."

Oh ! the joys of watering !

The Hettémas set to work at it as soon as ever the husband had come home and exchanged his office clothes for a Robinson Crusoe coat.   After dinner they were at it again, and long after dark, in the little garden from which rose the fresh scent of damp earth, one heard the creaking of the pump, the knocking together of the great cans, and loud pantings among the beds, with a trickling which seemed to fall from the workers' faces into their watering-pots ; then from time to time a shout of triumph.

"I've given the greedy peas thirty-two !"

" And I fourteen to the balsams !"

People who were not content with being happy, but liked

to look on at their own happiness, and seemed to enjoy the taste of it till it made one's mouth water; the husband especially, by the irresistible manner in which he related the joys of wintering in company:

"It is nothing now, but you'll see in December! One comes home muddy and wet, with all the worries of Paris on one's back, finds a good fire, a good light, the soup scenting the room, and under the table a pair of shoes stuffed with straw. No, look you, when one has filled one's self with a plate of cabbage and sausages, a bit of gruyère kept fresh in a cloth, when one has emptied on that a bottle of wine which did not come by way of Bercy, free of baptism and duty, how jolly it is to draw one's chair up to the fire, light a pipe, drink one's coffee with a dash of brandy, and then forty winks opposite one another, whilst the hoar-frost is coating the window-panes. Only forty winks, just to get the heavy part of the digestion over. Afterwards, one draws a bit, the wife clears the table, makes her little arrangements, the bed clothes, the hot water bottle, and when she is in bed and the place warmed, one tumbles in, and feels hot all over as if one had crept bodily into the straw of one's shoes."

He waxed almost eloquent on the subject, this shaggy giant with his heavy jaw, so timid ordinarily that he could not say two words without blushing and stammering.

This excessive timidity, in comical contrast with his black beard and huge proportions, had brought about his marriage and life of tranquillity. At twenty-five, overflowing with vigour and health, Hettéma had known neither love nor woman, when one day at Nevers, after a club-dinner, his comrades dragged him half drunk into a brothel and forced him to take his choice. He left there unsettled, returned, chose the same each time, paid her debts, carried her off, and, alarmed at the idea that some one might take her from

And then forty winks opposite one another.

him and that he would have to begin a fresh conquest,
finished by marrying her.

"A lawful couple, my dear," said Fanny, with a smile of
triumph to Jean, who listened, terrified. "And, of all I have
known, the most proper and respectable."

She affirmed it in the sincerity of her ignorance, the lawful couples into whose homes she had been able to penetrate
meriting no doubt no other opinion; and all her notions of
life were as false and as sincere as this one.

Quiet neighbours, those Hettémas, always even-tempered,
capable even of services which did not demand too much
exertion, with, above all, a horror of scenes, quarrels in which
they had to take one side, and, in general, of anything which
might disturb a good digestion. The wife tried to initiate
Fanny into the rearing of fowls and rabbits, the invigorating
joys of watering, but in vain.

Gaussin's mistress, bred in a town, and a frequenter of
studios, only liked the country for frolics, parties, as a place
where one can shout, roll, lose one's self with one's lover.
She detested exertion, work; and her six months as manageress having exhausted for a long time to come her active
faculties, she glided into a state of vague torpor, of intoxication resulting from perfect happiness and the open air,
and which hardly left her power to dress herself, do her hair,
even to open her piano.

The household cares being left entirely to a charwoman
from the neighbourhood, when in the evening she ran over
the events of the day so as to relate them to Jean, she had nothing to tell but a visit to Olympe, chats over the fence, and
cigarettes, heaps of cigarettes, the remains of which covered
the marble hearth. Six o'clock already! Hardly time to
change her dress, to pin a flower in her bosom, to go and
meet him on the green road.

But with the autumn fogs and rain, and the early twi-
lights, she had more than one pretext for not going out, and
often on his return he surprised her in one of her dressing-
gowns of white wool, falling in large folds, which she put on
in the morning, her hair looped up as when he had started.
He thought her charming thus, her neck still young, her
tempting and well cared-for flesh which he knew was ever
willing and free of obstacles. And yet this state of degradation shocked him, alarmed him as if it were a danger.

He himself, after a great effort of work to augment their
resources a little without having recourse to Castelet—nights
passed over plans, drawings of pieces of artillery, caissons,
rifles on a new model, which he drew on Hettéma's account—
felt himself invaded all at once by this enervating influence
of the country and solitude which attacks the strongest, the
most active, and of which his infancy spent in a remote
corner of nature had placed in him the deadening germ.

And the materialism of their huge neighbours aiding,
communicating itself to them in the perpetual goings and
comings from one house to the other, with a little of their
moral debasement and their enormous appetite added,
Gaussin and his mistress also found themselves gravely discussing the meals and the hour of going to bed. Césaire
having sent them a cask of his " frog's wine," they passed
one whole Sunday in bottling it, the door of their little cellar
opening out upon the last sun of the year, a blue sky where
clouds, rose-coloured like heather, were floating. The days
of the straw-stuffed shoes and the naps in front of the log-
fire were not far off. Happily they had a diversion.

He found her one evening very much upset. Olympe had
been telling her the story of a poor little child brought up
by its grandmother at Morvan. The father and mother,
wood merchants in Paris, had ceased to write, and had paid

nothing for months. The grandmother having died suddenly, some bargemen had brought the little brat by the Yonne canal to restore it to the parents; but they found no one. The wood-yard closed, the mother gone off with a lover, the father drunken, bankrupt, disappeared. A happy lot, those lawful couples! And there was the poor child, six years old, a little love, without bread, or clothes, or home.

She was moved to tears, then suddenly:

"Suppose we took it; will you?"

"What folly!"

"Why?" And then, nestling to him and coaxing him: "You know how I have wanted a child by you; we could bring him up, educate him. One comes to love these little ones that one picks up as much as if they were one's own."

She pleaded too the pleasant change that it would be for her, alone all day, worried with wretched thoughts. A child too is a safeguard. Then seeing him alarmed at the expense: "It's nothing, the expense. Just think, only six years old! we can dress him with your old clothes. Olympe, who knows all about that kind of thing, assured me that we should not even notice it."

"Why doesn't she take him then?" said Jean, with the ill-humour of a man who feels himself overcome by his own weakness. He tried, however, to resist by the aid of the decisive objection: "And when I'm no longer here?" He rarely spoke of this departure so as not to distress Fanny, but he thought of it, and employed it to give him confidence against the dangers of his life and De Potter's sad confidences. "What a complication a child would be, what a burden on you in the future!"

Fanny's face clouded:

"You are wrong, deary; it would be some one to whom I could talk of you, a comfort, a responsibility, too, which would give me strength to work, to take a pleasure in life again."

He reflected a moment, pictured her all alone in the empty house :

" Where is the child ? "

" At Bas-Meudon, with a bargeman who took him in for a few days. After that there is nothing for him but the almshouse, charity."

" Well, go and fetch him, since you have set your mind on it."

She threw her arms round his neck, and, pleased as a child, played and sang all the evening, joyous, full of spirits, transfigured. The next day in the train Jean spoke of their decision to Hettéma, who appeared to know all about the affair, and to be desirous of not being mixed up in it. Buried in his corner and in the perusal of the " Petit Journal," he stammered from behind his beard :

" Yes, I know, it's the ladies' affair, it doesn't concern me." And showing his head over the top of the paper : " Your wife appears to me to be very romantic," said he.

Romantic or not, there she was in the evening, dismayed, on her knees, a plate of soup in her hand, endeavouring to tame the little Morvandian lad, who, bolt upright, in a mistrustful attitude, his head hanging, an enormous head with hair like hemp, obstinately refused to talk, to eat, even to show his face, and repeated in a choked and monotonous voice :

" See Ménine ! see Ménine ! "

" Ménine, that's his grandmother, I suppose. For the last two hours I've been able to get nothing else out of him."

Jean took a turn, too, at trying to make him swallow the soup, but without success. And they remained there, both of them kneeling on a level with him, one holding the plate, the other the spoon, as before a sick lamb, repeating kind and encouraging words to win him over.

"Let's have dinner, perhaps we frighten him ; he will eat if we don't look at him."

But he remained motionless, dumbfounded, repeating his little savage's whine of "See Ménine," which melted their hearts, until he went to sleep, standing against the sideboard ; and so soundly, that they were able to undress him, and get him to bed in the heavy country cradle borrowed of a neighbour, without his opening his eyes a second.

"Look how pretty he is," said Fanny, very proud of her acquisition ; and she made Gaussin admire the stubborn face, the features refined and delicate under the sunburnt skin, the perfect little body, with its broad back, its thick arms, its legs like those of a little faun, long and sinewy, and already covered with down below the knee. She lost herself contemplating this childish beauty.

"Cover him up, he will be cold," said Jean, whose voice made her start as though awoke from a dream; and whilst she tucked him up tenderly, the little one kept fetching long sobbing sighs, a murmur of despair, in spite of his slumber.

In the night he began to talk to himself :

"*Guerlaude mé*, Ménine."

"What does he say ?   Listen."

He wanted to be "*guerlaudé*," but what did that peculiar dialect mean ?   At all events Jean stretched out his arm, and began to rock the heavy cradle ; by degrees the child became quiet, and went off to sleep again, holding in his little fat dimpled hand the hand which he believed was that of his "Ménine," dead a fortnight ago.

He was like a wild cat in the house, scratching, biting,

taking his meals apart from the others, and growling when anyone approached his porringer. The few words which they got out of him were in the barbarous jargon of Morvandian woodmen, which no one would have been able to understand but for the Hettémas, who came from the same part of the country. However, by dint of care and kindness, they succeeded in taming him a little. He consented to change the rags in which he had been brought for warm and clean clothes, the sight of which at first made him scream with rage, like a jackal whom one was trying to muffle in a greyhound's wrapper. He learnt to eat at table, the use of the fork and spoon, and to answer when he was asked his name, "*i li dision* Josaph," at home.

As to giving him education of the most elementary description, it was not to be thought of yet. Reared in the midst of the forest in a charcoal burner's hut, the sound of a rustling and swarming nature filled his hard little noddle, like the sound of the sea fills the windings of a shell; and it was vain to try and get anything else into it, or to keep him in the house even in the roughest weather. Amidst rain and snow, when the bare trees were standing like frosted coral, he was off, ranging the thickets, rummaging the burrows with the dexterous cruelty of a ferret, and when he came home, famished with hunger, he always had in his fustian jacket all torn in holes, in the pocket of his little trousers muddy up to the waist, some stupefied or dead animal, bird, mole, field mouse, or if not, beet-roots or potatoes pulled up in the fields.

Nothing could overcome these poaching and marauding instincts, to which was added a clownish mania for hiding all sorts of shining trifles, brass buttons, jet beads, silver paper, which Josaph laid hands upon and carried off to his magpie hiding-places. All this booty had for him a vague and generic name, "food;" and neither reasonings nor thrashings could prevent him collecting his "food" at the expense of everything and everyone.

The Hettémas alone could manage him, the draughtsman keeping within his reach—on the table round which the young savage attracted by the compasses and coloured pencils prowled—a dog-whip, which he flicked at his legs. But neither Jean nor Fanny would have used such threats, although the child showed himself cunning and mistrustful towards them, untamable even by tender spoilings, as if his "Ménine" in dying had deprived him of all further affection. Fanny, "because she smelt nice," succeeded in keeping him on her knees for a moment sometimes, whilst towards Gaussin, who was nevertheless very kind to him, he was always the same wild beast as on his arrival, with mistrustful look and extended claws.

This invincible and almost instinctive repulsion of the child, the curious malice of his little blue eyes with their white lashes, and especially the blind and sudden affection of Fanny for this stranger who had all at once entered into their life, troubled the lover with a fresh suspicion. It was a child of hers perhaps, brought up by a nurse or at her step-mother's; and Machaume's death which they heard of about this time seemed a coincidence to justify these torments. Sometimes, in the night, when he held the little hand which clutched his own (for the child, in the unconsciousness of sleeping and dreaming, always thought he had hold of "Ménine"), he asked withall his inward and secret trouble: "Where do you come from?" "Who are you?" hoping to find out, communicated by the heat of the little being, the mystery of his birth.

But his uneasiness disappeared at a remark of old Legrand, who came to ask them to help him to pay for his wife's

funeral, and who cried out to his daughter, on seeing
Josaph's cradle :

"Hullo! a youngster! you ought to be happy! You
who could never manage to have one."

Gaussin was so pleased that he paid for the funeral without asking to see the estimate, and kept old Legrand to
breakfast.

Employed on the tramway from Paris to Versailles,
drunken and apoplectical, but always robust and looking
well under his hat of waxed leather with its heavy band of
crape, which made it a true mute's head-gear, the old driver
appeared delighted at the reception his daughter's gentleman gave him, and he came from time to time to have a
meal with them. His white buffoon's hair falling over his
close-shaven and tumified face, his drunkenly majestic airs,
the respect which he had for his whip, striking attitudes
with it, depositing it carefully in a corner with motherly
precautions, impressed the child immensely ; and at once a
great intimacy sprang up between them. One day when
they were finishing dinner together, the Hettémas surprised
them :

"Ah ! excuse us, a family gathering," said the wife minc-
ing, and the word struck Jean in the face, humiliating as a
blow.

His family! This foundling who was rolling his head on the
table-cloth, this old pirate at home with his pipe in the corner
of his mouth, his guttural voice, explaining for the hundredth
time that two sous' worth of whip-cord lasted him six months,
and that for twenty years he had not changed the handle !
His family, that was too much ! no more so than she was
his wife, this Fanny Legrand, getting old and worn-out,
leaning on her elbows, half hidden in the smoke of her
cigarettes. Before a year was over, all this would have dis-

appeared out of his life, the same as chance acquaintances of travel and table-d'hôte.

But at other times, this idea of departure which he invoked as an excuse for his weakness when he felt himself sinking, being dragged down, this idea, instead of reassuring and solacing him, made him feel all the manifold bonds closing tightly around him; what a laceration this departure would be, not one separation but ten, and what it would cost him to let go the little child's hand which in the night surrendered itself in his. Even to La Balue, the oriole whistling and singing in the cage which was too small for him and was always going to be changed, and in which he bent his back like the old cardinal in his iron prison; yes, even La Balue had taken possession of a little corner in his heart, and it would be painful to remove him from it.

Yet this inevitable separation was approaching, and the splendid month of June, which was making all nature gay would probably be the last they would pass together. Was it that which made her nervous and irritable, or little Joseph's education, suddenly undertaken with ardour, to the great disgust of the young Morvandian who remained hours together over his letters, without looking at or pronouncing them, his face shut with a bar like the doors of a farm-yard? Day by day she was carried away in paroxysms of violence and tears ceaselessly renewed, although Gaussin did his best to be indulgent; but she was so insulting, there arose from her rage such spite and hatred against her lover's youth, his education, his family, the gap which life would increase between their destinies, she understood so well how to wound him in the tenderest spots, that at last he began to be angry and to reply.

But there was in his anger the reserve, the pity of a man who has been well brought up, blows which he did not strike

as being too painful and to the point, whilst she let loose all
the fury of a prostitute without responsibility or shame,
making a weapon of anything, watching with a cruel joy on
her victim's face the contraction of pain which she occasioned,
then suddenly falling into his arms and imploring his pardon.

The physiognomy of the Hettémas, witnesses of these
quarrels which almost always burst out at table, at the
moment of sitting down and uncovering the soup or carving
the joint, was a picture. They exchanged a look of comical
terror across the table. Could they begin eating, or was the
leg of mutton going flying out into the garden along with
the dish, the gravy and the haricot stew?

"And mind, no scenes!" said they, each time there was a
question of dining together; and with this remark they accepted an invitation to lunch in the forest which Fanny
gave them over the wall one Sunday. Oh, no! they would
not quarrel, the day was too fine! And she ran to dress
the child and fill the baskets.

Everything was ready, they were setting off, when the
postman brought a registered letter which delayed Gaussin.
He rejoined the party at the entrance to the forest, and said
in an undertone to Fanny:

"It's from uncle. He's delighted. A splendid crop, sold
as it stands. He returns Déchelette's eight thousand francs,
with lots of compliments and thanks for his niece."

"Yes, his niece! in the Gascon style. The old fool," said
Fanny, who no longer fancied these uncles from the South;
then, joyfully:

"We must invest this money."

He looked at her, astounded, having always thought her
most scrupulous in money matters.

"Invest? but it's not yours."

"Wait a bit, I never told you." She blushed, with that

look which betrayed the slightest prevarication. That good
fellow Déchelette, having learnt what they were doing for
Josaph, had written to her to say that this money would
help them to bring up the child. "But then, you know, if
you don't like that, we can send it back to him; he's in
Paris."

The voices of the Hettémas who had discreetly gone on
in front resounded under the trees :

"To the right or left?"

"To the right, to the right, towards the ponds !" cried
Fanny, then turning to her lover :   "Come now, you're not
going to start your foolish jealousy again ; we've been long
enough together, hang it ! "

She knew that trembling pallor of the lips, that glance at
the child, examining him from head to foot ; but this time
there was but a feeble attempt at jealous anger, he had got
to be cowardly by this time, to make concessions for the sake
of peace.   "What need to torment myself, to try and get to
the bottom of things ? If this child is hers, what more simple
than that she should take it, hiding the truth from me,
after all the scenes, the cross-questionings I have made her
go through? Is it not better to accept what is. and pass
quietly the few months that remain to us?"

And along the hilly forest paths he went, carrying their
portable breakfast in its heavy basket covered with a white
cloth, resigned and weary, his back bent like an old gardener's,
whilst in front of him walked the mother and child, Josaph
dressed out and awkward in a suit bought at La Belle-
Jardinière which prevented him from running, she in a bright
loose gown, her head and neck bare beneath a Japanese
parasol, her figure filled out, her walk languid, and in her
beautiful wavy hair a great white lock which she no longer
took the trouble to conceal.

In front of them and lower down, the Hettémas had sub-
sided in a dip in the path, their heads covered with gigantic
straw hats like those of the Touareg horseman, themselves
dressed in red flannel, loaded with eatables, fishing-rods,
nets; and the wife, to spare her husband, was carrying bravely
across her huge chest the hunting-horn without which the
draughtsman would never have dreamt of a walk in the
forest.   As they marched along, the couple sang:

> " At eve, I like to hear
>   The water's silvery song;
>   I love the frightened deer—"

Olympe's repertory contained an endless supply of these
everyday sentimentalities; and when one thought where she
had picked them up, in what shameful half-light of drawn
blinds, to how many men she had sung them, the serenity of
the husband accompanying her in thirds seemed truly grand.
. The remark of the grenadier at Waterloo: " They are too—"
was probably that of this man's philosophical indifference.

Whilst Gaussin was dreamily watching the enormous
couple plunge into a hollow which he was just entering behind them, the sound of wheels was heard coming along the
path, with a peal of mad laughter and childish voices;
and suddenly there appeared at a few steps from him a load
of young girls, their ribbons and hair flying, in a chaise
drawn by a little donkey which a girl hardly older than the
others was leading by the bridle along the rough way.

It was easy to see that Jean was one of the party whose
fantastic appearance, that of the fat lady girdled with a
hunting-horn especially, had animated the young folks with
an inextinguishable gaiety; and therefore the elder girl
tried to impose silence for a minute on the children.   But
the new Touareg hat provoked their merriment more than

Jean turned round to see this whirlwind of fair youth.

176.

ever, and, in passing before the man who drew himself up at the side of the path to make way for the little chaise, a pretty abashed smile begged his pardon and expressed a naive astonishment at finding the old gardener had such a young and sweet face.

He raised his hat timidly and blushed, ashamed, he knew not why; and the chaise stopping at the top of the hill by the cross ways, with a prattling of small voices who were reading aloud the names on the finger-post almost obliterated by the rain, "Route des Étangs, Chêne du Grand Veneur, Fausses Reposes, Chemin de Vélizy," Jean turned round to see disappear, in the green path carpeted with moss where the sun was peeping in, and where the wheels were rolling on velvet, this whirlwind of fair youth, this load of happiness, with its spring colours and peals of laughter echoing among the branches.

A furious blast from Hettéma's horn roused him abruptly from his dream. They were all settled by the side of the pond and busy unpacking the provisions; and from afar one could see reflected on the clear water the white cloth on the level sward, and the red flannel jackets glowing amongst the verdure like huntsmen's coats.

"Come along! you've got the lobster," cried the fat man; and then Fanny's sharp voice:

"Was it little Bouchereau who kept you?"

Jean started at this name of Bouchereau which took him back to Castelet by his sick mother's bedside.

"Yes, really," said the draughtsman, taking the basket out of his hands. "The tall one who was leading is the doctor's niece. His brother's daughter who lives with him. They stay at Vélizy during the summer. She's pretty."

"Oh! pretty; very impudent-looking rather." And

Fanny, who was cutting the bread, eyed her lover, uneasy at his absent gaze.

Madame Hettéma, very gravely unpacking the ham, found great fault with this custom of letting young girls wander about at liberty in the woods. "You may say it's the English way, and that this girl was educated in London, but all the same, it's not at all proper."

"No, but very convenient for adventures!"

"Oh! Fanny!"

"I beg pardon, I forgot; you believe in innocent girls."

"Come, suppose we have lunch," said Hettéma, who began to be alarmed. But she had to publish all she knew about young ladies. She had some beautiful stories on the subject; convents, schools, they were nice places. The girls left them, used up and faded, with a distaste for men; not even capable of bearing children. "And then it is that they are given to you, you precious simpletons. An innocent girl! As if there were such a thing; as if, ladies or not ladies, all girls did not know from their birth what's what. For my own part, at twelve, I had nothing more to learn, nor you either, eh, Olympe?"

"Of course," said Madame Hettéma, shrugging her shoulders; but the fate of the lunch made her uneasy, especially on hearing Gaussin who was getting angry, declare that there were girls and girls, and that one could still find in families—

"Oh! yes, families," retorted his mistress with a look of contempt, "let us talk of them; yours especially."

"Be quiet. I forbid you."

"Yokel!"

"Hussy! It's a good thing that there will soon be an end of this, I've not got much longer to live with you."

"Go, take your hook; it's I who'll be pleased."

They were throwing these insults in one another's teeth
before the mischievous curiosity of the child lying full
length on the grass, when a fearful trumpet blast, multiplied
a hundred-fold in echoes across the pond, in the upward-slop-
ing masses of forest, suddenly drowned their quarrel.

"Is that enough? Will you have some more?" And
purple, his neck swollen, fat Hettéma, finding only this means
of silencing them, waited, the mouth-piece to his lips, the
bell threatening.

CHAPTER IX.

As a rule, their differences did not last long, melting away
with a little music or Fanny's cajoleries ; but this time he
was seriously angry with her, and for several days he kept
the same gloomy face, the same spiteful silence, starting his
drawing directly after meals, and refusing to go out at all
with her.

It was like a sudden feeling of shame at the degradation
in which he was living, the fear of meeting the little chaise
again coming up the path and that limpid, youthful smile
on which his mind was constantly dwelling. Then, in a
confusion like that of a departing dream, of a fading fairy
transformation scene, the apparition became indistinct, lost
in the woody distance, and Jean saw it no more. There remained only with him a trace of sadness, of which Fanny
suspected the cause, and resolved to have satisfaction.

" It's done," said she to him one day, quite joyfully. " I've
seen Déchelette. I've given him back the money. He
thinks with you that it's better so, though I should like to
know why. At all events, it's done. Afterwards, when I'm
alone, he will give a thought to the little one. Are you
satisfied ? Are you angry with me still ? "

And she told him about her visit to the Rue de Rome, her
astonishment at finding, in place of the noisy and wild cara-
vansary, full of raving gangs, a quiet, homely house, guarded
by the most rigorous instructions. No more galas, no more
masked balls ; and the explanation of this change was found

Closed for glutinous reasons.

152.

in these words written in chalk at the little entrance to the studio by some parasite, furious at having been refused admittance: 'Closed for glutinous reasons.'"

"And that's the truth, dear. Déchelette, on arriving, was smitten with a girl he picked up at the rink, Alice Doré. He has been keeping her for a month at his place, absolutely at his place. A very pretty, gentle, little woman, a sweet little lamb. They hardly make a sound between them. I promised that we would go and see them; it will be a change for us after hunting-horns and barcarolles. It all comes to the same thing, doesn't it, philosophy and its theories? No morrow, no entanglement. Ah! didn't I chaff him!"

Jean let her take him to Déchelette's, whom he had not seen since their meeting at the Madeleine. He would have been much surprised then if anyone had said to him that he would come to associate without disgust with this cynical and disdainful lover of his mistress, to become almost his friend. From the very first visit he was astonished himself at feeling so much at his ease, charmed by the gentleness of this man, at his frank, childish laughter in his Cossack's beard, and an evenness of temper which not even the cruel liver attacks which leadened his face and eyes could affect.

And how well one could understand the love with which he inspired Alice Doré, with her long, soft, white hands, her insignificant flaxen beauty set off by the brilliancy of her Flemish skin as golden as her name; gold in her hair, her eyes, fringing her lids, and gilding her skin even beneath the nails.

Picked up by Déchelette from off the asphalt of the rink, amidst the coarse and brutal remarks of debauchery, the clouds of smoke which the man blows, as he names a price,

in the prostitute's painted face, his politeness had touched
and surprised her.   She found herself a woman again, from
the poor beast of pleasure which she had been, and when he
was going to send her off in the morning, in accordance with
his principle, with a good breakfast and a few louis, her
heart was so big, she asked him so sweetly, so longingly, " Let
me stay on," that he had not the courage to refuse.   Since
then, half out of a humane respect, half from lassitude, he
kept his door closed on this chance honeymoon which he
passed in the freshness and calm of his summer palace, so
well arranged with an eye to comfort ; and they lived thus
very happily, she in the tender consideration which she had
never known, he in the pleasure which he gave to this poor
being, and her naive gratitude ; being under the influence
too, without being able to account for it, and for the first
time, of the pervading charm of a woman's intimacy, the
mysterious spell of a joint existence, in a conformity of goodness and sweetness.

For Gaussin, the studio in the Rue de Rome came as a
diversion in the low and mean course his life was dragging,
the life of some petty clerk who keeps his woman ; he loved
the conversation of this man of science with his artistic
tastes, of this philosopher in his Persian robe, light
and lax as his doctrine ; these accounts of travels which
Déchelette sketched in the fewest possible words were so
fitting amongst the Oriental hangings, the gilded Buddhas,
the bronze monsters, the exotic luxury of the immense hall,
where the light entered through the lofty glass roof, the
true light of sylvan depths, agitated by the frail foliage of
the bamboo, the serrated fronds of the tree-ferns, and the
enormous leaves of the strilligias mingled with some philo-
dendrons thin and flexible like water plants, seeking shade
and damp.

On Sunday especially, with the deep bay-window looking on the deserted street of Paris in summer, the rustling of leaves, the fragrance of fresh earth at the foot of the plants, it was almost as much the country and the forest as Chaville, less the promiscuousness of the Hettémas and their horn. No one ever came there. Once, however, Gaussin and his mistress arriving for dinner, heard from the entrance the sound of several voices. The day was closing in, they were drinking raki in the conservatory, and the discussion seemed lively :

" And I think that five years at Mazas, one's name lost, life destroyed, is paying very dear for an act of passion and folly. I will sign your petition, Déchelette."

" It's Caoudal," said Fanny, in a low voice, and starting.

Some one answered with the snappish dryness of refusal : " And I will sign nothing, not wishing to accept any liability with the rascal."

" La Gournerie, now." And Fanny, clinging to her lover, murmured : " Let's go away if you don't care to see them."

" Why ? not at all ! " In reality, he scarcely knew what his impression would be when finding himself in the presence of these men, but he would not shrink from the trial, desirous perhaps of knowing the actual extent of this jealousy which was the prime cause of his wretched love.

" Come along ! " said he, and they appeared in the waning rose-coloured light, which illumined the bald heads and grizzly beards of Déchelette's friends, stretched on low divans round an Oriental table, on which was trembling, in five or six glasses, the milky and aniseed-flavoured liqueur which Alice was pouring out. The women kissed. " You know these gentlemen, Gaussin ? " asked Déchelette, with a lazy movement of his rocking-chair.

Did he know them ! Two at least were familiar to him

from having stared at their portraits for hours in the shop-
windows among other celebrities. What suffering had they
not caused him, what a hatred he had for them, successor's
hatred, a rage which tempted him to spring upon them,
to gnaw their faces when he met them in the street! But
Fanny had truly said that he would get over that; at present
they were to him the faces of acquaintances, of relations
almost, far-off uncles whom he had found again.

"Handsome still, the youngster!" said Caoudal, stretched
out at all his giant length, and holding a screen above his
eyes to protect them from the light. "And Fanny too."
He rose on his elbow and scanned her with the eyes of a
connoisseur: "The face will do still; but the figure—you
do well to lace it in; after all, take comfort, my child. La
Gournerie is even fatter than you."

The poet pursed his thin lips disdainfully. Seated Turkish
fashion on a pile of cushions (since his journey to Algeria he
professed not to be able to bear any other attitude), huge,
clammy, his face unintelligent, with the exception of his firm
forehead beneath a white forest, and his keen slave-driver's
glance, he affected towards Fanny an absent reserve, an exaggerated politeness, as if to teach Caoudal a lesson.

Two landscape painters, with sun-burnt and rustic faces,
completed the company; they, too, knew Jean's mistress,
and the younger one said as he shook hands with her:

"Déchelette has told us the story of the child; it was
very nice of you, my dear."

"Yes," said Caoudal to Gaussin, "quite the correct thing,
adoption. Not in the least provincial."

She seemed growing embarrassed at these praises, when
some one ran against a chair in the dark studio, and a voice
asked: "Is anyone there?"

"It's Ezano," said Déchelette.

Him Jean had never seen, but he knew the place that this fanciful Bohemian character, steady and married now, and a great light at the Beaux-Arts, had held in Fanny Legrand's existence, and he bethought him of a packet of impassioned and charming letters. A little hollow-faced, shrunken man came forward, his gait stiff, shaking hands at arm's length, holding people at a distance by a platform and administrative manner. He appeared much surprised to see Fanny, and especially at finding her still pretty after so many years.

"Why, it's Sappho!" And a faint blush coloured his cheeks.

This name of Sappho, which gave her back to the past, and placed her among all her old friends, caused a certain awkwardness.

"And Monsieur d'Armandy who has brought her," said Déchelette quickly, to warn the new-comer. Ezano bowed and they began to talk. Fanny, reassured at seeing how her lover was taking things, and proud of him, of his beauty, his youth, in the presence of these critical artists, was very lively and animated. Entirely given up to her present passion, she hardly recollected her connexions with these men; years of cohabitation for all that, of life in common which had imprinted on her in the contact habits and fancies which still survived, even to the way of making cigarettes which she had caught from Ezano, as well as his preference for Job paper and Maryland tobacco.

Jean noted without the least distress this little detail which formerly would have exasperated him, and experienced, at finding himself so calm, the joy of a prisoner who has filed his chain and feels that the least effort will set him free.

"Eh! my poor Fanny," said Caoudal in a joking voice and pointing at the others; "what a falling off! aren't they old, aren't they played out? we're the only two fit ones left.'

Fanny began to laugh: "Ah! excuse me, Colonel" (he was thus named sometimes on account of his moustaches), "it's not quite the same thing, I'm of another generation."

"Caoudal always forgets that he's ancestral," said La Gournerie; and at a movement of the sculptor whom he knew he was probing to the quick: "Medallist in 1840," he cried in his strident voice; "there's a date for you, my boy!"

There remained between these two old friends an aggressive tone, a silent antipathy, which had never caused a quarrel, but which showed itself in their looks, their lightest words, and that for the last twenty years, ever since the poet carried off the sculptor's mistress. Fanny went for nothing now, they had both of them experienced other pleasures, other mortifications, but the spite lived, hollowed out more deeply as the years passed.

"Look at us both now, and say honestly if it's I who am ancestral!" In a tight-fitting coat which showed off his muscles, Caoudal planted himself upright, arching his chest and shaking his head of flaming locks where never a white hair was to be seen:

"Medallist in 1840, fifty-eight years old and three months. And what does that prove? Is it a man's age that makes him old? It's only at the Comédie-Française and the Conservatoire that men are doddering at sixty, nodding, shuffling, their back bent, legs weak, tumbling about. At sixty, hang it all! I shall walk as firmly as at thirty, because I take care of myself; and the women go for one still, provided the heart remains young, and warms and influences the whole carcass.'

"Do you think so?" said La Gournerie, looking at Fanny and sneering. And Déchelette with his open smile:

"And yet you are eternally saying that there's nothing like youth."

"It's my little Cousinard who made me alter my opinion. Cousinard, my new model. Eighteen years old, plump and dimpled all over—a Clodion. And so lively and good-natured, smacking of the people, of the Paris of the Markets where her mother sells poultry. She says such stupid things one could kiss her for them. The other day in the studio she found one of Dejoie's novels, looked at the title 'Thérèse,' and threw it down with a pretty pout. 'If that had been called "Poor Thérèse," I would have read it all night!' I'm desperately smitten I can tell you."

"So you're hooked again? And in six months' time there'll be another separation, floods of tears, distaste for work, murderous rages." Caoudal's face clouded:

"It's true nothing lasts. One pairs, one separates."

"Then why pair?"

"And you? Do you think you've got a lifetime before you with your Flemish lady?"

"Oh, we, we've not started regular housekeeping; have we, Alice?"

"Certainly not," replied in a gentle and absent voice the young girl who had mounted a chair and was plucking bunches of wistaria and green leaves for the table. Déchelette continued:

"There will be no rupture between us, hardly a leave-taking. We made a two months' agreement to live together; on the last day there will be a separation, without despair and without surprise. I shall go back to Ispahan—I've just engaged my sleeping car—and Alice will return to her little rooms in the Rue Labruyère which she has kept on."

"On the third floor, most convenient for flinging oneself out of the window!"

Saying this, the young girl smiled, her face ruddy, the light of the falling day upon her, the heavy bunch of mauve flowers in her hand ; but her voice was so profound, so serious, that no one answered.   The wind freshened, the houses opposite seemed higher.

"Come, to table !" cried the Colonel.   "And let's have some festive conversation."

"Yes, that's it, '*gaudeamus igitur*,' let us enjoy ourselves whilst we are young, eh, Caoudal?" said La Gournerie with a false-sounding laugh.

As Jean was passing along the Rue de Rome again, a few days later, he found the studio closed, the great canvas curtain let down, a mournful silence from the cellar to the terraced roof.   Déchelette had gone at the time settled, the agreement having expired.   And he thought : "It is a grand thing to do as one likes in this life, to govern one's reason and one's heart.   Shall *I* ever have the courage?"

A hand was placed on his shoulder :

"Good day, Gaussin."

Déchelette, wearied-looking, more yellow and frowning than usual, explained to him that, detained in Paris by some business, he was not leaving just yet, that he was staying at the Grand-Hôtel, having a horror of the studio since that dreadful affair—

"What was that?"

"True, you don't know.   Alice is dead.   She committed suicide.   Wait whilst I see if there are any letters for me."

He returned almost at once, and as with trembling fingers he removed the newspaper wrappers, he talked in a hollow voice, like a somnambulist, without looking at Gaussin who was walking at his side :

"Yes, dead, threw herself from the window as she said that evening when you were there.   How could it be helped? I did not know, I could not suspect.   The day on which I

She threw herself from the window.

191.

was to have started she said to me quietly: 'Take me with you, Déchelette, do not leave me alone. I can no longer live without you.' I laughed at the idea. Fancy me with a woman out there among the Kurds, the desert, the fevers, the nights of bivouac. At dinner she repeated: 'I shall not be in your way, you will see how good I shall be.' Then, seeing that she was giving me pain, she insisted no longer. Afterwards we went to the Variétés, had a private box; all that was settled beforehand. She appeared satisfied, held my hand all the time and murmured: 'I am happy.' As I was leaving during the night, I took her home in my carriage; but we were both of us sad and did not speak. She did not even thank me for a little packet which I slipped into her pocket, sufficient to enable her to live quietly for a year or two. Arrived at the Rue Labruyère she asked me to come up. I would not. ' I entreat you— only to the door.' But there I made a stand, and did not enter her room. My place was engaged, my things packed, and then I had repeated too often that I was going. As I went downstairs, my heart rather swollen, I heard her call out to me something like, ' quicker than you,' but I only understood it when I was below, in the street—Oh !—"

He stopped—his eyes cast down—before the horrible vision which the pavement presented to him now, at every step that inert black mass which was groaning.

"She died two hours afterwards, without a word, without a complaint, gazing at me with her golden eyes. Did she suffer? Did she recognise me? We had laid her on the bed, all dressed, a large lace shawl covering one side of her head to hide the wound in her skull. Very pale, with a little blood on her temple, she was still pretty, and so calm. But as I bent over her to wipe away this drop of blood which returned always, inexhaustible, her look seemed to me to

take an indignant and terrible expression. A mute curse
which the poor girl was casting on me. And after all, what
difference would it have made to me to have remained a
few days longer, or to have taken her, so eager, so little in
the way, with me. No, pride, the obstinacy of abiding by
what I had said. Well, I did not yield ! and she is dead,
dead for me who yet loved her."

He grew excited and spoke in a loud voice, followed by
the astonishment of the people he elbowed as they walked
down the Rue d'Amsterdam ; and Gaussin, passing by his
old home with its balcony and verandah which he could see,
thought of Fanny and their own story, and felt himself
shudder as Déchelette continued :

"I followed her to Montparnasse cemetery, without friends,
without relations. I wished to be the only one to think of
her. And since then, here I have been, always dwelling on
the same thing, not feeling capable of going away with this
besetting idea on my mind, avoiding my house where I passed
two such happy months with her. I live out of doors, I go
about, I try to change my thoughts, to escape from that
dead girl's eye which rises up in judgment against me under
the trickling blood."

And stopping, struck by remorse, with two great tears
rolling down his little flat nose, so good-natured looking, so
enamoured of life, he said :

"Come, my friend ; after all I'm not wicked. It's most
extraordinary that I should have done such a thing."

Jean tried to console him, putting it down to chance, bad
luck ; but Déchelette repeated, shaking his head, and with
his teeth set :

"No, no, I shall never forgive myself. I should like to
punish myself."

This desire for expiation did not cease to haunt him, he

talked about it to all his friends, to Gaussin whom he would call for when the office closed.

"You must get away, Déchelette. Travel, work, that will occupy you," Caoudal and the others kept saying, a little uneasy at this fixed idea, this persistent wish to make them repeat that he was not wicked. Finally, one evening, either wishing to revisit the studio before his departure, or drawn thither by a settled project to have done with his trouble, he entered his house again, and in the morning some labourers passing along the street on their way to work picked him up on the pavement in front of his door, his skull split, dead by the same kind of suicide as the woman, with the same horrors, the same shattering of a despair flung into the street.

In the dimly lighted studio a crowd was pressing. Artists models, actresses, all the dancers, all the supper-eaters at the last balls. There was a sound of shuffling feet, of whispering, the murmur of a chapel beneath the short flames of the tapers. People were looking through the creepers and foliage at the body lying exposed in golden-flowered silk stuff, turbaned to hide the hideous wound on the head, stretched out at full length—the white hands in front betokening abandonment, the supreme release—on the low divan overshadowed by wistarias where Gaussin and his mistress first became acquainted on the night of the ball.

CHAPTER X.

People die then sometimes of these ruptures! Now, when they quarrelled Jean dared no longer speak of his going, he cried no more, exasperated : "Happily there will soon be an end of this." She would only have had to answer : ".Very good, go ; I shall kill myself; I shall do as the other one did." And this threat, which he fancied he could distinguish in the melancholy of her looks and the songs she sang, in her silent reveries, moved him to terror.

Yet he had passed the examination which terminates the ministerial stage ; for consular attachés having taken a good place, he was going to be appointed to one of the first vacant posts, and it was only an affair of weeks, of days! And around them, in this closing of the season and gradually decreasing sunshine, everything also was hastening towards the changes of winter. One morning Fanny, opening the window in the first mist, cried :

"Why, the swallows have gone."

One after another the private country houses closed their shutters ; along the Versailles road furniture vans followed in rapid succession, great omnibuses loaded with packages, and with plumes of green plants on the top, whilst the leaves were caught up in whirlwinds, scattered like the scudding clouds under the lowering sky, and the ricks rose in the bare fields. Behind the leafless orchard, looking smaller from lack of foliage, the closed cottages, the drying-houses of the laundries with their red tiled roofs appeared in groups in the cheerless landscape, and, on the other side of the house, the now exposed railway stretched its black track alongside the greyish forest.

What cruelty to leave her there all alone in this joyless scene ! He felt his heart relent in advance; never would he have courage for the parting. It was on this that she reckoned, waiting for it when the supreme moment came, and till then tranquil, making no remarks, faithful to her promise not to place obstacles in the way of this departure, long foreseen and agreed upon. One day he entered with the news :

"I am appointed."

"Ah ! where to ? "

She questioned him with an indifferent air, but with bloodless lips and eyes, and such a contraction of her whole face that he did not keep her longer in suspense. " No, no, not yet. I have given up my turn to Hédouin ; that will give us six months at least.

Then burst a storm of tears, laughter and mad kisses : "Oh ! Thanks, thanks. How happy I shall make your life now ! It was that, you know, that made me naughty, the idea of your going." She would prepare for it now, become resigned to it little by little. And then, in six months' time, they would no longer have the mournful autumn with them, giving greater force to the blow.

She kept her word. No more nervous attacks, no more quarrels ; and even, to avoid the vexations caused by the boy, she decided to put him to school at Versailles. He only got out on Sunday, and, if this new order of things did not soften at once his rebellious and savage nature, it taught him, at least, to be hypocritical. They lived peacefully, the dinners with the Hettémas enjoyed without storms, and the piano re-opened for their favourite songs.

But at heart Jean was more uneasy, more perplexed than ever, asking of himself where his weakness was leading, thinking sometimes of giving up the consular service, and entering the office. It would be Paris and the agreement with Fanny indefinitely renewed ; but also the dream of his youth dispelled, the despair of his relatives, the undoubted rupture with his father, who would never forgive him for this renunciation, and especially when he knew the cause of it.

And for whom ? For an aged and faded creature, whom he no longer loved—he had had a proof of it in the presence of her lovers. What sorcery then held him to this life ?

As he was getting into the train one morning, towards the end of October, a young girl's eyes lifted to his own recalled suddenly the meeting in the wood, the radiant beauty of the girl-woman, the remembrance of which had haunted him for months. She was wearing the same bright-coloured dress, which the sun had flecked so prettily under the branches, but covered by a large travelling-cloak ; and in the carriage, the books, the little bag, the bunch of great reeds and late flowers, told of the return to Paris, the end of the country stay. She too had recognised him by a half smile trembling in her eyes as limpid as spring-water ; and there was, during a second, the unexpressed accordance of the same thought in these two beings.

"How is your mother, Monsieur d'Armandy ?" asked suddenly old Bouchereau, whom the dazzled Jean had not seen at first, buried in his corner, reading, his pale face cast down.

Jean gave the latest accounts, very much touched at this recollection of him and his, and more moved still when the young girl inquired after the little twins, who had written her uncle such a pretty letter, thanking him for the care

Jean gave the latest accounts.

bestowed on their mother. She knew them? It filled him with joy; then, as he was apparently extraordinarily sensitive that morning, he became sad at once on learning that they were returning to Paris, that Bouchereau was starting his term at the School of Medicine. He would not have a chance of seeing her again. And through the windows, the flying fields, resplendent a moment ago, seemed to him dreary, and lying in the light of an eclipse.

There was a long whistle; they had arrived. He said good-bye and left them, but outside the station they met again, and Bouchereau, in the tumult of the crowd, informed him that from the next Thursday he would find him at home in the Place Vendôme, if he felt inclined for a cup of tea. She gave her uncle her arm, and it seemed to Jean that it was she who had invited him without speaking a word.

After having decided several times that he would call on the Bouchereaus, then that he would not—for why cause himself useless regrets?—he gave it out at home, nevertheless, that there would shortly be a grand gathering at the Ministry, at which he would have to be present. Fanny looked up his dress suit, had his white ties ironed; and then suddenly on the Thursday evening he no longer had the least inclination to go out. But his mistress reasoned with him on the necessity of this unpleasant duty, reproaching herself with having absorbed him too much, selfishly kept him to herself, and she finally decided him, playfully finished dressing him, touched up his cravat, his hair, laughed because her fingers smelt of the cigarette, which every moment she was taking from her mouth and putting on the chimney-piece, saying it would make his partners turn up their noses. And, seeing her so gay and good-tempered, he was remorseful at having lied, and would willingly have remained with her at the fireside, if Fanny had not forced him : " I insist, you must," and pushed him tenderly out into the dark road.

It was late when he came home; she was asleep, and the lamp lighting this fatigued slumber recalled to his mind a like scene, three years ago already, after the terrible revelations that he had heard. What a coward he had shown himself then! By what madness had that which should have broken his chain riveted it more securely? A loathing came over him. The room, the bed, the woman, all disgusted him equally; he took the light, carried it softly into the next room. He longed so to be alone, to think over what had happened to him—Oh! nothing, next to nothing—

He loved.

There is in certain words, which we employ ordinarily, a hidden spring, which suddenly throws them open, explains to us their true, innermost meaning; then the word refolds, regains its hackneyed shape, and becomes insignificant, worn out by mechanical usage. Love is one of these words; those who have once known its real meaning will understand the delicious anguish in which Jean had existed for the last hour, without being able, at first, to account for that which he was experiencing.

Away there, in the Place Vendôme, in that corner of the drawing-room where they had sat a long time talking to one another, he was conscious of nothing but perfect felicity, of a soft charm enwrapping him. It was only when outside, the door closed on him, that he had been seized with a mad joy, then with a weakness as if all his veins had opened: "What is the matter with me?" And the Paris which he was traversing on his way back seemed to him novel, fairy-like, grown larger, radiant. Yes, at this hour when the beasts of night are let loose and prowl about, when the ooze from the sewers rises, shows itself off, swarms under the yellow gas, he, Sappho's lover, eager for every debauchery, saw that Paris which may be seen by the young girl returning from a ball, her head filled with waltz tunes which she repeats to the stars from beneath her white attire, that chaste Paris, bathed in the moonlight in which virgin souls blossom forth, that was the Paris which he saw. And suddenly, as he ascended the broad staircase at the railway station, on the way to his wretched home, he surprised himself saying aloud : " Why, I love her, I love her ; " and it was thus that he had learnt it.

" Are you there, Jean ? Whatever are you doing ? "

Fanny wakes with a start, frightened at not feeling him at her side. He will have to go and kiss her, lie, tell her about the ball at the Ministry, whether there were any pretty dresses, and with whom he danced ; but to escape this inquisition, especially the dreaded caresses, full as he is of souvenirs of the other, he invents a pressure of work, drawings for Hettéma.

" There's no fire ; you will be cold."

" No, no."

" Leave the door open at least, so that I can see your lamp."

He must carry out the lie to the end, set out the table, the diagrams ; then, seated motionless, holding his breath, he thinks, calls up memories, and, to fix his dream, recounts it to Césaire in a long letter, whilst the night wind moves the branches which creak without any rustling of leaves, whilst the rumbling trains follow one after the other, and La Balue, disturbed by the light, moves about in his little cage, jumps from perch to perch with hesitating cries.

He tells all, the meeting in the wood, the railway carriage, his singular emotion on entering those rooms which appeared so melancholy and tragic the day of the consultation, with furtive whisperings in the doorways, and mournful looks exchanged from chair to chair, and which this evening were thrown open, animated and noisy, in long, illumined suite. Bouchereau himself wore no longer his set look, that dark, searching, disconcerting glance under the low eyebrows, but the tranquil and paternal expression of a good-natured old man who permits that one should enjoy one's self at his house.

"Suddenly she came up to me, and then I saw nothing more. Her name is Irène, she is pretty, good-natured looking, an Englishwoman's gold-brown hair, a child's mouth always ready to laugh. Oh! not that unmeaning laugh, so irritating in many women ; a true overflowing of youth and happiness. She was born in London ; but her father was French, and she has no accent, only a charming way of pronouncing certain words, of saying " uncle " which each time makes old Bouchereau's eyes beam with love. He adopted her to relieve his brother's family, which is numerous, and replace her sister, the eldest, who two years ago married his chief assistant. But she, oh, doctors do not suit her at all. How she amused me with that nonsense about the young savant who exacted from his betrothed, above all things, a formal and solemn engagement to bequeath their bodies to the Anthropological Society ! And she is a bird of passage. She loves ships, the ocean, the sight of a ship heading for the open sea stirs her soul. She told me this frankly as a comrade ; quite an English miss in manners, in spite of her Parisian grace ; and I listened, enraptured at her voice, her laugh, at the conformity of our tastes, the inward certainty that my life's happiness was there, at my side, and that I had only to seize it, to carry it off, far, far off, wherever my adventurous career might lead me—"

" Come to bed, deary."

He starts, stops, hides instinctively the letter he is writing : " Directly. Go to sleep, go to sleep."

He speaks angrily to her, and, straining himself, hears the regular breathing of sleep return, for they are quite near one another, and yet so far apart !

"—Whatever happens, this meeting, this love, will be my deliverance. You know my life ; you understand, although we never spoke of it, that it is the same as formerly, that I have not been able to free myself. But what you do not know is, that I was prepared to sacrifice fortune, future, all, to this fatal condition into which I was being dragged deeper day by day. Now, I have found the spring, the fulcrum which I wanted ; and, to give my weakness no chance, I have sworn not to return—you know where—but free and separated. To-morrow sees me escape—"

It was not the next day, nor the next. There must be a means of escape, a pretext, the climax of a quarrel when one cries : " I go," no more to return ; and Fanny was gentle and merry as in the first illusory days of their life together.

Should he write " it is all over " without further explanation ? But this violent woman would never yield thus, she would persist, would beard him in his hotel, his office. No, better to attack her face to face, convince her of the irrevocableness, the definitiveness of this separation, and, without pity as without anger, tell her the reasons.

But with these reflections returned the dread of Alice Doré's suicide. In front of their house, on the other side of the road, there was a lane running down to the railway, and closed by a gate ; the neighbours went through there on days when they were pressed for time, and followed the rails to the station. And the south countryman's imagination pictured his mistress, after the parting scene, rushing out across

the road, down the lane, and throwing herself under the
wheels of the train which was taking him away. This fear
oppressed him to such a degree that the mere sight of this
swinging gate between two ivy-covered walls made him
shrink from an explanation.

If he had only had a friend, someone to protect her, to
assist her in this first crisis ; but, buried by themselves like
marmots, they knew no one, and it was not the Hettémas,
those monstrous egoists shining and swimming in fat, besti-
alised yet more by the approach of their Esquimaux's hiber-
nation, that the unfortunate woman could call to her aid in
her despair and abandonment.

Yet the separation must be brought about, and quickly.
In spite of his promise to himself Jean had returned two or
three times to the Place Vendôme, more and more in love ;
and although he had said nothing yet, old Bouchereau's open-
armed reception of him, Irène's attitude, in which, mingled
with reserve, was a tenderness, an indulgence, and as it
were the timid awaiting of a declaration, all warned him
against delay. Then the anguish of lying, the excuses he
invented for Fanny, and the kind of sacrilege in turning from
Sappho's kisses to a discreet and timid courtship.

CHAPTER XI.

IN the midst of this dilemma, he found on his table at the Ministry the card of a gentleman who had already called twice during the morning, as the usher said with a certain awe at the following name :

C. GAUSSIN D'ARMANDY,

President of the Submersionists of the Rhone Valley,
Member of the Central Investigation and Vigilance Committee,
Departmental Delegate, &c., &c., &c.

Uncle Césaire in Paris !   Le Fénat a delegate, member of a Vigilance Committee !   He had not recovered from his stupefaction when his uncle appeared, still brown as a fir-cone, with his frolicsome eyes, his laugh at the corner of his temples, his conspirator's beard, but instead of the everlasting fustian jacket, a new frock-coat, buttoned down the front, and giving the little man a majesty truly presidential.

What brought him to Paris ?   The purchase of an elevator for the immersion of his new vineyards,—he pronounced the word "elevator" with a conviction which gave him greater importance in his own eyes,—and the order for his own bust which his colleagues had asked him for, to adorn the council room.

"You saw," he added, with a modest air, "that they have named me president.   My idea of submersion is the sensation of the South.   And to think it is I, Le Fénat, who am going

to save the vines of France !. There is nothing like us harebrained ones, you see."

But the chief object of his journey was the rupture with
Fanny. Seeing that the affair dragged, he had come to con-
clude it at a blow. "It is in my line, you know. When
Courbebaisse left his, on marrying—" Before embarking on
his story, he stopped, and unbuttoning his frock-coat he drew
out a small pocket-book with bulging sides :

"First of all, take this off my hands. Yes! money—it
will purchase your release." He mistook his nephew's gesture,
understood that he refused it from delicacy. "Take it !
take it ! I am proud to be able to repay the son a little of
what the father did for me. Besides Divonne will have it thus.
She knows all about the affair, and is so delighted that you
are thinking of marrying, of shaking off your old stick-
fast."

Jean thought this expression in Césaire's mouth, after the
service his mistress had rendered him, rather unjust, and it
was with a touch of bitterness that he answered :

"Take back your pocket-book, uncle ; you know better
than anyone that money questions are a matter of indifference
to Fanny."

"Yes, she was a good girl," said his uncle in the funeral
oration style, and winking his crows-footed eye, he added :

"Keep the money, at any rate. With the temptations
of Paris, I would rather it were in your hands than in mine ;
and besides it is necessary in ruptures as in duels."

Upon this, he rose, declaring that he was dying of hunger
and that this important question could be better discussed
fork in hand, at lunch. Always the same trifling levity of
the south countryman in the treatment of matters touching
the other sex.

"Between ourselves, my lad—" they were sitting in a

restaurant in the Rue de Bourgogne, and his uncle, up to his chin in napkin, was expanding, whilst Jean was picking at his food, too upset to eat, "—I think you take things too tragically. I know well that the first step is difficult and the explanation tiresome ; but if you don't feel equal to it, don't try it, do like Courbebaisse. Up to the morning of his marriage Mornas knew nothing. In the evening, on leaving his betrothed, he went to fetch the singer at her music-hall and took her home. You may say that that was an irregular proceeding and not very faithful either. But then, one hates scenes, and with such terrible women as Paola Mornas ! For nearly eighteen years had this great fine fellow trembled before this little blackamoor. To give her the slip he had to be artful and cunning." And this is how he managed it :

The day before the marriage, a fifteenth of August, the national fête day, Césaire proposed to her to go and catch a dish of fish in the Yvette. Courbebaisse was to join them at dinner ; and they would return on the evening of the next day when Paris had got rid of the stink of dust, rockets and lamp-oil. Happy idea. Behold them then both stretched on the grass by the side of the little river which dances and sparkles between its low banks, makes the fields so green and the willows so leafy. After fishing, a bathe. It was not the first time that they had swam about together, Paola and he, like good fellows, comrades. But that day, little Mornas, her bare arms and legs, her Maugrabin's body made in a mould which the damp bathing costume was plastering over, perhaps too the idea that Courbebaisse had given him carte blanche—Ah ! the rogue. She turned round, fixed him with her eyes :

" Now then, Césaire, no more of that."

He did not persist, from fear of spoiling his chance, and said to himself: " After dinner."

Very merry was the dinner on the wooden balcony of the inn, between the two flags which the landlord had run up in honour of the fifteenth of August. It was hot, the hay smelt sweetly, and they heard the drums, the crackers, and the band of the choral society which was marching about the streets.

"Isn't Courbebaisse a nuisance, not to come till to-morrow?" said Mornas, who was stretching her arms and looking as if the champagne had got into her head. "I should like to enjoy myself to-night."

"And I too!"

·He had come and leant by her side over the railing of the balcony, still hot from the sultry day, and slyly, to sound her, he passed his arm round her waist: "Oh, Paola, Paola." This time, instead of getting angry, the singer began to laugh, but so loudly, so heartily that he ended by doing likewise. The same attempt—repulsed in the same manner—in the evening, after returning from the fair where they had danced and played for macaroons; and as their bedrooms adjoined she sang to him through the partition: "You're too little, you're too little," with all sorts of unfavourable comparisons between himself and Courbebaisse. He restrained himself with difficulty from answering her, calling her widow Mornas; but it was too soon yet. The next morning, as he sat down to a good breakfast whilst Paola fidgeted, and got anxious at last, at not seeing her lover, it was with a certain satisfaction that he took out his watch and said solemnly:

"Twelve o'clock, the deed is done."

"What deed?"

"He is married."

"Who?"

"Courbebaisse."

Bang!

Bang!   Ah! my friend, what a smack!

211.

The singer, wrapped in one of the flags, was bawling out the Marseillaise!

214.

"Ah! my friend, what a smack! In all my gallant adventures I never received one like it. And then, suddenly, she is for setting off. But there is no train before four o'clock. And during this time the faithless one was flying along as fast as steam could take him towards Italy, with his wife. Then, in her rage, she claws, she overwhelms me with blows and scratches; this, my chance! I who had locked the door; then she turns on the crockery, and finally falls into frightful hysterics. At five o'clock, they carry her to bed, watch her, whilst I, scratched all over as if I had just come out of a briar bush, I run to fetch the doctor from Orsay. In those sorts of affairs it is like a duel, and it would be advisable always to have a doctor with one. Picture me on the way, fasting, and in a broiling sun! It was night when I brought him back. All at once, on approaching the inn, we heard the murmur of a crowd, there is a mob of people under the window. Ah! heavens, she has committed suicide? She has killed some one? With Mornas this was the more likely. I rush forward, and what do I see? The balcony hung with Venetian lanterns, and the singer standing there, consoled and superb, wrapped in one of the flags, and bawling out the "Marseillaise," in the midst of the imperial fête, above the heads of the applauding people.

"And that is how Courbebaisse's connexion terminated, my boy; I don't say that it was all over at once. After ten years of imprisonment one must always reckon on a little supervision. But, at any rate, I came in for the worst of it; and I will do as much for you if you like."

"Ah! uncle, this is a different sort of woman."

"Go along," said Césaire, opening a box of cigars and holding them up to his ear to find out if they were dry, "you are not the first one to leave her."

"That is true enough."

And Jean recovered his ease at this idea, which would
have broken his heart a few months before. To tell the
truth, his uncle had reassured him a little with his comical
tale, but what he could not bear the idea of was the double,
deceit during months, the hypocrisy, the divided attentions;
he could never make up his mind to it, and had put things
off too long already.

"Then what do you propose doing?"

Whilst the young man was writhing in this state of un-
certainty, the member of the Vigilance Committee was
smoothing his beard, practising smiles, effects, ways of
holding the head; then he asked carelessly:

"Does he live far from here?"

"Who?"

"Why, that artist, that Caoudal whom you spoke to me
about, with regard to my bust. We might go and see about
the cost while we are together."

Caoudal, though celebrated, and a great squanderer of
money, still occupied in the Rue d'Assas the studio where
he had first made his name. Césaire, as they walked along,
made inquiries about his standing as an artist; true, he
would pay the price, but the gentlemen of the Committee
were anxious to have a first class work.

"Oh, don't be afraid, uncle, if Caoudal once takes it in
hand." And he enumerated the sculptor's titles, Member of
the Institute, Commander of the Legion of Honour, and of a
crowd of foreign orders. Le Fénat opened his eyes wide.

"And you are friends?"

"Intimate friends."

"Ah, see what Paris can do, see what fine friends one
makes there."

Gaussin would have been somewhat ashamed all the
same in confessing that Caoudal had been Fanny's lover,

and that he had made his acquaintance through her. But it would seem that Césaire was thinking of this:

"He is the author of that Sappho which we have at Castelet? Then he knows your mistress, and might be useful in the separation. The Institute, the Legion of Honour, all that has weight with a woman."

Jean did not answer, wondering too, perhaps, how he might utilize the influence of the first lover.

And his uncle continued with a hearty laugh:

"By-the-bye, do you know, the bronze is no longer in your father's room. When Divonne knew, when I had the misfortune to tell her that it represented your mistress, she would no longer have it there. With the consul's whims, his objection to the least change, it was not an easy matter, especially without causing any suspicion of the reason. Oh, the women! She worked it so well that at the present moment Monsieur Thiers presides on your father's chimney-piece, and poor Sappho, covered with dust, lies in the 'Windy Chamber,' in company with the fire-dogs and disused furniture; she even got a jolt in the moving, her chignon and lyre broken. Divonne's spite, no doubt, had caused her this misfortune."

They arrived in the Rue d'Assas. On seeing the modest and working look of this city of artists, these studios with great numbered doors opening out into the two sides of a long yard terminating in the common-looking buildings of a Communal school, with its perpetual hum of reading, the president of the submersionists had fresh doubts about the talent of a man so ordinarily housed; but no sooner had he entered Caoudal's studio than he knew what he had to expect.

"Not for a hundred thousand francs, not for a million!" thundered the sculptor at Gaussin's first word; and raising his great body from the divan on which he was stretched out in the disorder and desolation of the studio: "A bust! yes, I daresay; look down there at that plaster smashed into a thousand pieces; my statue for the next Salon which I have just been demolishing with a mallet. That's what I think of sculpture, and however tempting be the physiognomy of Monsieur—"

"Gaussin d'Armandy, President—"

Uncle Césaire was firing off all his titles, but there were too many of them. Caoudal interrupted him, and turning towards the young man: "You are staring at me, Gaussin. You find me aged?"

It was true that he looked his full age in this light falling from above on the scars, the hollows and bruises of his debauched and jaded face, his lion's mane showing shabby spots like an old carpet, his hanging, flabby cheeks, and his moustache the colour of fading gilt, which he no longer took the trouble to curl or dye. What was the good? Cousinard, the little model, had just left him. "Yes, my dear fellow, with my moulder, a savage, a brute, but twenty!"

His accents enraged and ironical, he strode up and down the studio, kicking over a stool which stood in his way. He stopped, suddenly, before a garlanded mirror hanging above the divan, and looked at himself with a hideous grimace: "I hope I'm ugly enough, broken up enough, skinny and wrinkled as an old cow!" He clasped his neck with his hand, then in the lamentable and comical voice of an old beau who bemoans himself: "And to think that I shall be regretting even this, next year!"

Uncle Césaire was amazed. This an Academician, who was letting his tongue run, and relating his low amours! There were fools everywhere then, even at the Institute; and his admiration for the great man diminished with the sympathy which he felt for his weaknesses.

"How is Fanny? Are you still at Chaville?" asked Caoudal, suddenly calmed and coming to sit at Gaussin's side, familiarly tapping him on the shoulder.

"Ah, poor Fanny, we have not much longer to live together now!"

"You are going away?"

"Yes, soon; and I am going to be married first. I must leave her."

The sculptor laughed ferociously:

"Bravo! I am glad. Avenge us, my lad, avenge us on the jades. Forsake them, deceive them, and let them weep, the wretches! You will never do them as much harm as they have done to others."

Uncle Césaire was delighted.

"You see, this gentleman does not take things so tragically as you. Fancy, the innocent youth, what prevents him from leaving her is the fear that she will commit suicide!"

Jean confessed very simply the impression which Alice Doré's suicide had made on him.

"But that is not the same thing," said Caoudal, eagerly. "She was a melancholy creature with no spirit in her, a poor doll without sufficient sawdust. Déchelette was mistaken in thinking that she died on his account; it was because she was sick and tired of life. Whilst Sappho, ha, ha!—Commit suicide! She is too much enamoured of love and will burn down to the end, down to the socket. She is like those actors who play the parts of lovers and no others, and who go down to the grave, toothless, hairless, but still lovers Look at me. Am I going to kill myself? It is no use my being distressed; I know well that this one gone I shall get another, and that so it will continue. Your mistress will do as I do, as she has done before. Only as she is no longer young, it will be a more difficult matter."

Césaire continued, triumphant : "Now are you satisfied, eh ?"

Jean said nothing, but his scruples were overcome and his resolution taken. They were going away, when the sculptor called them back to show them a photograph he had picked up from amongst the dust on the table, and was wiping with his sleeve. "Look, there she is ! Isn't she pretty enough to worship, the jade? Look what legs, what a throat !" And the contrast was terrible between those longing eyes, that impassioned voice, and the senile trembling of the broad fingers holding the delicious image with its dimpled charms of Cousinard the little model.

CHAPTER XII.

"Is it you? How early you are!"

She came from the bottom of the garden, her skirt full of fallen apples, and ran quickly up the steps, uneasy at the look, at once embarrassed and stubborn, which her lover wore.

"Whatever is the matter?"

"Nothing, nothing, it's the weather, the sun. I wanted to take advantage of the last fine day to take a turn in the forest, both of us. Will you come?"

"Oh! luck!" she cried—the street urchin's exclamation which she used every time she was delighted. For more than a month they had not been out, confined to the house by November rains and storms. It was not always enjoyable in the country; as well live in the ark with Noah's beasts. She had a few orders to give in the kitchen, as the Hettémas were coming to dinner; and as he waited outside on the Pavé des Gardes, Jean looked at the little house suffused in the soft light of late summer, at the country road with its broad, mossy flags, with that caressing, lingering gaze which we have for spots we are about to quit.

Through the widely opened window of the dining-room he heard the oriole warbling and Fanny's orders to the woman: "Mind you don't forget, dinner for half-past six. Serve the guinea-fowl first. Ah! I must give you some table-linen." Her voice rang clear and joyous amidst the chirping in the kitchen and the cries of the bird singing himself hoarse in the sun. And he, knowing that their companionship had only two hours longer to last, was oppressed by these festive preparations.

He felt inclined to go in and tell her all, there and then, at one blow ; but he was afraid of her screams, of the fearful scene which the whole neighbourhood would hear, of a scandal which would raise all Chaville. He knew that once let loose, no considerations restrained her, and he adhered to his idea of taking her into the forest.

" Come along, I'm ready."

She took his arm playfully, warning him to speak low and walk quickly as they passed in front of their neighbour's house, for fear lest Olympe should want to accompany them and thus spoil their walk. She was not easy until, the road and railway bridge passed, they turned to the left into the woods.

It was a mild and lovely day; the sun, slightly shaded by a silvery floating vapour, bathed the whole atmosphere, clung to the copses where, amongst the still surviving russet leaves of a few trees, might have been seen magpies' nests and clumps of green mistletoe in the lofty branches. One heard the continuous cry of a bird, like the sound of filing, and blows of beaks on the trees answering to the woodman's chopping.

They walked slowly, leaving their footprints on the ground softened by the autumnal rains. She was hot through having come so quickly, her cheeks flushed, her eyes brilliant, and she stopped to take off the large blond lace shawl, a present from Rosa, which she had thrown over her head when they came out, a fragile and costly relic of past splendours. For the last three years he had known the dress she had on, a poor garment of black silk, giving way under the arms and at the waist : and when she lifted it because of some puddle as she walked in front of him, he saw the heels of her boots were wearing down.

How cheerfully she had accepted this half misery, without a regret or complaint, concerned for him, for his comfort, never happier than when she was nestling against him, her hands crossed on his arm. And Jean asked himself, as he looked at her rejuvenated by this spring-tide of sunshine and love, what flow of sap there could be in such a creature, what marvellous faculty of forgetfulness and pardon, to preserve so much gaiety and indifference after a life of passion, of crosses and tears, all stamped on her face, but fading away at the slightest touch of gaiety.

" It's a good one ; I tell you it's a good one."

She plunged into the wood up to her knees in dead leaves, came back, her hair all down, rumpled by the brambles, and showed him the small network at the foot of the mushroom which distinguishes the esculent boletus. " You see, it has got the net ! " And she was delighted.

He did not listen to her, being absent-minded, and asking himself : " Is this the moment ? Must I ? " But his courage failed him, she was laughing so heartily, or the spot was not favourable ; and he drew her further and further away, like an assassin who meditates his blow.

He was going to make up his mind when, at a turn in the path, someone came and disturbed them, the keeper Hoche-corne whom they met occasionally. Poor fellow, he had lost one after the other, in the little cottage which the State allowed him on the edge of the pond, two children and his wife, and all of the same deadly fever. After the first death, the doctor declared the situation unhealthy, too near the water and its emanations ; and, in spite of certificates and recommendations, he had been left there two, three years, the time to see all his dear ones die, with the exception of a little girl with whom he had at last come to live in a new house at the entrance to the wood.

Hochecorne, with the face of an obstinate Breton, light, courageous-looking eyes, and a receding forehead beneath his keeper's cap, was the true type of fidelity, of superstitious obedience to orders; he had the strap of his gun slung over one shoulder, while on the other reclined the head of his slumbering child whom he was carrying.

"How is she?" asked Fanny, smiling at the little four-year-old girl, pale and wasted with fever, who woke up and opened her large eyes encircled with red. The keeper sighed.

"Not well. In vain I take her about with me everywhere; now she will eat nothing, has no taste for anything; it must be that it was too late when we moved, and that she had already taken the fever. She's so slight, look, madame, like a leaf. One of these days she'll go off like the others. Good heavens!"

This "good heavens!" murmured in his beard, was his only protest against the cruelty of red-tapeism.

"She is trembling; it looks as though she was cold."

"It's the fever, madame."

"Wait a moment, we will warm her." She took the shawl which was hanging on her arm and wrapped the little one in it. "Yes, yes, do let me; it will come in for her wedding veil, later on."

The father smiled, heartbroken, and touching the child's little hand as she fell asleep again, pale as a corpse in all this white, he made her thank the lady and then disappeared, with a "Good heavens!" which was lost in the cracking of the branches under his feet.

Fanny, no longer merry, pressed closely to Jean with all the timid fondness of a woman whose emotion, fear, or joy, causes her to approach more closely him whom she loves.

Jean said to himself: "What a good girl!" but without allowing his resolution to give way; on the contrary, he strengthened himself in it, for on the slope of the path they were taking arose Irène's form, the remembrance of the bright smile which had greeted him there and which had taken possession of him, before even he recognised its profound charm, its inmost fount of intelligent sweetness. He reflected that he had waited until the last moment, that this was Thursday. "Come, it must be done," and seeing an opening at a little distance, he assigned it as the utmost limit.

It was a clearing in the midst of trees lying surrounded by chips, stripped bark, faggots, and holes for the charcoal burning. A little further down was the pond from which a white mist was rising, and on its bank the little deserted cottage with falling roof and broken windows flying open— the Hochecornes' plague-house. Beyond, the woods stretched towards Vélizy, a great hillside of ruddy foliage, of dense and dreary forest. He stopped abruptly:

"Supposing we rest a short time?"

They sat down on a long tree which had been felled, an old oak on which the marks of the axe showed where the branches had been. It was a warm nook enlivened by the pale sunlight and a perfume of hidden violets.

"How lovely it is!" she said, leaning languidly on his shoulder and seeking for a place on his neck to kiss. He drew back a little, took her hand. Then, seeing the sudden expression of sternness on his face, she became terrified.

"What is the matter with you?"

"Bad news, my poor girl. Hédouin, you know, he who took my place—" He spoke painfully, in a hoarse voice, the sound of which astonished even himself, but which grew firmer towards the end of his story made up beforehand—

Hédouin fallen ill on reaching his post and himself ordered to replace him. He had thought that easier to say, less cruel than the truth. She listened to the end without interrupting him, her face of a grey pallor, her eyes fixed. "When do you start?" she asked, withdrawing her hand.

"This evening—to-night." And, his voice unreal and mournful, he added: "I reckon to spend twenty-four hours at Castelet and then embark at Marseilles."

"Enough! no more lies!" she cried with a savage burst and springing up; "no more lies; you aren't up to it. The truth is, you are going to be married. Your family has been working at this long enough. They are frightened to death that I should keep hold of you, that I should prevent you from going out to catch typhus or yellow fever. Well, they are satisfied now. It is to be hoped the lady is to your taste. And when I think of your bows I used to tie on Thursdays! What a fool I must have been, eh?"

She gave a woeful, atrocious laugh, a laugh which contorted her mouth and showed on one side a gap caused by the breaking—quite recent, no doubt, for he had not seen it before—of one of her beautiful enamelled teeth which she was so proud of, and this, the missing tooth in this hollow, cadaverous, distracted face, gave Gaussin a horrible shock.

"Listen to me," he said, taking hold of her and seating her by force at his side. "It is true, I am going to be married. My father wished it, as you know well; but what difference can that make to you since I have to go?"

She loosed herself, nursing her wrath:

"And it was to tell me this that you've dragged me miles into the forest? You said to yourself: 'At least, no one will hear her if she screams.' No, look you, there shall be no outburst—not a tear. In the first place, I've had enough of you, handsome youth that you are; you can go your way, and it isn't I who will call you back. Away with you then abroad, and take your wife with you, your little one as they say in your part of the country. She must be a beauty too, the little one, ugly as a gorilla or else in the family way. For you are as great a simpleton as those who chose her for you."

She no longer restrained herself, launching out into a torrent of insults and abuse, until finally she was brought to the point of being able only to stammer, " coward, liar, coward," which she threw exasperatingly in his teeth, as a threatening fist.

It was Jean's turn to listen without saying a word, without an effort to silence her. He preferred her thus, insulting, vile, the true daughter of old Legrand : the separation would be less cruel. Did this strike her? All at once she ceased, fell headforemost on her lover's knees, with a great sob which shook her frame, and a broken wailing :

" Pardon, mercy—I love you, I've only you—My love, my life, do not do this—don't leave me—what do you think is to become of me ? "

His feelings were overcoming him ; ah, this was what he had feared. Her tears infected him, and he threw his head back to keep them in his swimming eyes, trying to calm her with foolish words, and ever the reasonable argument : " But since I had to go."

She raised herself, with this cry which discovered all her hope :

" Ah ! but you would not have gone. I should have said, 'Stay, let me love you still.' Do you think it can happen to one twice to be loved as I love you ? You've time enough to marry, you're so young, whilst I—I shall soon be finished, done for, and then we shall separate as a matter of course."

He wished to get up, and had courage to do this and to

tell her that all that she could do was vain; but clinging to
him, trailing on her knees in the mud lingering in this
hollow, she forced him to sit down again, and in front of
him, between his knees, with the breath of her lips, the
voluptuous closing of her eyes, with childish endearments,
her hands on his stern face, her fingers amongst his hair, in
his mouth, she tried to stir into a blaze the cold cinders of
their love, repeated to him softly their past delights, the
languid awakenings, the bliss of their Sunday afternoons.
All that was nothing to what she would give him in the
future; she knew of other caresses, other intoxications, she
would invent new ones for him.

And as she whispered these words, words such as men
hear at the doors of low dens, great tears trickled down her
agonised and terror-stricken face, as she writhed and cried
in a wailing voice: "Oh! this must not be; tell me it is
not true that you are going to leave me." And then came
more sobs, groans, cries for help, as if she saw a knife in his
hand.

The executioner was hardly braver than the victim. He
feared her anger not more than her caresses; but he was
defenceless against this despair, this clamour which filled
the wood and spent itself over the stagnant and fever-breed-
ing water above which the joyless blood-red sun was setting.
He had made up his mind to suffer, but not with this acute-
ness; and it needed all the dazzling attractions of the new
love to prevent him from lifting her up in his arms and
saying: "I will stay, be quiet; I will stay."

How long had passed in this exhausting struggle? The
sun was no more than an ever diminishing bar of light on
the horizon; the pond was taking a slaty tint, and one would
have said its unhealthy exhalations were invading the waste
land and the woods and hills opposite. In the dusk which

Is that you, Gaussin?

was creeping on them he saw only the pale face lifted to his, the open mouth moaning ceaselessly. Shortly after night had fallen the cries became hushed. Then arose the sound of floods of tears, unending as the incessant rain accompanying the crashings of the storm, with from time to time a deep and hollow " Oh ! " at some horrible object which she was driving away and which was constantly returning.

Then, silence. It is all over, the beast is dead. A cold wind rises, shaking the branches, and wafting along the echo of some distant clock.

"Come, get up, don't stop there."

He raises her gently, feels her limp in his hands, obedient as a child and convulsed with great sighs. She appears to preserve a fear, a respect for the man who has just shown himself so strong. She walks at his side, in his step, but timidly, without taking his arm ; and to look at them thus reeling and dejected, guided along the paths by the yellow reflection of the soil, one would have thought they were a couple of peasants returning home worn out by the long day's work in the open air.

At the border of the wood a light appears—Hochecorne's open door—showing the forms of two men. " Is that you, Gaussin ? " asks Hettéma's voice, as he comes with the keeper to meet them. They were beginning to be uneasy at not seeing them return and at the moans they heard in the wood. Hochecorne was going to take his gun and set out to look for them.

"Good evening, sir ; good evening, madame. The little one's delighted with her shawl ! I had to put her to bed in it."

Their last action in common, the charity of a short while back, their hands clasped for the last time round the body of the little dying child.

"Good-bye, good-bye, Hochecorne." They hasten all three towards home, Hettéma still very much puzzled by the sound which had filled the wood. "It rose and fell, one would have said it was some beast being killed. But how was it you heard nothing?"

Neither answers.

At the corner of the Pavé des Gardes Jean hesitates.

"Stop to dinner," said she, in a low supplicating voice. "Your train has gone, you can catch the nine o'clock one."

He goes in with them. What is there to fear? Such a scene could not occur twice, and it is the least he can do to give her this little consolation.

The room is warm, the lamp burns brightly, and the sound of their steps in the lane has warned the servant, who is placing the soup on the table.

"Here you are at last!" says Olympe who has already taken her seat, and tucked her napkin up under her short arms. She is uncovering the soup and stops short with a cry: "Good gracious, my dear!"

Wan, looking ten years older, her eyes swollen and blood-shot, mud on her dress, on her hair even, the scared and disordered appearance of some low prostitute just escaped from the hands of the police—such was Fanny. She breathes a moment, her poor burning eyes blink at the light, and then by degrees the warmth of the little house, the table gaily set out, provoke the remembrance of the happy days and a new outburst of sobs in which one distinguishes the words:

"He is leaving me. He is going to be married."

Hettéma, his wife, the country woman who waits on them, look at one another, at Gaussin. "Let's have dinner, any way," says the fat man who is furious apparently; and the sound of the greedy spoons is mingled with the splashing of water in the next room where Fanny is bathing her face. When she returns, smothered with powder, in a white woollen dressing-gown, the Hettémas look at her in agony, expecting some new outburst, and are very much astonished to see her, without a word, throw herself gluttonously on her food like a shipwrecked sailor, filling up the hollow of her grief and the gulf of her cries with everything within her reach, bread, cabbage, a guinea fowl's wing, apples. She eats and eats.

They talk constrainedly at first, then more freely, and as the Hettémas have no sympathy but with what is dull and material, of how pancakes can be eaten with preserves, or if hair is better than feathers to sleep on, they arrive without a hitch at the coffee, which the huge couple flavour with burnt sugar and sip leisurely, their elbows on the table.

It is a pleasure to see the confiding and placid look which these unwieldy companions of crib and litter exchange. They have no wish to part, these two Jean surprises this look, and in this room abounding with souvenirs and familiar objects, the torpor of fatigue, of digestion, of comfort, creeps over him. Fanny, who is watching him, has softly moved her chair up to his, glided on to his knee, slipped her arm under his.

"Hark!" he says, suddenly. "Nine o'clock; quick, good-bye. I will write to you."

He is up, outside, across the road, groping in the dark to open the gate in the lane. Two arms enfold him: "Kiss me at least."

He feels himself within the folds of the dressing-gown, next to her skin, pervaded by the odour, the heat of a woman's flesh, agitated by this parting kiss which leaves in his mouth a taste of fever and tears; and she, under her breath, feeling him give way: "One more night, only one."

A signal on the line.   It is the train !

How had he the strength to free himself, to rush to the station the lamps of which were shining through the leafless branches ? He was wondering still, breathless in a corner of the carriage, watching through the window for the shining lights of the cottage, for a white form at the gate. "Adieu ! adieu !" And this cry removed the silent terror which he had felt at the curve in the line, of seeing his mistress in the place she had occupied in his ghastly dream.

His head outside, he watched their little house, the light from which was scarcely more than that of a lost star, fade, diminish, and become confused amongst the trees and fields. All at once he was conscious of an immense joy and relief. How freely one breathed, how lovely it was, all this valley of Meudon and the great black hills forming in the distance a triangle twinkling with innumerable lights, disposed towards the Seine in regular lines ! Irène was awaiting him there, and he was going to her with all the swiftness of the train, all his lover's longing, all his enthusiasm for a chaste and youthful life.

Paris ! He took a cab to go to the Place Vendôme. But in the gaslight he saw his clothes, his boots covered with mud, a thick heavy mud, all his past life which clung closely and filthily to him. "Oh ! no, not to-night." And he regained his old lodging-house in the Rue Jacob, where Le Fénat had ordered a room for him near his own.

CHAPTER XIII.

THE next day, Césaire, who had taken upon himself the delicate mission of going to Chaville to fetch his nephew's books and other effects and consummating the rupture by the removal, came back very late, just as Gaussin was beginning to distress himself with all sorts of foolish and sinister suppositions. At last a cab, heavy as a hearse, turned the corner of the Rue Jacob, loaded with corded boxes and an enormous trunk which he recognised as his, and his uncle entered, mysterious and heart-broken.

"I've been a long time collecting everything so as to make one journey of it and not be obliged to go there again." Then, pointing to the packages which two servants were bringing into the room: "There is the linen, the clothes, and there the papers and books. Nothing is wanting but your letters; she entreated me to leave her them to read over again, and have something of yours. I thought there would be no danger in that. She is such a good girl."

He sat for a long time on the trunk, puffing and blowing, and sponging his face with his unbleached silk handkerchief as big as a napkin. Jean did not dare to ask for particulars, what sort of a state he had found her in ; his uncle gave him none for fear of distressing him. And they filled this uncomfortable silence, big with unexpressed thoughts, by remarks about the sudden change in the weather, which had become cold since the day before, the mournful aspect of this deserted and bare suburb of Paris, studded with chimneys of manufactories and those enormous metal cylinders, the cisterns, of the market-gardeners.

"She did not give you anything for me, uncle?" asked Jean after a while.

"No, you can rest easy. She will never worry you, she has accepted her position with much resolution and dignity."

How was it that Jean saw in these words an implied censure, a reproach for his harshness?

"All the same," continued his uncle, "taking one thing with another, I should prefer Mornas's claws to this unfortunate creature's despair."

"Did she cry much?"

"Ah, my lad. And so well, with such feeling that I wept myself in front of her, without strength to—" He snorted, shook off his emotion as an old goat shakes its head. "After all, what could one do? It isn't your fault; you couldn't pass all your life there. You have done the thing very handsomely, you have left her money and furniture. And now, have done with all this sort of thing! Get this marriage affair settled quickly. Too serious a business for me, that. The consul comes in there. My line is in left-handed settlements." And seized suddenly with a fit of melancholy, his face against the window-pane, staring at the lowering sky and the trickling roofs. "All the same, the world is getting sad. In my time separations took place more gaily than that."

Le Fénat gone, followed by his elevator, Jean, deprived of this happy and prattling temperament, had a long week to pass, a feeling of emptiness and solitude, all the dark bewilderment of widowerhood. In such a condition, even without the regret for a lost love, one searches for, one feels the want of a companion; for existence shared with another, the cohabitation of table and bed creates a tissue of invisible and subtle bonds the strength of which reveals itself only in grief, in the effort of breaking them. The influence of contact and habit is so miraculously penetrating, that two beings living the same life come even to resemble one another.

His five years with Sappho had not yet moulded him to this extent, but his body nevertheless preserved the marks of the chain and experienced its weighty influence. And even, as happened several times, his steps turned of themselves towards Chaville on leaving the office, and he often found himself in the morning seeking on the pillow at his side those heavy masses of black hair, innocent of a comb, where fell his first kiss.

The evenings especially seemed to him interminable in this lodging-house bedroom, which reminded him of the first days of their life together, the presence of a different, a delicate and silent mistress, whose little card scented his glass with the perfume of an alcove and with the mystery of her name—Fanny Legrand. At these times he would set out to tire himself, to walk, to be dazed with the music and lights of some second-rate theatre, until old Bouchereau gave him permission to pass three evenings a week with his betrothed.

It had all been finally settled. Irène loved him; uncle was willing; the marriage was fixed for the beginning of April, at the end of the term. Three months of winter to see, to understand, to long for one another, to paraphrase lovingly that first look which knits souls, and that first avowal which troubles them.

The evening of the signing of the marriage contract, on returning home without the least inclination for sleep, Jean felt a desire to make his room look orderly and workman-like, with that natural instinct of bringing our life into accordance with our ideas. He arranged his table and his books, as yet unpacked and stowed away at the bottom of one of the hastily made boxes, the law books between a pile of handkerchiefs and a garden jacket. From the leaves of a dictionary of commercial law—the book he used the most— fell a letter, without envelope, in his mistress's hand-writing.

Fanny had trusted it to the chance of future labours, unwilling to rely on Césaire's too brief sensibility, and judging that it would arrive more safely by this means. He was disinclined to open it at first, but gave way on seeing the first words, which were very gentle and reasonable, and in which her agitation was only discoverable by the trembling of the pen and the uneven lines. She asked one favour, only one, that he would go and see her from time to time. She would say nothing, reproach him with nothing, neither his marriage, nor this separation which she knew to be absolute and definite. Only to see him!

"Just think what a terrible blow for me, and so unexpected, so sudden. I feel as if there had been a death or a fire, not knowing what to make of it. I weep—I wait. I look at the place where I was so happy. Only you could reconcile me to this new situation. It is a charity, come and see me, so that I may not feel so lonely; I am afraid of myself."

These wailings, this suppliant appeal, ran through the whole letter, ending always in the same way: "Come! come!" It made him think he was in the glade in the middle of the forest, with Fanny at his feet, and in the dusk, that poor face lifted up to his, all swollen and tear-stained, and the lips opening in a cry. It was that which pursued him all night, that which disturbed his sleep, and not the blissful intoxication he had enjoyed with her. It was that aged and withered face which he saw again, in spite of all his efforts to place between himself and it that countenance with its pure lines, like a carnation in flower, which the avowal of love tinged with little rose-coloured flames beneath the eyes.

This letter was eight days old; eight days that the unhappy creature had been waiting for a word or a visit, the encouragement to resignation which she asked for. But why had she not written since? Perhaps she was ill; old fears came over him again. He thought Hettéma might be able to give him some news, and, relying on the regularity of his habits, he went and waited for him in front of the Comité d'Artillerie.

The last stroke of ten was sounding from the church of Saint-Thomas d'Aquin, when the fat man came round the corner of the little square, his collar turned up, his pipe in his mouth and held with both hands to warm his fingers. Jean watched him coming from afar, and was much moved at the recollections which he awakened; but Hettéma greeted him with hardly disguised ill-temper: " You here! Haven't we just cursed you this week! we who went to live in the country to be quiet! "

And as he finished his pipe at the door, he related how the preceding Sunday they had invited Fanny to dinner, and the child whose day out it was, by way of diverting her mind from her wretched thoughts. And, to tell the truth, they were merry enough at table, and she had even given them a little singing at dessert; they separated about ten, and the Hettémas were about to tumble deliciously into bed, when suddenly there came a knocking at the shutters, and little Josaph's voice calling out terrified:

"Come quick! mamma is going to poison herself." Hettéma rushed off and arrived in time to take a bottle of

laudanum from her by force.   There was a fearful struggle ;
he had to seize her by the waist, hold her and defend himself against the blows and the comb with which she tore his
face.   In the struggle the bottle broke, the laudanum over-
flowed everything, and it ended by his clothes being stained
and tainted with the poison.   "But you can well understand
what such scenes, all this varied drama, are for quiet people.
And we've had enough of it ; I've given notice ; next month
I move."   He put his pipe in its case, and, with an undis-
turbed good-bye, disappeared under the low arch of a little
court-yard, leaving Gaussin all upset at what he had heard.

He pictured the scene in that room which had been their
room, the terror of the child calling for help, the brutal
struggle with the huge man, he seemed to taste the opium
flavour, the sleepy bitterness of the spilt laudanum.   The
horror of it remained with him all the rest of the day,
aggravated by the idea of the solitude in which she would
now be left.   The Hettémas gone, who would stay her hand
from fresh attempts?

A letter came which reassured him a little.   Fanny
thanked him for not being so hard-hearted as he would
appear, since he still took an interest in the poor forsaken
creature : "You were told, were you not ?   I wished to die ;
it was at feeling so lonely.   I tried, I could not, they stopped
me, my hand trembled perhaps—the fear of suffering, of
becoming ugly.   Oh, that little Doré, however had she the
courage ?   After the first shame at having failed, I was
joyful to think that I could write to you, love you from a
distance, see you again ; for I have not lost hope that you
will come some day, as one visits an unhappy friend, a house
of mourning, from pity, only from pity."

From henceforward there arrived from Chaville every two
or three days a capricious correspondence, long, short, a

He had to seize her by the waist.

journal of grief which he had not the strength to send back, and which enlarged in this tender heart the raw spot of a pity without love, no longer for the mistress, but for the human being suffering on his account.

One day it was the departure of her neighbours, those witnesses of her past happiness, who carried away with them so many remembrances. Now she had nothing left to recall him but the furniture, the walls of their little house, and the serving-woman, a poor wild animal, as little interested in things as the oriole all shivering with the winter cold, perched sad and ragged-looking in a corner of his cage.

Another day, a pale sunbeam falling on the window, she awoke joyous at this idea : he will come to-day ! Why ? She could not say, a fancy. She began at once to make the house look nice, and the woman coquettish in her Sunday dress and the cap he liked ; then until evening, until the last glimmer of light, she counted the trains from the dining-room window, listened for him coming along the Pavé des Gardes. Must she not have been mad !

Sometimes only a line : "It rains, it is gloomy; I am alone, mourning for you." Or else she contented herself with putting in an envelope a poor flower, all saturated and stiff with hoar frost, the last in their little garden. More plainly than all her bewailings this flower, plucked from beneath the snow, told of winter, solitude, abandonment; he saw the spot, at the end of the walk, and, along the flower-borders, a woman's skirt, soaked to the hem, going backwards and forwards in a solitary promenade.

This pity which rent his heart caused him to live with Fanny still, in spite of their separation. He thought of her and pictured her every moment ; but by a singular failure of memory, although it was only five or six weeks since their parting, and the smallest details of their home were still pre-

sent to his mind's eye—La Baluc's cage opposite a wooden
cuckoo-clock won at a country fète, even to the branches of
the nut-tree, which at the least wind beat against their
dressing-room windows—the woman herself appeared no
longer distinct. He saw her in a dim mist, with one sole
prominent and distressing detail, the deformed mouth, the
smile marred by that tooth which was wanting.

Thus aged, what would become of the poor creature by
whose side he had slept so long? The money, which he had
given her, spent, where would she go, to what depth would
she sink? And all at once there rose up in his mind the
recollection of the wretched street-walker met that evening
in the tavern, dying of thirst over her smoked salmon.
That would be her fate; she whose care, whose passionate
and faithful tenderness he had so long accepted. This idea
made him desperate. Yet what could he do? Because he
had had the misfortune to meet this woman, to live some
time with her, was he condemned to keep her always, to
sacrifice his happiness to her? Why he and not the others?
In the name of what justice?

Whilst forbidding himself to see her again, he wrote to
her, and his letters, purposely dry and practical, betrayed
his emotion under their good advice. He recommended her
to take Josaph from school and have him with her to occupy
and amuse her; but Fanny refused. Why bring the child
into the presence of her grief and discouragement? It was
quite enough on Sunday when the little one rambled from
chair to chair, wandered from house to garden, seeing that
some great misfortune had desolated the place, and no longer
daring to ask for news of "Papa Jean" since he had been
told with sobs that he had gone away, that he would never
return.

"All my papas go away, then!"

These words of the forsaken child, coming in the midst of a miserable letter, fell heavy on Gaussin's heart. Soon, this thought of her at Chaville oppressed him to such a point that he advised her to return to Paris, to mix with the world. With her unhappy experience of men, Fanny saw only in this offer a fearful selfishness, a desire to rid himself of her forever by one of those sudden caprices familiar to her; and she frankly expressed her feelings on this point.

"You know what I told you before. I shall remain your wife in spite of all—your loving and faithful wife. You are wrapped up with our little home, and I would not leave it for all the world. What should I do in Paris? I am filled with disgust at that past life of mine which is driving you away; and besides, think of what you would expose us to. You fancy you are very firm, then? Come and see me but once, you naughty boy, only once."

He did not go; but one Sunday afternoon as he was alone and working, he heard two little knocks on his door. He started, recognizing her old way of announcing herself. Fearing to find some order to the contrary below, she had mounted at one breath without asking any questions. He approached, his footsteps deadened by the carpet, hearing her breath through the cracks of the door.

"Jean, are you there?"

Oh! that humble and broken voice! Once more, not loudly: "Jean!" then a plaintive sigh, the rustling of a letter, the kiss of adieu which she threw him.

Not till she had descended the staircase, step by step, slowly, as if expecting to be recalled, did Jean pick up the letter and open it. They had buried the little Hochecorne that morning at the hospital for sick children. Fanny had come with the father and a few people from Chaville, and had not been able to resist coming up to see him or to leave

these lines written beforehand. "Did I not tell you! if I
lived in Paris I should never leave your staircase. Adieu,
deary; I am going home."

On reading it, his eyes filled with tears; he recalled the
same scene in the Rue de l'Arcade, the grief of the discarded
lover, the letter slipped under the door, and Fanny's heart-
less laugh. She loved him then more than he loved Irène!
Or else is it that a man, being more interested than a woman
in life and its affairs, has not like her the exclusiveness of
love, the forgetfulness and indifference for everything which
does not concern her absorbing and unique passion?

This torture, this painful feeling of pity from which he
suffered, was only soothed at Irène's side. Here alone was
his anguish alleviated and melted away under the glance of
her soft eyes. There remained only an immense weariness,
a temptation to lay his head on her shoulder and remain
there speechless, motionless, sheltered.

"What ails you?" she would say. "Are you not happy?"

Oh! yes; so happy. But why was he so sad and tearful
in his happiness? And at times he felt inclined to tell her
all, as he would tell a kind and intelligent friend, without
thinking, poor fool, of the distress which such confidences
occasion in young hearts, of the incurable wounds which
they may make in a trustful affection. Ah! if he could
only have borne her away, fled with her! he felt that that
would have put end to his tortures; but old Bouchereau
would not abate an hour of the time fixed upon. "I am old,
I am ill. I shall see my child no more; do not rob me of
these last days."

Beneath his harsh exterior, this great man was the best
of men. Condemned without reprieve by the heart disease
whose progress he followed and noted, he spoke of it with an
admirable coolness, continuing his lectures half suffocated,

examining patients less unhealthy than himself. One sole weakness there was in this vast mind, and one denoting clearly the Tourangeau's peasant origin ; his respect for titles, for nobility. And the remembrance of the little turrets at Castelet, the ancient name of Armandy, had had a share in his readiness to accept Jean as his niece's husband.

The marriage was to take place at Jean's home, which would avoid the moving of his poor mother, who sent her future daughter every week a tender, affectionate letter dictated to Divonne or one of the little twins. And he was glad to be able to talk to Irène about his people, to feel Castelet in the Place Vendôme, all his affections grouped around his dear betrothed.

But he was dismayed at feeling so old, so weary compared to her on seeing her take a childish joy in things which no longer amused him, in the pleasures—already discounted by him—of married life. Thus, the list of all the things which they would have to take to the consulate, furniture, materials to choose, a list, in the middle of which he came to a stop one evening, his pen hesitating, terrified at the recommencement of the life in the Rue d'Amsterdam, of all the sweet delights used up, exhausted by those five years spent with Fanny, in a travesty of marriage and married life.

CHAPTER XIV.

" Yes, my dear fellow, he died last night in Rosa's arms I have just been taking him to be stuffed."

De Potter the composer, whom Jean had met coming out of a shop in the Rue du Bac, fixed himself on to him with an effusiveness very little suited to his hard, business-like features, and related to him the martyrdom of poor Bichito, killed by the Paris winter, shrivelled up with cold in spite of lumps of wadding and the spirit lamp lit for the last two months under his little nest, like as for children born before their time. Nothing kept him from shivering, and the night before, whilst they were all around him, a last shudder shook him from head to tail and he died like a good Christian, thanks to floods of holy water which mamma Pilar sprinkled on his rough skin where life was ebbing away in ever-changing waves and prismatic movements, saying as she did so, her eyes raised to heaven : " *Dios loui pardonne !* "

" I laugh over it, but my heart is sad all the same ; especially when I think of the grief of my poor Rosa whom I left in tears. Fortunately Fanny was with her—"

" Fanny ? "

" Yes ; it was a long time since we had seen her. She arrived this morning in the midst of the drama, and the good girl stayed to console her friend." He added, without noticing the impression caused by his words : " It is all over, then ? You are no longer together ? Do you remember our conversation on the lake at Enghien. You, at least, profit by the lessons one gives you." And there was a shade of envy in his approbation.

Gaussin, his brows knitted, felt a real uneasiness at thinking that Fanny had returned to Rosario; but he was vexed with himself for this weakness, having no longer any right or responsibility in her existence.

De Potter stopped in front of a house in the Rue de Beaune, a very old street in that once aristocratic part of Paris, which they had just entered. It was here that he lived, or was reputed to live, for propriety's—for the world's sake, for in reality his time was spent between the Avenue de Villiers and Enghien, and he only appeared occasionally under the conjugal roof in order that his wife and child might not appear too forsaken.

Jean was pursuing his way, desirous of being alone, but De Potter retained his hand in his own long hands, tough from constant playing, and, without the least embarrassment, like a man who feels no impropriety in his vice, said :

"Do me a favour, come up with me. I am supposed to dine at home to-day, but I cannot really leave my poor Rosa all alone in her despair. You will serve as a pretext for my going out, and save me tiresome explanations."

The composer's study in the splendid and cold-looking suite of rooms on the second floor, offered all the desolate appearance of a room no longer used for work. Everything in it was too neat, there was none of that disorder, that feverish activity which communicates itself to the furniture and the various objects. Not a book, not a leaf of paper on the table, majestically occupied by an enormous bronze inkstand dry and shining as in the shop window ; not a sign of music on the old piano shaped like a spinet which had inspired his first works. And a white marble bust, the bust of a young woman with delicate features and a sweet expression, pale-looking in the light of the waning day, rendered more cold still the screened and fireless grate, seemed to look sadly at the walls covered with gilded and ribbonned crowns, medals, commemorative frames, the whole glorious and vain collection generously left to his wife as compensation, and which she preserved as the ornaments on the tomb of her happiness.

Hardly had they entered, when the study door opened and Madame de Potter appeared :

"Is that you, Gustave ?"

She thought he was alone, and seeing a stranger, stopped short with evident embarrassment. Elegant, pretty, and tastefully dressed, she appeared more refined than her bust, her soft features wearing a look of nervous and courageous resolution. In society opinions were divided as to her character. Some blamed her for enduring her husband's undisguised contempt, his other connection which was known to all the world ; others, on the contrary, admired her silent resignation. And the general opinion put her down as a quiet woman loving her own tranquillity above everything, and finding sufficient consolation for her widowhood in the love of a beautiful child and the pleasure in bearing the name of a great man.

But while the composer introduced his companion and made up some sort of falsehood to avoid dining at home, Jean could detect by the uneasiness on this young womanish face, by the fixedness of the vacant look which saw, which heard nothing more, as if absorbed in grief, that some great sorrow lay buried. alive beneath the worldly exterior. She appeared to accept this tale which she did not believe, and contented herself with saying gently :

"Raymond will cry, I had promised him that we would dine at his bedside."

" How is he ? " asked De Potter, absent-mindedly, and with a touch of impatience.

" Better, but he coughs still.   Will you not come and see him ? "

He muttered a few words in his moustache, pretending to look round the room for something : " Not now—in a great hurry—appointment at the club at six."   What he wanted to avoid was being alone with her.

" Good-bye, then," said the young woman suddenly composed, her features calm again like some sheet of pure water which has just been disturbed to its depths by a stone. She bowed and disappeared.

" Let's be off ! "

And De Potter having regained his liberty hurried off Gaussin who watched this sinister personage, blinded by his passion, stiff and correct in his English-cut overcoat, descending the stairs in front of him, who had been so moved when he took his mistress's chameleon to be stuffed, and yet who was going away without kissing his sick child.

" All that, my dear fellow," said the composer as if in response to his friend's thought, " all that is the fault of those who made me marry.   A true service they rendered me and that poor woman in doing so !   What folly to wish to make a husband and father of me !   I was Rosa's lover, so I have remained, and so I shall remain till one or other of us dies.   A vice which gets hold of you at the right moment, which holds you firmly, can you ever free yourself from it ?   And you yourself, are you sure that if Fanny had wished—? "   He hailed an empty cab which was passing, and as he got in :

"Speaking of Fanny, you know the news ?   Flamant has been pardoned, has left Mazas.   It was Déchelette's petition.

Poor Déchelette ! he will have benefited some one even after his death."

Standing motionless, with a mad desire to run after, to catch hold of those wheels which were rolling away at full speed along the gloomy street where the gas was being lit, Gaussin was surprised to find himself so moved. " Flamant pardoned, released from Mazas ; " he repeated these words in a low voice, saw in them the reason of Fanny's silence for the last few days, of her lamentations so suddenly interrupted, appeased beneath the caresses of a consoler ; for the first thought of the wretched man free at last must have been for her.

He recalled the amorous correspondence dated from the prison, the obstinacy of his mistress in defending him only when she was so indifferent about the others ; and instead of congratulating himself over an occurrence which logically should have freed him from all uneasiness, all remorse, an unaccountable anguish kept him awake and feverish during a part of the night. Why ? He loved her no longer, but he thought of his letters remaining in this woman's hands, which she would read to the other man perhaps, and of which —who knows ?—under some bad influence, she might make use one day to disturb his quiet, his happiness.

Real or false, or containing without him suspecting it a care of another kind, this anxiety about his letters forced him to take an imprudent step, the visit to Chaville which he had always stubbornly set his face against. But to whom could he entrust such a private and delicate mission ? One morning in February he took the ten o'clock train, very calm in mind and heart, and fearing only to find the house shut up, and the woman disappeared with her forger.

At the curve in the line, the open shutters and the curtains in the cottage windows reassured him ; and remember-

"Why, it's Joseph," he said to himself.

254.

ing his emotion when he saw the little light twinkling in the gloom disappearing behind him, he laughed at himself and his short-lived impressions. He was not the same man, and assuredly he would no more find the same woman. Yet it was only two months since. The trees along the line had not put on fresh leaves, they had the same rusty look as on the day of the rupture, of her echoing cries.

He was the only one to get out at the station in the cold and penetrating fog, and, taking the little footpath all slippery with frozen snow, passing under the railway arch, he met no one until he arrived at the Pavé des Gardes, on turning into which a man and child appeared, followed by a railway porter, pushing before him his barrow loaded with trunks.

The child, muffled up in a scarf, and with his cap down over his ears, stifled an exclamation as they passed close by. "Why, it's Josaph," he said to himself, rather astonished and sad at this ingratitude on the little boy's part; and having turned round he met the eyes of the man who was leading the child by the hand. That intelligent and delicate face, paled by imprisonment, those ready-made clothes bought the day before, that fair, stubbly beard which had not had time to grow since leaving Mazas—they were Flamant's of course! And Josaph was his son.

It was a revelation at one flash. He recalled, understood everything, from the letter written in prison in which the handsome engraver confided to his mistress the child he had in the country, to the mysterious arrival of the little one, and Héttema's embarrassment in speaking of the adoption, and Fanny's glances at Olympe; for they had all conspired together to make him support the forger's son. Oh, the fool! and how they must have laughed! A disgust at all this shameful past came upon him, a longing to flee far away ; but there were things troubling him about which he would have liked to know. The man and child had gone, why not she ? And then, his letters, he must have his letters, leave nothing belonging to him in this lurking-place of uncleanness and misfortune.

"Madame! Here's master!"

"Who, master?" naively asked a voice from within the bedroom.

"I," said Jean.

He heard a cry, a hasty bound, then : "Wait, I am getting up, I am coming."

Still in bed, past midday ! Jean fancied he knew why, he knew the causes of these shattered, jaded mornings. And whilst he waited in the dining-room where the least objects were familiar to him, the whistle of the up-train, the trembling bleat of a goat in a neighbouring garden, the plates and dishes lying about the table, carried him back to the old mornings, the hasty little breakfast before starting.

Fanny entered and rushed towards him ; then, stopping short at his cold reception, they remained a second astonished, hesitating, like when one meets after those broken intimacies, at either end of a destroyed bridge, some distance from bank to bank, and between one the immense space of rolling and swallowing floods.

"Good day," she said, in a low tone, without moving.

She found him altered, grown pale. He was astonished at seeing her so young, a little fatter only ; not so tall as he had pictured her, but bathed in that peculiar radiance, that brilliancy of the complexion and eyes, that sweetness of a cool grass-plot as she was after nights of ardent caresses. She had remained in the wood, then, in the depths of the valley filled with dead leaves, she whose remembrance consumed him with pity.

" One gets up late in the country," he said, ironically.

She made excuses, affected a headache, and, like him, spoke impersonally, not knowing how to address him; then, seeing a mute interrogation in his eyes at the finished meal : " It's the child, he breakfasted there this morning before going—"

" Going ? Where ? "

He affected an extreme indifference of voice, but the flash in his eyes betrayed him. And Fanny answered :

" The father has turned up again ; he came to take him away."

" On leaving Mazas, eh ? "

She started, but did not attempt to tell a lie.

" Well, yes. I had promised, I have performed. How often I longed to tell you, but dared not ; I was afraid you would send him away, poor little fellow." And she added timidly : " You were so jealous."

He laughed disdainfully. Jealous—he, of that convict ; get along ! And, feeling his anger rising, he changed the subject, and said quickly what brought him. His letters ! Why had she not given them to Césaire ? That would have obviated an interview painful to both of them.

" That's true," she said, still very meek, " but I will give you them now ; they are there."

He followed her into the bedroom, saw the tumbled bed, the clothes thrown hastily over the two pillows, inhaled that smell of cigarette smoke, mingled with the perfumes of a woman's toilet, which he recognized as well as the little mother-of-pearl box on the table. And the same thought striking them both : " There are not many of them," she said, opening the box; " we should not run any risk of setting the place on fire."

He was silent, agitated, his mouth parched, hesitating to approach this rumpled bed before which she was turning

over the letters for the last time, her head bent forward, her
neck firm and white beneath the tied up masses of hair, and
her voluptuous figure looking stouter in its abandoned pose
beneath the folds of the floating woollen gown.

"There ! they're all here."

Having taken the packet and put it abruptly into his
pocket, for his thoughts were elsewhere, Jean asked :

"Then, he has taken away his child ? Where are they
going to ?"

"To Morvan, his native place, to conceal himself, and do
his engraving which he will send to Paris under a false
name."

"And you ? Do you intend to remain here ?"

She turned away her eyes to avoid his, saying confusedly
that it would be very melancholy. So she thought—she
would, perhaps, go away soon—a little trip.

"To Morvan, no doubt ? A family party !" And, pouring out his jealous fury : "Confess at once that you are
going to join your thief, that you are going to live together.
You have been wanting to do so long enough. Go back to
your lair. Strumpet and forger, they go well together, it
was very good of me to try and lift you out of the mire."

She preserved her unmoved muteness, a gleam of triumph
shot from under her half-closed eyes. And the more he
lashed her with his savage, insulting irony, the prouder she
seemed, and more marked became the quivering at the
corners of her mouth. Now he spoke of his own happiness,
of young and chaste love, the only real love. Oh ! what a
soft pillow to rest on, the heart of a virtuous woman. Then,
abruptly, his voice lowered as if he was ashamed :

"I just met him, your Flamant, he passed the night here?"

"Yes, it was late and snowing. He had a bed made up
on the sofa."

She clasped him in her arms.

200.

" You lie, he slept there ; one has only to look at the bed, at you."

" Well, and if he did ?" She brought her face close to his, her great grey eyes blazing with libertine flames. " Did I know that you were coming? With you gone, what difference did all the rest make to me? I was sad, lonely, disgusted—"

" And then, the flavour of prison ! From the time that you have been living with an honest man that must have seemed tasty to you, eh? What a feast you must have had ! Ah ! slut ! there—"

She saw the blow coming without trying to avoid it, received it full in her face, then, with a dull murmur of pain, of joy, of victory, she sprang upon him, clasped him in her arms : " Deary, deary, you love me still," and they rolled together on the bed.

The roar of a passing express woke him with a start towards evening ; and, with open eyes, he remained a few moments without recognising where he was, all alone in the great bed where his limbs, stiff as if from excessive walking, seemed to be laid one against the other, jointless, strengthless. A great deal of snow had fallen during the afternoon. In the desert-like silence one could hear it melting, rustling on the walls, down the window-panes, dripping on the false roof, now and then on the coke fire, and splashing the hearth.

Where was he? What was he doing there? Little by little, from the reflection of the small garden, the room appeared to him all white, lit up from below, the large portrait of Fanny rising up before him, and the remembrance of his fall came upon him without causing the least astonishment. From the moment he had entered, in face of this bed, he had felt himself recaptured, lost ; these sheets attracted him like a gulf, and he said to himself : "If I fall into it, it will be without remission and for always." It was done ; and beneath the melancholy disgust at his cowardice he had a kind of solace in the idea that he would emerge no more from this state of degradation, the pitiful comfort of the wounded man, who, losing his blood, dragging his sores along, has thrown himself on a dung-heap to die there and, weary of suffering, of struggling, all his veins open, thrusts himself deliciously into the soft and fetid warmth.

That which remained for him to do now was horrible, but very simple. Return to Irène after this treason, risk a life like De Potter's ? Low as he had fallen, he had not come to that. He would write to Boucheieau, the great physiologist who was the first to study and describe diseases of the will, submit to him a terrible case, the history of his life since first meeting this woman, when she had laid her hand on his arm, until the day when, believing himself saved, in the full swing of happiness, of transport, she seized him again by the magic of the past, that horrible past in which love went for so little, only cowardly habit and vice which had eaten into his bones.

The door opened. Fanny walked very quietly into the room so as not to wake him. From between his closed eye-lids he watched her, alert and strong, youthful again, warming at the fire her feet soaked with the snow of the garden, and from time to time turning towards him with the little smile which she had worn that morning, during the quarrel. She came and took the packet of Maryland from its accustomed place, made a cigarette, and was going away, but he detained her.

"You aren't asleep then ?"

"No, sit down there, and let us talk."

She sat down on the edge of the bed, a little surprised at this seriousness.

"Fanny. We will both go—"

She thought at first that he was joking to put her to the test. But the precise details which he gave quickly undeceived her. There was a post vacant, that of Arica; he would apply for it. It was a matter of a fortnight, the time to get their trunks ready.

"And your marriage?"

"Not a word on that subject. What I have done is irreparable. I see plainly that it is all over, that I can never leave you again."

"Poor baby," said she, with a sad and slightly scornful tenderness.

Then having taken two or three whiffs:

"Is it far, this country you mention?"

"Arica? very far, in Peru." And in a low voice: "Flamant will not be able to rejoin you."

She remained thoughtful and mysterious in the clouds of tobacco smoke. He was still holding her hand, stroking her bare arm, and lulled, by the trickling of the water all around the little house, he closed his eyes, and sank gently into the mire.

CHAPTER XV.

Nervous, trembling, under steam, already on the way, like all those who are preparing for a voyage, Gaussin has been for the last two days in Marseilles, where Fanny is to come and embark with him. Everything is ready, their berths taken, two first-class cabins for the vice-consul of Arica travelling with his sister-in-law ; and he is here pacing the discoloured tiles of the hotel bedroom, feverishly awaiting his mistress and the sailing of the vessel.

He is obliged to walk about and fidget on the premises, as he dare not go out. The street embarrasses him as if he were a criminal, a deserter, this confused and swarming Marseilles street, where, so it seems to him, his father and old Bouchereau will appear at every corner and place their hands on his shoulder to capture him and take him back.

He shuts himself up, has his meals there, without even going down to the table-d'hôte, reads without fixing his eyes, throws himself on his bed, beguiles his vague siestas with the " Wreck of the Pérouse " and the " Death of Captain Cook," which, all fly-marked, are hanging on the walls, and for hours together leans over the balcony of worm-eaten wood shaded by a yellow awning, patched like the sail of a fishing boat.

His hotel, the Hôtel du Jeune Anacharsis, whose name, chosen at hazard in the directory, tempted him when he agreed upon a place of meeting with Fanny, is an old inn by no means luxurious, and not even very clean, but which faces the port, is on the sea, on the voyage. Under its windows are parrots, cockatoos, foreign birds with their low interminable warbling—all the stock-in-trade out in the open air of a bird-fancier, whose cages, piled one above the other, salute the breaking day with a sound as of a virgin forest, short, and drowned as the day advances by the noise of the busy port, regulated by the great bell of Notre-Dame de la Garde.

There is a confusion of oaths in every language, the cries of boatmen, of porters, of shell hawkers, mingled with the blows of the hammers in the dry-dock, the creaking of the cranes, the din of the weighing machines, bounding on the pavement, ships' bells, machine whistles, the regular sound of pumps, capstans, bilge-water being discharged, steam escaping—all this tumult redoubled and thrown back by the echoing sea close by, from which arises from time to time the hoarse roar, like some marine monster's breathing, of a great transatlantic liner putting out to sea.

And the smells, too, call up distant lands, quays more sunny and hot than this one ; cargoes of sandal-wood and log-wood being discharged, lemons, oranges, pistachio-nuts, beans, ground nuts, the acrid odour from which escapes' mounts up with clouds of exotic dusts into an atmosphere saturated with brackish water, and the burning herbs and greasy fumes of the cook-shops.

At evening these sounds are hushed, these dense vapours descend and evaporate ; and as Jean, reassured by the darkness, lifts the blinds and looks at the port asleep and black beneath the maze of masts, yards, and bowsprits, whilst the silence is only broken by the lapping waves, the distant barking of a dog on board some ship, out, far out at sea, the Planier light, which, as it revolves, throws a long red or white flame, tears aside the shadows and shows in a lightning flash the outlines of islands, forts, and rocks. And this luminous glance, guiding thousands of lives on the horizon, is his voyage again inviting and making signs to him, calling him in the voice of the wind, the murmurs of the open ocean, and the hoarse din of a steamboat ever groaning and breathing in some part of the roads.

Still twenty-four hours to wait; Fanny is not to join him till Sunday. These three days he was to have passed with his friends, to have devoted to the dear ones whom he will not see for several years, whom he may never see again; but on the first evening of his arrival at Castelet, when his father knew that the marriage was broken off and had guessed the cause, a violent, a terrible explanation took place.

What are we then, what are our tenderest affections, those most near to our heart, that a feeling of anger coming between two beings of the same flesh, the same blood, tears, wrenches, sweeps away their love, nature's feelings with their deep and delicate roots, with the blind, irresistible force of one of those typhoons of the China seas which the hardiest sailors dare not call to remembrance, but say as they turn pale : "Don't let us speak of it—"

He will never speak of it, but he will remember all his life that fearful scene on the terrace at Castelet, where his happy childhood was spent, before that splendid, calm horizon, those pines, those myrtles, those cypresses which, motionless and shuddering, were witnesses of the father's curse. He will always see that tall old man, his cheeks convulsed and twitching, approaching him with that mouth, that look of hatred, speaking words which can never be forgiven, driving him from home and from honour : "Away, go with your vile woman, you are dead to us!" And the

After a long gaze, he fled away in despair.

little twins crying, on their knees on the terrace, asking pardon for their big brother, and Divonne's pallor, without a look, without an adieu for him ; whilst above, behind the window-pane, the invalid's sweet and anxious face was asking the reason of all this disturbance, and why Jean was going off so quickly without kissing her.

This idea that he had not kissed his mother made him turn back when he was half-way to Avignon ; he left Césaire with the carriage in the valley, took a cross-road, and entered Castelet through the home farm, like a thief. The night was dark ; his feet got entangled in the dead vines, and finally he even lost his way, seeking the house in the shadow, a stranger already in his own home. The whiteness of the plastered walls guided him at last with their pale reflection ; but the entrance door was locked, the lights in all the windows extinguished. Ring, call ? He dared not, from fear of his father. Two or three times he made the tour of the house, hoping to get in through some shutter not properly fastened. But Divonne had made her evening rounds with her lantern ; and after a long gaze at his mother's room, an adieu with all his heart to the home of his childhood which is casting him off too, he fled away in despair, with a remorse which clings to him for ever.

As a rule, before these long absences, these voyages with their dangers of sea and wind, the parents, the friends, prolong their adieux until the final embarking ; they pass the last day together, visit the ship, the traveller's cabin, so as better to follow him on his journey. Several times during the day Jean sees these affectionate parties passing by the hotel, numerous and noisy sometimes ; but he is especially touched by one family group on the floor above him. An old man, an old woman, country people in easy circumstances, with jackets of cloth and yellow cambric, have come to accompany their boy, to be with him until the vessel starts ; and leaning out of the window, in the idleness of waiting, one sees them all three, holding one another's arms, the sailor in the middle, close together.   They do not speak ; they embrace.

As he looks at them, Jean thinks of the beautiful parting he might have had.   His father, his little sisters, and, leaning on him with her soft, trembling hand, she whose keen spirit and adventurous soul were urged on by the sight of a ship ploughing the deep.   Barren regrets.   The crime is accomplished, his destiny on its journey ; it only remains for him to go and to forget.

How slow and cruel the hours of the last night appeared to him !   He turned and turned in his bed in the hotel, watched for day on the window-panes with their slow changes from black to grey, then to the white of dawn, which the lighthouse pricked still with a red spark fading away before the rising sun.

Then only he goes to sleep, awakes again with a start at the flood of light in his room, the confused cries in the bird-fancier's cages, and the innumerable chimes of the Marseilles Sunday sounding over the quiet quays, the machinery at rest, the oriflammes floating at the mast heads.   Ten o'clock already !   And the Paris express arrives at mid-day.   Quickly he dresses himself to go to meet his mistress ; they will breakfast looking at the sea, then the luggage will be taken on board, and at five o'clock, the signal.

A glorious day, a deep sky across which the gulls pass like white patches, the sea of a darker blue, of a mineral blue, on which, on the horizon, sails, smoke, everything is visible, everything glistens and dances ; and, as the natural music of these rivers of sun in the transparency of the atmosphere and water, some harps are playing, under the windows of the hotel, an Italian air of a divine fluency, but whose notes dragged out on the strings, cruelly rack the nerves. It is more than music, it is the winged interpretation of these Southern joys, life and love full, flowing over in tears. And the memory of Irène passes into the vibrating, wailing melody. How far off it is! What a lovely country lost, what an everlasting regret for things broken, irreparable!

Come!

As he goes out, Jean meets a young waiter at the door.

"A letter for the consul. It came this morning, but the consul was sleeping so soundly!" Travellers of distinction are rare at the Hôtel du Jeune Anacharsis; so these good Marseilles folks sound their guest's title at every opportunity. Who can have written to him? No one knows his address but Fanny. And, examining the envelope more closely, he becomes terrified, he understands.

"Well, no! I cannot go; it is too great a folly, for which I feel I have not the strength. For such undertakings, my poor boy, one must have youth, which I lack, or the blindness of a mad passion, which neither of us have. Five years ago, in the happy days, a sign from you would have made me follow you to the other end of the earth, for you cannot deny that I loved you passionately. I gave you all I had; and, when it was necessary to tear myself away from you, I suffered as I never before did for any man. But, look you, a love like that wears one out. To feel you are so handsome, so young, to be always trembling lest I should lose you! Now, I have done, you have given me too much of life, of suffering, I can bear no more.

"Under these circumstances, the prospect of this long voyage, of this transplanting of life, fills me with fear. I who cannot bear to stir, and who have never been further

than Saint-Germain, think of that ! And then women age
so quickly in the sun, and you would not be thirty before I
was as yellow and worn out as mamma Pilar ; then it is that
you would begrudge me your sacrifice, and poor Fanny
would have to bear the blame for all. Listen, there is an
Eastern country, I read it in one of your "Tour du Mondes,"
where, when a woman is unfaithful to her husband, they
sew her up alive with a cat in a raw hide, then they throw
the bundle, howling and struggling, on the shore in the
blazing sun. The woman shrieks, the cat claws, it is a
death struggle between the two, whilst the skin shrinks and
contracts on this horrible combat of prisoners, until the last
groan, the last palpitation of the sack. That is the kind of
fate which would await us two—"

He stopped a minute, crushed, stupefied. As far as the
eye could reach the blue sea sparkled. "*Addio*," carolled
the harps, and mingled with them, another voice hot and passionate as they, "*Addio*." And the emptiness of his ruined
life, laid waste, wrecked and mournful, appeared to him, the
field bare, the harvest gathered without hope of return, and
for this woman, who was slipping away from him.

"I ought to have told you this before, but I did not dare,
seeing you so determined, so resolved. Your enthusiasm
seized me ; and then my woman's vanity, my natural pride
at having re-captured you after the rupture. But, in my
heart of hearts, I felt there was something wanting, gone,
exploded. How could it be otherwise after such shocks ?
And do not fancy that it is because of the wretched
Flamant. For him, as for you and all the others, all is
over, my heart is dead ; but there is the child, whom 1 cannot do without, and who leads me back to the father, the
poor man who ruined himself for love, and who came back
to me from Mazas as ardent and tender as at our first

He stopped a minute, crushed, stupefied.

meeting. Only fancy, when we came together again, he passed the whole night weeping on my shoulder; you see there was not much to distress yourself about.

"I have told you, my dear boy, I have loved too much, I am broken. For the future, I have need of someone to love me in my turn, to worship me, to admire me, to soothe me. He will be always at my feet, will never see in me a wrinkle or a grey hair; and, if he marries me, as he intends to do, it will be a favour on my part. Compare—And above all, no folly. My precautions are taken to prevent you from ever finding me again. From the little station café, where I am writing this, I can see through the trees the house where we have spent such happy, and such cruel hours, and the card swinging on the door, awaiting new inmates. You are free now, you will never hear of me more. Adieu, one kiss, the last, on the neck, deary—"

THE END.

42, CATHERINE STREET, STRAND,
NOVEMBER, 1885.

VIZETELLY & CO.'S
NEW BOOKS,
AND NEW EDITIONS.

NEW WORK BY THE AUTHOR OF "SIDE-LIGHTS ON ENGLISH SOCIETY."

In large post 8vo, 434 pp., cloth gilt, price 10s 6d.

IMPRISONED IN A SPANISH CONVENT:
AN ENGLISH GIRL'S EXPERIENCES.
BY E. C. GRENVILLE-MURRAY.

ILLUSTRATED WITH NUMEROUS PAGE AND OTHER ENGRAVINGS.

" Instead of the meek cooing dove with naked feet and a dusty face who had talked of dying for me, I had now a bright-eyed rosy-cheeked companion who had cambric pocket-handkerchiefs with violet scent on them and smoked cigarettes on the sly."—*Page* 75.

(*For other works by* MR. GRENVILLE-MURRAY, *see pages* 7, 8, *and* 9.)

In crown 8vo, 5s.

UNDER THE SUN.

ESSAYS MAINLY WRITTEN IN HOT COUNTRIES.

FORMING THE SECOND VOLUME OF THE CHOICER MISCELLANEOUS WORKS
OF GEORGE AUGUSTUS SALA.

Illustrated with an etched Portrait of the Author, and Twelve Page Engravings.

A SMALL NUMBER OF COPIES OF THE ABOVE WORK HAVE BEEN PRINTED IN DEMY OCTAVO,
ON HAND-MADE PAPER, WITH THE ILLUSTRATIONS ON INDIA PAPER MOUNTED.

(For other works by MR. G. A. SALA, see pages 11 and 12.)

NEW STORY BY THE AUTHOR OF THE CHEVELEY NOVELS.

In Crown 8vo, tastefully bound, price 3s. 6d.

HIS CHILD FRIEND.

By the Author of "A MODERN MINISTER," "SAUL WEIR," "SOULS AND CITIES," &c

" By the aid of the chimney with the register up Mrs. Lupscombe's curiosity was, to a
certain extent, gratified."—*Page* 10.

In post 8vo, cloth gilt, price 3s. 6d.

NO ROSE WITHOUT A THORN,

AND OTHER TALES.

By F. C. BURNAND, H. SAVILE CLARKE, R. E. FRANCILLON, &c.

Illustrated with numerous Page and other Engravings from Designs by R. CALDECOTT,
LINLEY SAMBOURNE, M. E. EDWARDS, F. DADD, &c.

" There is much that is original and clever in these ' Society ' tales."—*Athenæum.*
" Many of the stories are of the greatest merit."—*Daily Telegraph.*

In post 8vo, cloth gilt, price 3s. 6d.

THE DOVE'S NEST,
AND OTHER TALES.

By JOSEPH HATTON, RICHARD JEFFERIES, H. SAVILE CLARKE, &c.

Illustrated with numerous Page and other Engravings from designs by

R. CALDECOTT, CHARLES KEENE, M. E. EDWARDS, ADELAIDE CLAXTON, &c.

"We strongly advise the reader to begin with 'How one ghost was laid,' and to follow it up with 'Jack's wife,' with whom by the way as portrayed both by artist and author he cannot fail to fall in love. These two graceful little extravaganzas will put him into so excellent a temper that he will thoroughly enjoy the good things that follow."—*Life.*

In crown 8vo, neatly bound, price 6s.

PRINCE ZILAH.
By JULES CLARETIE.

Translated from the 57th French edition, and forming Vol. XI. of
VIZETELLY'S ONE-VOLUME NOVELS.
"M. Jules Claretie has of late taken a conspicuous place as a novelist in France."—*Times.*

NEW VOLUMES OF ZOLA'S REALISTIC NOVELS.

In crown 8vo, illustrated with Tinted Page Engravings, price 6s. each.

I.

THE RUSH FOR THE SPOIL (LA CURÉE).
TRANSLATED FROM THE 34TH FRENCH EDITION.

II.

THE LADIES' PARADISE.
TRANSLATED FROM THE 50TH FRENCH EDITION.

III.

THÉRÈSE RAQUIN.
The above works are also published, without the Engravings, price 5s. each.

THE BOULEVARD NOVELS,
In small 8vo, attractively bound, 2s. 6d.

I.

NANA'S DAUGHTER.
A STORY OF PARISIAN LIFE.

By ALFRED SIRVEN and HENRI LEVERDIER.
From the 35th French Edition.

VIZETELLY'S SIXPENNY SERIES OF AMUSING BOOKS.

In picture cover, with many Engravings, price 6d.

MATRIMONY BY ADVERTISEMENT;

AND OTHER ADVENTURES OF A JOURNALIST.

BY CHARLES G. PAYNE.

Contains the Author's experiences in a Madhouse as an "Amateur Maniac," and on a hansom as an "Amateur Cabby," as well as the details of a pretended search for a wife through the agency of the Matrimonial Journals, and other amusing articles.

She pressed herself against his ponderous side as he walked along. It was a trick that she had learned from a precocious kitten.

Uniform with the above, and by the same Author.

VOTE FOR POTTLEBECK!

THE STORY OF A POLITICIAN IN LOVE.

Illustrated with a Frontispiece and numerous other Engravings.

In paper cover, 1s. ; or in parchment binding, gilt on side, 2s. 6d.

ADMIRABLY SUITED FOR PRIVATE REPRESENTATION.

THE PASSER-BY:

A COMEDY IN ONE ACT.

BY FRANÇOIS COPPÉE, of the French Academy.

TRANSLATED, WITH THE AUTHOR'S SANCTION, FROM THE 41ST FRENCH EDITION,
By Letos, Author of "The Red Cross," &c.

"A translation exceedingly well done."—*Whitehall Review.*

NEW SATIRICAL POEM, BY A WELL-KNOWN POET.

In crown 8vo, price 1s.

LUCIFER IN LONDON,

AND HIS REFLECTIONS ON LIFE, MANNERS, AND THE PROSPECTS OF SOCIETY.

"Shows a good deal of observation, and reflects the spirit of the age in making Lucifer intellectually curious and easily bored."—*Pall Mall Gazette.*
"Decidedly witty and original."—*Sunday Times.*

In paper cover, 1s. ; or cloth gilt, 2s. 6d.

PATTER POEMS,

HUMOROUS AND SERIOUS, FOR READINGS AND RECITATIONS,

BY WALTER PARKE.

With Illustrations by J. Leitch.

"'Patter Poems' include many sparkling and merry lays, well adapted for recitation, and sure of the approval of the audience. We hope Mr. Parke will continue to produce humours as delightful as 'The Wonderful What's-his-name,' and the pleasant and truthful sketch of 'The Demon Tragedian.'"—*Saturday Review.*

NEW VOLUMES OF DU BOISGOBEY'S SENSATIONAL NOVELS.

In scarlet covers, 1s. each.

"M. du Boisgobey gives us no tiresome descriptions or laboured analyses of character; under his facile pen plots full of incident are quickly opened and unwound. He does not stop to moralise; all his art consists in creating intricacies which shall keep the reader's curiosity on the stretch, and offer a full scope to his own really wonderful ingenuity for unravelling."—*Times.*

THE DAY OF RECKONING. 2 Vols.

THE SEVERED HAND.

BERTHA'S SECRET.

"A most effective romance, depending for its interest on the skilful weaving and unweaving of mysteries. 'Bertha's Secret' is very well worth perusal."—*Times.*

WHO DIED LAST? OR, THE RIGHTFUL HEIR.

THE CRIME OF THE OPERA HOUSE. 2 Vols.

WORKS BY E. C. GRENVILLE-MURRAY.

NEW AND CHEAPER EDITION.

Two Vols. large post 8vo, attractively bound, price 15s.

UNDER THE LENS:

SOCIAL PHOTOGRAPHS.

BY E. C. GRENVILLE-MURRAY.

ILLUSTRATED WITH ABOUT 300 ENGRAVINGS BY WELL-KNOWN ARTISTS

CONTENTS OF VOL. I.

JILTS:—Mrs. Pinkerton—A Western County Belle—Zoe, Lady Tryon—An Inconsolable Jilt—A Jilted Drysalter—Love and Pickles—An Entr'acte—Mrs. Prago and Miss Daisy Caunter—A Widow with a Nice Little Estate—An Unmercenary Pair of Jilts.

ADVENTURERS AND ADVENTURESSES:—Of the Genus Generally—Matrimonial Adventurers—The Joint Stock Company Chairman—A Financial Adventurer—A Professional Greek—The Countess D'Orenbarre—Lady Goldsworth—Mirabel Hildacourse—Lily Gore—Bella Martingale—Pious Mrs. Palmhold—Mrs. Decoy—Mrs. Lawkins.

PUBLIC SCHOOLBOYS AND UNDERGRADUATES:—Drawbacks of Eton—Of Various Eton Boys—Rugby and Rugbeians—Harrow, Winchester, Westminster—Oxford Undergraduates—University Discipline—Sporting and Athletic Undergraduates—Reading and Religious Undergraduates.

CONTENTS OF VOL. II.

SPENDTHRIFTS:—Prefatory—The Gambletons—Lord Charles Innynges—Lord Luke Poer—Lord Rottenham—Lord Barker—The Marquis of Malplaquet—The Lords Lumber—Sir Calling Earley—Tommy Dabble—Dicky Duff.

HONORABLE GENTLEMEN (M.P.'s):— Preliminary — Erudite Members — Crotchety Members — Free Lances — The Irish Contingent—Very Noble M.P.'s—Money Bags—Beery M.P.'s—Workingmen M.P.'s—Party Leaders—A Seatless Member.

SOME WOMEN I HAVE KNOWN:—An Ex-Beauty—Miss Jenny—Mademoiselle Sylvie—Miss Rose—Madame de l'Esbrouffe-Tourbillon.

ROUGHS OF HIGH AND LOW DEGREE:—How Roughs are Made—The Nobleman Rough—The Foreign Garrison Rough—The Clerical Rough—The Legal Rough—Medical Roughs—The Rough Flirt—The Wife-Beating Rough—Vandal Roughs—The Tourist Rough—The Nautical Rough—The Professional Bruiser—The Low-Class Rough—Women Roughs.

" Brilliant, highly-coloured sketches. . . . contains beyond doubt some of the best writing that has come from Mr. Grenville-Murray's pen."—*St. James's Gazette.*

" Limned audaciously, unsparingly, and with much ability."—*World.*

" Distinguished by their pitiless fidelity to nature."—*Society.*

" Extremely personal. The author, brilliant as were his parts, appears to have laboured under a delusion which obliged him to mistake personal abuse for satire, and ill-nature for moral indignation."—*Athenæum.*

" Some of Mr. Murray's trenchant blows do real service to the cause of public morality and order."—*Daily Telegraph.*

" Includes unvarnished portraits of various characters who have made a flutter in recent times in this little world of ours."—*Vanity Fair.*

Second Edition, in large 8vo, handsomely bound, with gilt edges, price 10s. 6d.

PEOPLE I HAVE MET.

By E. C. GRENVILLE-MURRAY.

Illustrated with 54 tinted Page Engravings, from Designs by FRED. BARNARD.

CONTENTS :—

The Old Earl.	The Rector.	The Doctor.	The Bachelor.
The Dowager.	The Curate.	The Retired Colonel.	The Younger Son.
The Family Solicitor.	The Governess.	The Chaperon.	The Grandmother.
The College Don.	The Tutor.	The Usurer	The Newspaper Editor.
The Rich Widow.	The Promising Son.	The Spendthrift.	The Butler.
The Ornamental Director.	The Favourite Daughter.	Le Nouveau Riche.	The Devotee.
The Old Maid.	The Squire.	The Maiden Aunt.	

THE RICH WIDOW (reduced from the original engraving).

"Mr. Grenville-Murray's pages sparkle with cleverness and with a shrewd wit, caustic or cynical at times, but by no means excluding a due appreciation of the softer virtues of women and the sterner excellences of men. The talent of the artist (Mr. Barnard) is akin to that of the author, and the result of the combination is a book that, once taken up, can hardly be laid down until the last page is perused."—*Spectator.*

"Mr. Grenville Murray's sketches are genuine studies, and are the best things of the kind that have been published since 'Sketches by Boz,' to which they are superior in the sense in which artistically executed character portraits are superior to caricatures."—*St. James's Gazette.*

"From first to last, as might be expected, the book is well written."—*Standard.*

"No book of its class can be pointed out so admirably calculated to show another generation the foibles and peculiarities of the men and women of our times."—*Morning Post.*

"All of Mr. Greville Murray's portraits are clever and life-like, and some of them are not unworthy of a model who was more before the author's eyes than Addison—namely, Thackeray."—*Truth.*

An Edition of "PEOPLE I HAVE MET" is published in small 8vo, with Frontispiece, price 3s. 6d.

A BUCK OF THE REGENCY: *from "DUTCH PICTURES."*

" 'Mr. Sala's best work has in it something of Montaigne, a great deal of Charles Lamb—made deeper and broader—and not a little of Lamb's model, the accomplished and quaint Sir Thomas Brown. These 'Dutch Pictures' and 'Pictures Done With a Quill' should be placed alongside Oliver Wendell Holmes's inimitable budgets of friendly gossip and Thackeray's 'Roundabout Papers.' They display to perfection the quick eye, good taste, and ready hand of the born essayist—they are never tiresome.' —*Daily Telegraph.*

GEORGE AUGUSTUS SALA'S WORKS.

Second Edition, in demy 8vo, cloth gilt, price 12s. 6d.

A JOURNEY DUE SOUTH;

TRAVELS IN SEARCH OF SUNSHINE.

By GEORGE AUGUSTUS SALA.

ILLUSTRATED WITH 16 FULL-PAGE ENGRAVINGS BY VARIOUS ARTISTS.

CONTENTS :—

I.—A Few Hours in the Delightful City.
II.—Life at Marseilles.
III.—Southern Fare and Bouillabaisse.
IV.—Nice and its Nefarious Neighbour.
V.—Quite Another Nice.
VI.—From Nice to Bastia.
VII.—On Shore at Bastia.
VIII.—The Diligence come to Life again.
IX.—Sunday at Ajaccio.
X.—The Hotel too soon.
XI.—The House in St. Charles Street, Ajaccio.
XII.—A Winter City
XIII.—Genoa the Superb: the City of the Leaning Tower.
XIV.—Austere Bologna.
XV.—A Day of the Dead.
XVI.—Venice Preserved.
XVII.—The Two Romes. I. The Old.
XVIII.—The Two Romes. II. The New.
XIX.—The Two Romes. II. The New (*cont.*).
XX.—The Roman Season.
XXI.—In the Vatican: Mosaics.
XXII.—With the Trappists in the Campagna.
XXIII.—From Naples to Pompeii.
XXIV.—The Show of a Long-buried Past.
XXV.—The "Movimento" of Naples.
XXVI.—In the Shade.
XXVII.—Spring Time in Paris.
XXVIII.—"To All the Glories of France."
XXIX.—Le Roi Soleil and La Belle Bourbonnaise.
XXX.—A Queen's Plaything.

" In ' A Journey due South' Mr. Sala is in his brightest and cheeriest mood, ready with quip, and jest, and anecdote, brimful of allusion ever happy and pat."—*Saturday Review.*

In crown 8vo, price 5s.

DUTCH PICTURES, and PICTURES DONE WITH A QUILL.

Illustrated with a Frontispiece and other Page Engravings.

FORMING THE FIRST VOLUME OF THE

CHOICER MISCELLANEOUS WORKS OF GEORGE AUGUSTUS SALA.

A SMALL NUMBER OF COPIES OF THE ABOVE WORK HAVE BEEN PRINTED IN DEMY OCTAVO, ON HAND-MADE PAPER, WITH THE ILLUSTRATIONS ON INDIA PAPER MOUNTED.

The Graphic remarks: " We have received a sumptuous new edition of Mr. G. A. Sala's well-known ' Dutch Pictures.' It is printed on rough paper, and is enriched with many admirable illustrations."

Eighth Edition, in crown 8vo, 553 pages, attractively bound, price 3s. 6d., or gilt at the side and with gilt edges, 4s.

PARIS HERSELF AGAIN.

By GEORGE AUGUSTUS SALA.

WITH 350 CHARACTERISTIC ILLUSTRATIONS BY FRENCH ARTISTS.

" On subjects like those in his present work, Mr. Sala is at his best."—*The Times.*

" This book is one of the most readable that has appeared for many a day. Few Englishmen know so much of old and modern Paris as Mr. Sala."—*Truth.*

" ' Paris Herself Again' is infinitely more amusing than most novels. There is no style so chatty and so unwearying as that of which Mr. Sala is a master."—*The World.*

' It was like your imperence to come smouchin' round here, looking after de white folks' washin."

VIZETELLY'S ONE-VOLUME NOVELS.

"The idea of publishing cheap one-volume novels is a good one, and we wish the series every success."—*Saturday Review.*

In crown 8vo, good readable type, and attractive binding, price 6s. each.

THE THREATENING EYE.

By E. F. KNIGHT,

AUTHOR OF "A CRUISE IN THE FALCON."

"There is a good deal of power about this romance."—*Graphic.*
"One of those books that once begun is sure to be read through with avidity."—*Society.*
"Full of extraordinary power and originality. The story is one of quite exceptional force and impressiveness."—*Manchester Examiner.*

The Book that made M. Ohnet's reputation, and was crowned by the French Academy.

SECOND EDITION.

PRINCE SERGE PANINE.

By GEORGES OHNET,

AUTHOR OF "THE IRONMASTER,"

TRANSLATED, WITHOUT ABRIDGMENT FROM THE 110TH FRENCH EDITION.

"This excellent version is sure to meet with large success on our side of the Channel."—*London Figaro.*

THE FORKED TONGUE.

By R. LANGSTAFF DE HAVILLAND, M.A.,

AUTHOR OF "ENSLAVED," &c.

"In many respects the story is a remarkable one. Its men and women are drawn with power and without pity; their follies and their vices are painted in unmistakable colours, and with a skill that fascinates."—*Society.*
"Mr. de Havilland writes vigorously, and his story is full of incident and action."—*Pictorial World.*

BETWEEN MIDNIGHT AND DAWN.

By INA L. CASSILIS,

AUTHOR OF "SOCIETY'S QUEEN," "STRANGELY WOOED: STRANGELY WON," &c.

"An ingenious plot, cleverly handled."—*Athenæum.*
"The interest begins with the first page, and is ably sustained to the conclusion."—*Edinburgh Courant.*

In small 8vo, price 3s. 6d. each.

SIXTH EDITION, CAREFULLY REVISED, AND WITH A SPECIAL PREFACE,

A MUMMER'S WIFE. A Realistic Novel.

By GEORGE MOORE, Author of "A Modern Lover."

"A striking book, different in tone from current English fiction. The woman's character is a very powerful study."—*Athenæum.*
"'A Mummer's Wife,' in virtue of its vividness of presentation and real literary skill, may be regarded as in some degree a representative example of the work of a literary school that has of late years attracted to itself a good deal of the notoriety which is a very useful substitute for fame."—*Spectator.*
"'A Mummer's Wife' holds at present a unique position among English novels. It is a conspicuous success of its kind."—*Graphic.*

"Kiss me, dear," said Athénaïs.

In large crown 8vo, beautifully printed on toned paper, price 5s., or handsomely bound with gilt edges, suitable in every way for a present, 6s.

An Illustrated Edition of M. Ohnet's Celebrated Novel,

THE IRONMASTER; OR, LOVE AND PRIDE.

CONTAINING 42 FULL-PAGE ENGRAVINGS BY FRENCH ARTISTS, PRINTED SEPARATE FROM THE TEXT.

ZOLA'S POWERFUL REALISTIC NOVELS.

In crown 8vo, price 6s. each.

NANA:

TRANSLATED WITHOUT ABRIDGMENT FROM THE 127TH FRENCH EDITION.

Illustrated with Twenty-four Tinted Page Engravings, by French Artists.

Mr. HENRY JAMES on "NANA."

"A novelist with a system, a passionate conviction, a great plan—incontestable attributes of M. Zola—is not now to be easily found in England or the United States, where the story-teller's art is almost exclusively feminine, is mainly in the hands of timid (even when very accomplished) women, whose acquaintance with life is severely restricted, and who are not conspicuous for general views. The novel, moreover, among ourselves, is almost always addressed to young unmarried ladies, or at least always assumes them to be a large part of the novelist's public.

"This fact, to a French story-teller, appears, of course, a damnable restriction, and M. Zola would probably decline to take *au sérieux* any work produced under such unnatural conditions. Half of life is a sealed book to young unmarried ladies, and how can a novel be worth anything that deals only with half of life? These objections are perfectly valid, and it may be said that our English system is a good thing for virgins and boys, and a bad thing for the novel itself, when the novel is regarded as something more than a simple *jeu d'esprit*, and considered as a composition that treats of life at large and helps us to *know*."

THE "ASSOMMOIR;"

(The Prelude to "NANA.")

TRANSLATED WITHOUT ABRIDGMENT FROM THE 97TH FRENCH EDITION.

Illustrated with Sixteen Tinted Page Engravings, by French Artists.

"After reading Zola's novels it seems as if in all others, even in the truest, there were a veil between the reader and the things described, and there is present to our minds the same difference as exists between the representations of human faces on canvas and the reflection of the same faces in a mirror. It is like finding truth for the first time."—*Signor de Amicis.*

PIPING HOT!

("POT-BOUILLE.")

TRANSLATED FROM THE 63RD FRENCH EDITION.

Illustrated with Sixteen Page Engravings by French Artists.

GERMINAL; OR, MASTER AND MAN.

TRANSLATED WITHOUT ABRIDGMENT FROM THE 47TH FRENCH EDITION.

The above Works are published without Illustrations, price 5s. each.

In preparation. Uniform with the above Volumes.

ABBÉ MOURET'S TRANSGRESSION.

BY EMILE ZOLA.

SAPPHO.

By ALPHONSE DAUDET.   FROM THE 100TH FRENCH EDITION.

THE ARRIVAL OF THE ELEVEN YOUNG MEN AT NANA'S EVENING PARTY,

New Illustrated Edition, in large octavo, of
M. EMILE ZOLA'S CELEBRATED REALISTIC NOVELS.
*Each Volume contains about 100 Engravings, half of which are page-size.
The price is 7s. 6d. per volume.*

1. NANA.   2. THE ASSOMMOIR.   3. PIPING HOT.

DESIGNS BY BELLENGER, BERTALL, CLAIRIN, ANDRÉ GILL, KAUFFMANN, LELOIR, VIERGE, &c.

Second Edition, in small 8vo, price 3s. 6d.
A MODERN LOVER.

BY GEORGE MOORE, AUTHOR OF "A MUMMER'S WIFE."

"Mr. Moore has a real power of drawing character, and some of his descriptive scenes are capital."—*St. James's Gazette.*

"It would be difficult to praise too highly the strength, truth, delicacy, and pathos of the incident of Gwynnie Lloyd, and the admirable treatment of the great sacrifice she makes. The incident is depicted with skill and beauty."—*Spectator.*

In small 8vo, price 3s. 6d.
CAROLINE BAUER AND THE COBURGS.
FROM THE GERMAN.

ILLUSTRATED with TWO carefully engraved PORTRAITS of CAROLINE BAUER.

"Caroline Bauer's name became in a mysterious and almost tragic manner connected with those of two men highly esteemed and well remembered in England—Prince Leopold of Coburg, the husband and widower of Princess Charlotte, afterwards first King of the Belgians, and his nephew, Prince Albert's trusty friend and adviser, Baron Stockmar."—*The Times.*

"Caroline Bauer was rather hardly used in her lifetime, but she certainly contrived to take a very exemplary revenge. People who offended her are gibbeted in one of the most fascinating books that has appeared for a long time."—*Vanity Fair.*

In large crown 8vo, handsomely printed and bound, price 6s.
THE AMUSING
ADVENTURES OF GUZMAN OF ALFARAQUE.
A SPANISH NOVEL. TRANSLATED BY EDWARD LOWDELL.

ILLUSTRATED WITH HIGHLY-FINISHED ENGRAVINGS ON STEEL FROM DESIGNS BY STAHL.

"The wit, vivacity and variety of this masterpiece cannot be over-estimated."—*Morning Post.*
"A very well executed translation of a famous 'Rogue's Progress.'"—*Spectator.*

In post 8vo, price 2s. 6d.
THE CHILDISHNESS AND BRUTALITY OF THE TIME:

BY HARGRAVE JENNINGS, Author of "The Rosicrucians," &c.

"Mr. Jennings has a knack of writing in good, racy, trenchant style. His sketch of behind the scenes of the Opera, and his story of a mutiny on board an Indiaman of the old time, are penned with surprising freshness and spirit."—*Daily News.*

In crown 8vo, price 6s., the Third and Completely Revised Edition of

THE STORY OF
THE DIAMOND NECKLACE.

By HENRY VIZETELLY.

AUTHOR OF "BERLIN UNDER THE NEW EMPIRE," "PARIS IN PERIL," &c.

Illustrated with an Exact Representation of the Diamond Necklace, from a contemporary Drawing, and a Portrait of the Countess de la Motte, engraved on Steel.

"Had the most daring of our sensational novelists put forth the present plain unvarnished statement of facts as a work of fiction, it would have been denounced as so violating all probabilities as to be a positive insult to the common sense of the reader. Yet strange, startling, incomprehensible as is the narrative which the author has here evolved, every word of it is true." —*Notes and Queries.*

In square 8vo, paper cover, 1s., or cloth gilt, 2s. 6d.

THE COMIC GOLDEN LEGEND.

By WALTER PARKE.

WITH HUMOROUS ILLUSTRATIONS BY J. LEITCH.

"Shows much facility in turning a verse, and some talent for parody. The burlesque of Dolores is clever in its way."—*Graphic.*

"The stories are told in bright and luminous verses in which are dexterously wrought parodies of a good many present and some past poets."—*Scotsman.*

"We have had no such imitations of the idiosyncrasies of modern poets since the days of the gifted brothers James and Horace Smith."—*Lady's Pictorial.*

Uniform with the above.

SONGS OF SINGULARITY.

By WALTER PARKE.

ILLUSTRATED WITH 60 ENGRAVINGS.

In crown 8vo, price 3s. 6d.

A NEW EDITION, COMPRISING MUCH ADDITIONAL MATTER, OF

IN STRANGE COMPANY.

By JAMES GREENWOOD (the "Amateur Casual").

ILLUSTRATED WITH A PORTRAIT OF THE AUTHOR, ENGRAVED ON STEEL.

In large 8vo, 160 pages and 130 Engravings, price 1s.

GORDON AND THE MAHDI.
An Illustrated Narrative of the Soudan War.

"This wonderfully good shilling's worth should command a wide sale."—*Illustrated News.*

In small post 8vo, ornamental scarlet covers, 1s. each.

THE GABORIAU AND DU BOISGOBEY SENSATIONAL NOVELS.

> " Ah, friend, how many and many a while
>   They've made the slow time fleetly flow,
> And solaced pain and charmed exile,
>   BOISGOBEY and GABORIAU ! "
>
> *Ballade of Railway Novels in " Longman's Magazine."*

IN PERIL OF HIS LIFE.

"A story of thrilling interest, and admirably translated."—*Sunday Times.*

"Hardly ever has a more ingenious circumstantial case been imagined than that which puts the hero in peril of his life, and the manner in which the proof of his innocence is finally brought about is scarcely less skilful."— *Illustrated Sporting and Dramatic News.*

THE LEROUGE CASE.

"M. Gaboriau is a skilful and brilliant writer, capable of so diverting the attention and interest of his readers that not one word or line in his book will be skipped or read carelessly."—*Hampshire Advertiser.*

OTHER PEOPLE'S MONEY.

"The interest is kept up throughout, and the story is told graphically and with a good deal of art."—*London Figaro.*

LECOQ THE DETECTIVE. Two Vols.

"In the art of forging a tangled chain of complicated incidents involved and inexplicable until the last link is reached and the whole made clear, Mr. Wilkie Collins is equalled, if not excelled, by M. Gaboriau. The same skill in constructing a story is shown by both, as likewise the same ability to build up a superstructure of facts on a foundation which, sound enough in appearance, is shattered when the long-concealed touchstone of truth is at length applied to it."—*Brighton Herald.*

THE GILDED CLIQUE.

"Full of incident, and instinct with life and action. Altogether this is a most fascinating book."—*Hampshire Advertiser.*

THE MYSTERY OF ORCIVAL.

"The Author keeps the interest of the reader at fever heat, and by a succession of unexpected turns and incidents, the drama is ultimately worked out to a very pleasant result. The ability displayed is unquestionable." —*Sheffield Independent.*

DOSSIER NO. 113.

" The plot is worked out with great skill, and from first to last the reader's interest is never allowed to flag."—*Dumbarton Herald.*

THE LITTLE OLD MAN OF BATIGNOLLES.

THE SLAVES OF PARIS. Two Vols.

"Sensational, full of interest, cleverly conceived, and wrought out with consummate skill."—*Oxford and Cambridge Journal.*

THE CATASTROPHE. Two Vols.

"A plot vigorously and skilfully constructed, leading through a series of surprising dramatic scenes and thrilling mysteries, and culminating in a sudden and complete exposure of crime and triumph of innocence. 'The Catastrophe' does ample credit to M. Gaboriau's reputation as a novelist of vast resource in incident and of wonderful ingenuity in constructing and unravelling thrilling mysteries."—*Aberdeen Journal.*

INTRIGUES OF A POISONER.

"The wonderful Sensational Novels of Emile Gaboriau."—*Globe*.

THE COUNT'S MILLIONS. Two Vols.

"To those who love the mysterious and the sensational, Gaboriau's stories are irresistibly fascinating. His marvellously clever pages hold the mirror up to nature with absolute fidelity; and the interest with which he contrives to invest his characters proves that exaggeration is unnecessary to a master."—*Society*.

THE OLD AGE OF LECOQ, THE DETECTIVE. Two Vols.

"The romances of Gaboriau and Du Boisgobey picture the marvellous Lecoq and other wonders of shrewdness, who piece together the elaborate details of the most complicated crimes, as Professor Owen with the smallest bone as a foundation could reconstruct the most extraordinary animals."—*Standard*.

IN THE SERPENTS' COILS.

"This is a most picturesque, dramatic, and powerful sensational novel. Its interest never flags. Its terrific excitement continues to the end. The reader is kept spellbound."—*Oldham Chronicle*.

THE DAY OF RECKONING. Two Vols.

"M. du Boisgobey gives us no tiresome descriptions or laboured analyses of character: under his facile pen plots full of incident are quickly opened and unwound. He does not stop to moralise; all his art consists in creating intricacies which shall keep the reader's curiosity on the stretch, and offer a full scope to his own really wonderful ingenuity for unravelling."—*Times*.

THE SEVERED HAND.

"The plot is a marvel of intricacy and cleverly managed surprises."—*Literary World*.
"Readers who like a thoroughly entangled and thrilling plot will welcome this novel with avidity."—*Bristol Mercury*.

BERTHA'S SECRET.

"'Bertha's Secret' is a most effective romance. We need not say how the story ends, for this would spoil the reader's pleasure in a novel which depends for all its interest on the skilful weaving and unweaving of mysteries, but we will repeat that 'Bertha's Secret' is very well worth perusal."—*Times*.

WHO DIED LAST? OR THE RIGHTFUL HEIR.

"Travellers at this season of the year will find the time occupied by a long journey pass away as rapidly as they can desire with one of Du Boisgobey's absorbing volumes in their hand."—*London Figaro*.

THE CRIME OF THE OPERA HOUSE. Two Vols.

"We are led breathless from the first page to the last, and close the book with a thorough admiration for the vigorous romancist who has the courage to fulfil the true function of the story-teller, by making reflection subordinate to action."—*Aberdeen Journal*.

WAYWARD DOSIA, & THE GENEROUS DIPLOMATIST.
By HENRY GRÉVILLE.

"As epigrammatic as anything Lord Beaconsfield has ever written."—*Hampshire Telegraph.*

A NEW LEASE OF LIFE, & SAVING A DAUGHTER'S DOWRY. By E. ABOUT.

"'A New Lease of Life' is an absorbing story, the interest of which is kept up to the very end."—*Dublin Evening Mail.*

"The story, as a flight of brilliant and eccentric imagination, is unequalled in its peculiar way."—*The Graphic.*

COLOMBA, & CARMEN. By P. MÉRIMÉE.

"The freshness and raciness of 'Colomba' is quite cheering after the stereotyped three-volume novels with which our circulating libraries are crammed."—*Halifax Times.*

"'Carmen' will be welcomed by the lovers of the sprightly and tuneful opera the heroine of which Minnie Hauk made so popular. It is a bright and vivacious story."—*Life.*

A WOMAN'S DIARY, & THE LITTLE COUNTESS. By O. FEUILLET.

"Is wrought out with masterly skill, and affords reading which, although of a slightly sensational kind, cannot be said to be hurtful either mentally or morally."—*Dumbarton Herald.*

BLUE-EYED META HOLDENIS, & A STROKE OF DIPLO-MACY. By V. CHERBULIEZ.

"'Blue-eyed Meta Holdenis' is a delightful tale."—*Civil Service Gazette.*

"'A Stroke of Diplomacy' is a bright vivacious story pleasantly told."—*Hampshire Advertiser.*

THE GODSON OF A MARQUIS. By A. THEURIET.

"The rustic personages, the rural scenery and life in the forest country of Argonne, are painted with the hand of a master. From the beginning to the close the interest of the story never flags."—*Life.*

THE TOWER OF PERCEMONT, AND MARIANNE. By GEORGE SAND.

"George Sand has a great name, and the 'Tower of Percemont' is not unworthy of it."—*Illustrated London News.*

THE LOW-BORN LOVER'S REVENGE. By V. CHERBULIEZ.

"'The Low-born Lover's Revenge' is one of M. Cherbuliez's many exquisitely written productions. The studies of human nature under various influences, especially in the cases of the unhappy heroine and her low-born lover, are wonderfully effective."—*Illustrated London News.*

THE NOTARY'S NOSE, AND OTHER AMUSING STORIES.
By E. ABOUT.

"Crisp and bright, full of movement and interest."—*Brighton Herald.*

DOCTOR CLAUDE ; OR, LOVE RENDERED DESPERATE.
By H. MALOT. Two Vols.

"We have to appeal to our very first flight of novelists to find anything so artistic in English romance as these books."—*Dublin Evening Mail.*

THE THREE RED KNIGHTS ; OR, THE BROTHERS' VENGEANCE. By P. FÉVAL.

"The one thing that strikes us in these stories is the marvellous dramatic skill of the writers."—*Sheffield Independent.*

In demy 4to, handsomely printed and bound, with gilt edges, price 12s.

A HISTORY OF CHAMPAGNE;

WITH NOTES ON THE OTHER SPARKLING WINES OF FRANCE.

BY HENRY VIZETELLY.

CHEVALIER OF THE ORDER OF FRANZ-JOSEF.
WINE JUROR FOR GREAT BRITAIN AT THE VIENNA AND PARIS EXHIBITIONS OF 1873 AND 1878.

Illustrated with 350 Engravings,

FROM ORIGINAL SKETCHES AND PHOTOGRAPHS, ANCIENT MSS., EARLY PRINTED
BOOKS, RARE PRINTS, CARICATURES, ETC.

"Mr. Henry Vizetelly's handsome book about Champagne and other sparkling wines of France is full of curious information and amusement. It should be widely read and appreciated." —*Saturday Review.*

MR. HENRY VIZETELLY'S POPULAR BOOKS ON WINE.

"Mr. Vizetelly discourses brightly and discriminatingly on crus and bouquets and the different European vineyards, most of which he has evidently visited."—*The Times.*

Price 1s. 6d. ornamental cover; or 2s. 6d. in elegant cloth binding.

FACTS ABOUT PORT AND MADEIRA,

GLEANED DURING A TOUR IN THE AUTUMN OF 1877.

BY HENRY VIZETELLY.

WINE JUROR FOR GREAT BRITAIN AT THE VIENNA AND PARIS EXHIBITIONS OF 1873 AND 1878.
With 100 Illustrations from Original Sketches and Photographs.

BY THE SAME AUTHOR.

Price 1s. 6d. ornamental cover; or 2s. 6d. in elegant cloth binding.

FACTS ABOUT CHAMPAGNE

AND OTHER SPARKLING WINES,

COLLECTED DURING NUMEROUS VISITS TO THE CHAMPAGNE AND OTHER VITICULTURAL DISTRICTS OF FRANCE AND THE PRINCIPAL REMAINING WINE-PRODUCING COUNTRIES OF EUROPE.

Illustrated with 112 Engravings from Sketches and Photographs.

Price 1s. ornamental cover; or 1s. 6d. cloth gilt.

FACTS ABOUT SHERRY,

GLEANED IN THE VINEYARDS AND BODEGAS OF THE JEREZ, & OTHER DISTRICTS.
Illustrated with numerous Engravings from Original Sketches.

Price 1s. in ornamental cover; or 1s. 6d. cloth gilt.

THE WINES OF THE WORLD.

CHARACTERIZED AND CLASSED.